INDIAN TALES AND OTHERS

INDIAN TALES

AND OTHERS

BY

JOHN G. NEIHARDT

University of Nebraska Press
Lincoln and London

Copyright 1907, 1915, 1926 by the John G. Neihardt Trust
All rights reserved
Manufactured in the United States of America

First Bison Book printing: 1988
Most recent printing indicated by the first digit below:
1   2   3   4   5   6   7   8   9   10

Library of Congress Cataloging-in-Publication Data
Neihardt, John Gneisenau, 1881–1973.
  Indian tales and others / by John G. Neihardt.
    p. cm.
  "Bison book."
ISBN 0-8032-3318-3. ISBN 0-8032-8358-X (pbk.)
  1. Indians of North America—Fiction. 2. Frontier and pioneer
life—Fiction. 3. Western stories.   I. Title.
PS3527.E35I53 1926
813'.52—dc19   CIP 88-14337

Reprinted by arrangement with the John G. Neihardt Trust

CONTENTS

THE SINGER OF THE ACHE

The Old Omaha Speaks

NOW this is the story of one who walked not with his people, but with a dream.

To you I tell it, O White Brother, yet it is not for you, unless you also have followed the long trail of hunger and thirst—the trail that leads to no lodge upon the high places or the low places, by flowing streams or where the sand wastes lie.

It shall be as the talking of a strange tribe to you, unless you also have peered down the endless trail, with eyes that ached and dried up as dust, and felt your pony growing leaner and shadow-thin beneath you as you rode, until at last you sat upon a quiet heap of bones and peered and peered ahead.

Moon-Walker was he called—he who walked for the moon. But that was after he had called his pony from the grazing places and mounted for the long ride. Yet was there a time when he ran about among the lodges laughing very merrily with many boys and girls, who played with hoop and spear, made little bloodless wars upon unseen peoples, and played in little ways the big, sad games of men.

And then he was called by many names, and all of the names, though different, meant that he was happy.

But once his mother and his father saw that a man began to look out of his eyes, began to hear a man talking in his throat; and so they said: "It is the time for him to dream."

So they sent him at nightfall to the hill of dreams —as is the custom of our people.

Wahoo! the bitter hill of dreams!

And he of the many names went up into the hill of dreams and dreamed. And in through the mists that strange winds blow over the hills of sleep burst a white light, as though the moon had grown so big that all the sky was filled from rim to rim, leaving no place for sun and stars. And upon the surface of the white light floated a face, an awful face —whiter than the light upon which it floated; and so beautiful to see that he of the many happy names ached through all his limbs, and cried out and woke. Then leaping to his feet, he gazed about, and all the stars had grown so small that he looked twice and hard before he saw them; and the world was shrunken.

And frightened at the strangeness of all things, he fled down the hillside into the village. His mother and his father he wakened with bitter crying.

"How came the dream?" they whispered; for

upon the face of him who went up a boy they saw that which only many years should bring; and in his eyes there was a strange light.

"A face! a face!" he whispered. "I saw the face of the Woman of the Moon! Whiter than snow, it was, and over it a pale flame went! Oh, never have I seen so fair a face; and there was something hidden in it swift as lightning; something that would be thunder if it spoke; and also there was something kind as rain that falls upon a place of heat. Into the north it looked, high up to where the lonesome star hangs patient.

"And there was a dazzle of white breasts beneath, half-hidden in a thin blanket of mist. And on her head, big drifts of yellow hair, not hanging long as does your hair, O mother, but heaped like clouds that burn above the sunset. My breast aches for something I cannot name. And now I think that I can never play again!"

And there was a shaking of heads in that lodge, and a wondering, for this was not good. Not so had others, big in deeds, dreamed upon the hill in former times. Always there had been a coming of bird, or beast, or reptile, wrapped in the mystery of strange words; or there had been the cries of fighting men, or there had been a stamping of ponies, or the thin, mad song of arrows.

But here it was not so, and the mother said: "Many times the false dreams come at first, and then at last the true one comes. May it not be so with him?"

And the father said: "It may be so with him."

So once again up the hill of dreams went the boy. And because of the words of his father and mother, he wept and smeared his face with dust; his muddy hands he lifted to the stars. And he raised an earnest voice: "O Wakunda! send me a man's dream, for I wish to be a big man in my village, strong to fight and hunt. The woman's face is good to see, but I cannot laugh for the memory of it. And there is an aching in my breast. O Wakunda! send me the dream of a man!"

And he slept. And in the middle of the night, when shapeless things come up out of the hills, and beasts and birds talk together with the tongues of men, his dream came back.

Even as before the moon-face floated in a lake of cold white fire—a lake that drowned the stars. And as he reached to push it from him, lo! like a white stem growing downward from a flower, a body grew beneath it! And there was a flashing of white lightning and the Woman of the Moon stood before him.

Then was there a burning in the blood of the boy, as she stooped with arms held wide; and he was wrapped about as with a white fire, through which the face grew down with lips that burned his lips

The Singer of the Ache

as they touched, and sent pale lightnings flashing through him.

And as the dream woman turned to run swiftly back up the star-trails he who dreamed reached out his arms and clutched at the garments of light that he might hold the thing that fled, for dearer than life it seemed to him now.

And he woke. His face was in the dust. His clutching hands were full of dust.

Wahoo! the bitter hill of dreams! Have you climbed it, O White Brother, even as I?

And in the morning he told the dream to his father, who frowned; to his mother—and she wept. And they said: "This is not a warrior's dream, nor is it the dream of a Holy Man; nor yet is it the vision of a mighty bison hunter. Some strange new trail this boy shall follow—a cloudy, cloudy trail! Yet let him go a third time to the hill—may not the true dream linger?"

And the boy went up again; his step was light; his heart sang wildly in his breast. For once again he wished to see the Woman of the Moon.

But no dream came. And in the morning the pinch of grief was upon his face and he shook his fists at the laughing Day. Then did he and a great Ache walk down the hill together. All things were little and nothing good to see. And in among his people he went, staring with eyes that burned as with a fever, and lo! he was a stranger walking there! Only the Dream walked with him.

And the sunlight burned the blue, much-beaded tepee of the sky, and left it black; and as it burned and blackened, burned and blackened, he who dreamed the strange dream found no pleasure in the ways of men. Only in gazing upon the round moon did he find pleasure. And when even this was hidden from him for many nights and days he went about with drooping head, and sorrow was in his eyes.

And in these days he made wild songs; for never do the happy ones make songs—they only sing them. Songs that none had heard, he made; not such as toilers make to shout about the camp fires when the meat goes round. Yet was the thick, hot dust of weary trails blown through them, and cries of dying warriors, and shrieks of widowed women, and whimpering of sick *zhinga zhingas;* and also there was in them the pang of big man-hearts, the ache of toiling women's backs, the hunger, the thirst, the wish to live, the fear to die!

So the people said: "Who is this *nu zhinga* who sings of trails he never followed, of battles he never fought? No father is he—and yet he sings as one who has lost a son! Of the pain of love he sings —yet never has he looked upon a girl!"

And it was the way of the boy to answer: "I seek what I do not find, and so I sing!"

The Singer of the Ache

And the nights and days made summers and winters, and thus it was with the Singer of the Ache. He grew tall even to the height of a man—yet was he no man. For little did he care to hunt, and the love of battles was not his. Nor his the laughter of the feast fires. Nor did he look upon the face of any maiden with soft eyes.

And the father and mother, who felt the first frosts upon their heads, said: "Our son is now a man; should he not build a lodge and fill it with a woman? Should we not hear the laughter of *zhinga zhingas* once again before we take the black trail together?"

And because his father had many ponies, many maidens were brought before him for his choosing. But he looked coldly upon them and he said: "The stars are my sisters and my brothers, and the Moon is my woman, giving me songs for children. Soon shall there be a long trail for me."

Thereat a cry went up against him and more and more he walked a stranger. Only the Dream walked with him; and he sang the songs that ache.

Harsh words the father spoke: "Does the tribe need songs? Can hungry people eat a silly shout, or will enemies be conquered with a singing?"

But the mother wept and said: "Say not so of him. Do not his songs bring tears, so strange and sweet they are at times? Does a man quarrel with

the vessel from which he drinks sweet waters, even
if it be broken and useless for the cooking?"

And the father frowned and said: "Give me
many laughers, and I will conquer all the enemies
and fill all the kettles of the feasts! Let the weep-
ers and makers of tears drag wood with the women.
Always have I been a fighter of battles and a killer
of bison. This is not my son!"

And it happened one night that the Singer stood
alone in the midst of his people, when the round
moon raised a shining forehead out of the dark,
and grew big and flooded all the hills with white
light. And the Singer raised his arms to it and sang
as one who loves might sing to a maiden coming
forth flashing with many beads from her tepee.

And the people laughed and a mutter ran about:
"To whom does the fool sing thus?"

Soft, shining eyes he turned upon them, and he
said: "Even to the Woman of the Moon! See
where she looks into the North with white face
raised to where the lonesome star hangs patient!"

And the people said: "This is the talk of a fool
—no woman do we see!"

And then the Singer sang a new song through
which these words ran often: "Only he sees who
can—only he sees who can!"

So now he walked a fool among his people, singing the songs that ache.

Wahoo! bitter it is to be a fool! And yet, O

The Singer of the Ache

White Brother, only they who have been fools are wise at last!

And it happened one summer that the village was builded in the flat lands by the Big Smoky Water. And there came snorting up the stream a *monda geeung,* the magic fire-boat of the palefaces. Up to the shore it swam, and they who guided it tied it to the sand, for its fires were hungry and there was much wood in our lands.

And all the villagers gathered there to see the magic swimmer of the palefaces; and among them came the lonesome singing fool.

And it happened that a woman of the palefaces came forth and stood high up, and looked upon us, smiling. White as a snowfall in the late spring was her face, and her hair was like the sun upon a cloud. And we all stared wide-mouthed upon her, for never before had her kind come into the prairies.

Also stared the fool. Even long after all the people had gone he stared; even until the smoky breath of the fire-boat writhed like a big black serpent out of the place where the stream runs out of the sky.

And then he laid his head upon his knees and wept; for a longing, bigger than the wish to live, or the fear to die, had come upon him.

Very early in the morning, when the sleep of all things is deepest, he arose from sleepless blankets. He called his pony from the grazing places, and he mounted for a long ride. Into the North he rode, and as he rode he talked to himself and to the silence that clung about him: "It was the Woman of the Moon! Into the North she went, even unto the quiet place where the lonesome star hangs patient. There shall I ride—there shall I ride! For there do all my songs take wings and fly; and there at last their meanings await me. There shall I ride—there shall I ride!"

And the fires of the day burned out the stars and died; downward and inward rushed the black, black ashes of the night. And still he rode toward the North.

And like the flashing of a midnight torch through a hole in a tepee flashed the days and passed. And still he rode.

Through many villages of strange peoples did he ride, and everywhere strange tongues and strange eyes questioned him; and he answered: "Into the North I ride to find the Woman of the Moon!"

And the people pitied him, because he seemed as one whose head was filled with ghostly things; and they fed him.

Farther and farther into the waste places he pushed, making the empty spaces sweet and sad with his singing; and the winter came. Thin and lean he grew, and his pony grew lean and thin.

And the white, mad spirits of the snow beat about

the two. And now and then snow ghosts writhed up out of the ground and twisted and twirled and moaned, until they took on the shape of her he sought. And ever he followed them; and ever they fell back into the ground. And the world was bitter cold.

Wahoo! the snow ghosts that we follow, O White Brother!

And the time came when the pony was no longer a pony, but a quiet heap of bones; and upon this sat the man who walked for the moon. Then did the strength go out of him, and he turned his sharp face to the South. He sang no more for many days, for his body was as a lodge in which a fair woman lies dead with no mourners around. And at last he wakened in a strange lodge in a village of strangers.

And it happened when the green things pushed upward into the sun again that a young man who seemed very old, for he was bent, his face was thin, his eyes were very big, hobbled back into the village of his people.

And he went to a lodge which was empty, for the father with his frowning and the mother with her weeping had taken the long trail, upon which comes no moon and never the sun rises—but the stars are there.

Many days he lay within the lonesome lodge. And it happened that a maiden, one whom he had pushed aside in other days, came into the lodge with meat and water.

So at last he said: "I have sought and have not found; therefore will I be as other men. I will fill this lodge with a woman—and this is she. Henceforth I shall forget the dream that led me; I shall be a hunter of bison and a killer of enemies; for after all, what else?"

And this he did.

So all the village buzzed with kindly words. "The fool has come back wise!" they said.

And as the seasons passed there grew the laughter of *zhingas zhingas* in the lodge of the man who walked no more for the moon.

But a sadness was upon his face. And after a while the dream came back and brought the singing. Less and less he looked upon the woman and the children. Less and less he sought the bison, until at last Hunger came into that lodge and sat beside the fire.

Then again the old cry of the people grew up: "The fool still lives! He sings while his lodge is empty. His woman has become a stranger to him, and his children are as though a stranger had fathered them! Shall the fool eat and only sing?"

And a snarling cry grew up: "Cast out the fool!"

And it was done.

So out of the village stumbled the singing fool, and his head was bloody with the stones the people

The Singer of the Ache

threw. Very old he seemed, though his years were not many. Into the North he went, and men saw his face no more.

But lo! many seasons passed and yet he lived and was among all peoples! For often on hot dusty trails weary men sat down to sing his songs; and women, weeping over fallen braves, found his songs upon their lips. And when the hunger came his strange wild cries went among the people. And all were comforted!

And this, O White Brother, is the story of the fool who walked for the moon!

THE LOOK IN THE FACE

IT was after one of the Saturday night feasts at No-Teeth Lodge that I drew my old friend, Half-a-Day, to one side where the shadows were not broken by the firelight.

"Tell me another story, Half-a-Day," I said.

He grunted and puffed at his pipe in silence.

"Have I not given much meat to the feast and did I not throw silver on the drums?"

"Ah," he assented.

"Then I wish to hear a story."

"You are my friend," he began with majestic deliberation, speaking in his own tongue; "for we have eaten meat together from the same kettle and looked upon each other through the pipe smoke. It will therefore make me glad to tell you a story about buffalo meat——"

"Ah, about a hunt?"

"And a *me-zhinga* [girl]——"

"Oh, a love story!"

"And a man whom I wished to kill."

"Good! And did you kill him?"

"My brother is like all his white brothers, who

The Look In the Face

leap at things. Never will they wait. If I said yes or no, then would I have no story."

"Then give me a puff at the pipe, Half-a-Day, and I will be patient."

Half-a-Day gave me the pipe and began, with eyes staring through the fire and far away down the long trail that leads back to youth.

"Many winters and summers ago I was a young man; now I am slow when I walk and my head looks much to the ground. But I remember, and now again I am young for a little while. I can smell the fires in the evening that roared upward then, even tho' they are cold these many moons and their ashes scattered. And I can see the face of Paezha [flower], the one daughter of Douba Mona, for my eyes are young too. And Douba Mona was a great man.

"Paezha was not so big as the other squaws, and could never be so big, because she was not made for building tepees and bringing wood and water. She was little and thin and good to see like some of your white sisters, and there was no face in the village of my people like her face. Her feet touched the ground like a little wind from the south; her body bent easily like a willow; I think her eyes were like stars."

I smiled here, because the simile has become so trite among us white lovers. But Half-a-Day saw me not; he looked down the long trail that leads back to youth, leading through and beyond the fire.

"And I looked upon her face until I could see nothing else—not the sunrise nor the sunset nor the moon and stars. Her face became a medicine face to me; because I was a young man and it was good to see her. And also, I was a poor young man; my father had few ponies, and her father had as many as one could see with a big look.

"But I was strong and proud and in the long nights I dreamed of Paezha, till one day I said: 'I will have her and I will fight all the braves in all the villages before I will give her up. Then afterwards I will get many ponies like her father.'

"So one evening when the meat boiled over the fires, I went down to the big spring and hid in the grass, for it was the habit of Paezha to bring cold water to her father in the evenings, carrying it in a little kettle no bigger than your head covering, for she was not big.

"And I lay waiting. I could not hear the bugs nor the running of the spring water nor the wind in the willows, because my heart sang so loud.

"And I heard a step—and it was Paezha. She leaned over the spring, and looked down; then there were two Paezhas, so my wish for her was doubled and had the strength of two wishes.

"I arose from the grass. She looked upon me and fear came into her eyes; for there was that in

The Look In the Face

my face which wished to conquer, and I was very strong. Like the *tae-chuga* [antelope] she leaped and ran with wind-feet down the valley. I was without breath when I caught her, and I lifted her with arms too strong, for she cried."

Half-a-Day reached toward me for the pipe and puffed strongly.

"Then as I held her, I looked upon her face and saw what I had never seen before: a look in the face that was sad and weak and frightened, begging for pity. Only it was not all that; it was shining like the sun through a cloud, and it was stronger than I, for I became weak and could hold her no longer. A little while she looked with wide eyes upon me; and then I saw what makes the squaws break their backs carrying wood and water and *zhinga zhingas* [babies]; also what makes men fight and do great deeds that are not selfish.

"Then she ran from me and I fell upon my face and cried like a *zhinga zhinga* at the back of a squaw —I know not why."

Half-a-Day puffed hard at his pipe, then sighing handed it to me.

"Have you seen that look in the face, White Brother?" he said, staring upon me with eyes that mastered me.

"I am very young," I answered.

"But when you see it, it will make you old," continued Half-a-Day; "for when I arose and went back to the village I was old and nothing was the same. From that time I could look into the eyes of the biggest brave without trembling, for I was a man and I had seen the look.

"And it was in the time when the sunflowers die, the time for the hunting of bison. So the whole tribe made ready for the hunt. One morning we rode out of the village on the bison trail; and we were so many that the foremost were lost in the hills when the last left the village. And we all sang, but the ponies neighed at the lonesome lodges, for they were leaving home.

"Many days we travelled toward the evenings, and there was song in me even when I did not sing; for always I rode near Paezha, who rode in a blanket swung on poles between two ponies, for she was the daughter of a rich man. And I spoke gentle words to her, and she smiled—because she had seen my weakness in the valley of the big spring. Also I picked flowers for her, and she took them.

"But one day Black Dog rode on the other side of her and spoke soft words. And a strange look was on the face of Paezha, but not the look I had seen. So I drove away the bitterness of my heart and spoke good words to Black Dog. But he was sullen, and also he was better to look upon than I. I can say this now, for I have felt the winds of many winters.

"Many sleeps we rode toward the places of the

The Look In the Face

evening. The moon was thin and small and bent like a child's bow when we started, and it hung low above the sunset. And as we travelled it grew bigger, ever farther toward the place of morning, until it was like a white sun. Then at last it came forth no more, but rested in its black tepee after its steep trail.

"And all the while we strained our eyes from many lonesome hilltops, but saw no bison. Scarcer and scarcer became the food, for the summer had been a summer of fighting; we had conquered and feasted much, hunted little.

"So it happened that we who were strong took less meat that the weaker might live until we found the bison. And all the time the strength of Paezha's face grew upon me, so that I divided my meat with her. It made me sing to see her eat.

"One day she said to me: 'Why do you sing, Half-a-Day, when the people are sad?' And I said: 'I sing because I am empty.' And Black Dog, who rode upon the other side, he did not sing. So she said to him: 'Why do you not sing, Black Dog? Is it because we do not find the bison?' And Black Dog said: 'I do not sing because I am empty.'

"All day I was afraid that Paezha had judged between us, seeing me so light of thought and deed.

"One evening we stopped for the night and there was not enough meat left to keep us three sleeps longer. The squaws did not sing as they pitched the tepees. They were empty, the braves were empty, and the *zhinga zhingas* whined like little baby wolves at their mothers' backs, for the milk they drank was thin milk. No one spoke. The fires boomed up and made the hills sound as with the bellowing of bulls, and the sound mocked us. The dark came down; we sat about the fires but we did not speak. We groaned, for we were very empty, and we could not eat until we had slept. Once every sleep we ate, and we had eaten once.

"That night the wise old men gathered together in the tepee of the chiefs and sang medicine songs that Wakunda [God] might hear and see our suffering; then might he send us the bison.

"I heard the songs and I felt a great strength grow up out of my emptiness. Then I said: 'I will go to the fathers and they will send me in search of the bison; and I will find the bison for Paezha that she may not starve.' I had forgotten myself and my people. I knew only Paezha, for that day I had heard her moan, having nothing more to give.

"And I went to the big tepee. I stood amongst the fathers and lifted a strong voice in spite of my emptiness: 'Give me a swift pony and a little meat and I will find the bison!'

"And the old men sighed as they looked upon me. And Douba Mona, her father, being one of the wise men, said: 'I see a light in his eye and hear a strength in his voice. Give him the swift pony and the little meat. If he finds the bison, then shall he have Paezha, for well I see that there is something between them. Also he shall have many ponies; I have many.'

"And these words made me full as though I had sat at a feast.

"So the next morning I took the swift pony and the little meat and galloped toward the evening. The people did not take the trail that day, for toil makes hunger.

"Two sleeps I ròde, singing songs and dreaming dreams of Paezha. And on the evening of the third sunlight I stopped upon a hill, and turned my pony loose to feed. I was sick and weak because my emptiness had come back upon me and I had not yet found the bison. I fell upon my face and moaned, and my emptiness sent me to sleep.

"When I awoke, someone sat beside me—and it was Black Dog. He breathed soft words. 'I have come to watch over Half-a-Day,' he said, 'because I am older and a bigger man.'

"I spoke not a word, but my heart was warm toward Black Dog, for my dreams of Paezha had made me kind.

" 'Well I know,' he said, and his voice was soft as a woman's; 'well I know what Half-a-Day dreams about. And I have come to watch over him that his dream may come true.'

"Then being a young man and full of kindness, I

[21]

told Black Dog of the look I had seen in the face of Paezha. And he bit his lips and made a sound far down in his throat. And I fell to sleep wondering much.

"When I awoke, the ponies were gone, the meat was gone, Black Dog was gone. I grew strong as a bear. I shrieked into the stillness! I shook my fists at the sun! I cursed Black Dog! I stumbled on over the hills and valleys, shouting, singing, hurling big words of little meaning into the yellow day.

"Before night came I found the body of a dead wolf, and I fell upon it like a crow. I tore its flesh with my teeth. I called it Black Dog. I ate much. It smelled bad. I found a little stream and drank much. It was almost lost in the mud. I slept and dreamed of Paezha. I awoke, and it was day again. I found the dead wolf again. I ate. Then I was stronger and I went on into the yellow prairie.

"Toward evening I heard a thundering, yet saw no cloud. It was the dry time. Still it thundered, thundered—yet no cloud. I ran to the top of a hill and gazed.

"Bison! Bison! The prairie was full of bison, and they were feeding slowly toward the camp of my people.

"I turned, I ran! I did not make a sound, tho' I wished to cry out. I needed all my strength for running, for I had no pony. I ran, ran, ran. I fell, I got up, I fell. Night came; I walked. Morning came; still I walked. Night came; I stumbled. And in the morning I was creeping.

"I do not know when I reached the camp of my people. I remember only a shouting and a sudden moving of the tribe. And then, after many bad dreams, I was awake again and the people were feasting. They had found the bison.

"Then, when we were on the home trail, I learned of the treachery of Black Dog. He had told my people how he had found Half-a-Day dead upon the prairie, but was too weak to bring him back. And the people believed for a time. And Black Dog spoke soft words to Paezha, brave words to Douba Mona, until I was almost forgotten.

"But now I was a great man among my people, and Black Dog could not raise his head, for he had seen hate in the people's eyes.

"And in the time of the first frosts we reached our village and Paezha became my squaw. Also I got the ponies."

Here Half-a-Day paused to fill his pipe.

"It is a good story, Half-a-Day," I said. Half-a-Day lit his pipe, stared long into the glow of the embers, for the fires had fallen, and sighed.

"I have not spoken yet," he said; "for one day in the time of the first snow, Paezha lay dead in my lodge, and my breast ached. Black Dog had killed her at the big spring. At the same place where I had first seen the look, there he killed her.

Indian Tales and Others

"I remember that I sat beside her two sleeps and cried like a *zhinga zhinga*. And my friends came to me, whispering bitter words into my ears. 'Kill Black Dog,' they said. And I said: 'Bring him here to me, and I will kill him; my legs will not carry me.'

"But the fathers of the council would not have it so. And when they had buried her on the hill above the village, I awoke as from a long sleep, a very long sleep, and I was full of hate. They kept me in my lodge. They would not let me kill. I wished to kill! I wished to tear him as I tore the stinking wolf with my teeth! *I wished to kill!*"

Half-a-Day had risen to his feet, his fists clenched, his eyes shining with a cold light.

"Come, Half-a-Day," I said, "it is long past, and now it is only a story."

"It is more than a story!" he said. "I lived it. I wished to kill!"

He sat down again, and a softer light came into his eyes.

"And the time came," he went on with a weary voice, "when Black Dog should be cast forth from the tribe, according to the old custom. I said, 'I will follow Black Dog, and I will see him die.' And he was cast forth. I followed, and it was very cold. The snow cried under my feet, and I followed in the night.

"But Black Dog did not know I followed. I was

ever near him like a shadow. I did not sleep; I watched Black Dog. I meant to see him die.

"In his first sleep I crept upon him. I stole his meat; I stole his weapons. Now he would die, and I would be there to see. I would laugh, I would sing while he died.

"In the cold, pale morning I lay huddled in a clump of sage and I saw him get up, look for his meat and weapons, then stagger away into the lonesome places of the snow. And I sang a low song to myself. The time would come when I should see Black Dog die. I did not feel the cold; I did not grow weary; I was never hungry. And in the evenings I was ever near enough to hear him groan as he wrapped himself in his blankets. Often I crept up to him and looked upon his face in the light of the stars, and I saw my time coming, for his face was thinner and not so good to look upon as in the time when the sunflowers died.

"I could have killed him, but then he could not have heard me sing, he could not have heard me laugh. So I waited and followed and watched. I ate my meat raw that Black Dog might not see my fire. Also I watched to see that he found nothing to eat; and he found nothing.

"One day I lay upon the summit of a hill and saw him totter in the valley. Then I could be quiet no longer. I raised my voice and shouted: 'Fall, Black

Dog! Even so Half-a-Day fell when Black Dog stole his meat and his pony!'

"And I saw him get up and stare about, for I was hidden. Then his voice came up to me over the snow; it was a thin voice: 'I know you, Half-a-Day! Come and kill me!'

" 'Half-a-Day never killed a sick man nor a squaw,' I shouted, and then I laughed. Then Black Dog shook his fists at the four corners of the sky and stumbled off into the hills, and I followed. Now my time was very near, for Black Dog felt my nearness and he knew that he would die and I should see him.

"And one evening my time came. Black Dog was in the valley by a frozen stream, and he fell upon his face, sending forth a thin cry as he fell. He did not get up.

"I ran down to where he lay—and I laughed. I heard him groan. I rolled him over on his back and looked upon his face.

"He opened his eyes and they were very dim and sunken. His face was sharp. I sat down beside him. I said, 'Now die, and I will sing about it.'

"Then his face changed. It became a squaw's face—*and it had the look!*—a look that was sad and weak and frightened and begging for pity. And it seemed to me that it was not the face of Black Dog any more. *It had the look!* I had seen it in the face of Paezha by the spring!

The Look In the Face

I grew soft. There was a great springtime in my breast. The ice was breaking up. I wrapped my blankets about him. I gave him meat. He stared at me and ate like a wolf. I spoke soft words. I made a fire from the brush that was on the frozen stream. I warmed him and he grew stronger. All night I watched him and in the morning I said: 'Take my bow and arrows, Black Dog; I wish to die. Go on and live.' For I had lost the wish to kill; I only wished to die. And he said no word; but his eyes were changed.

"I staggered away on the back trail. I had no meat, I had no blankets, I had no weapons. I meant to die.

"But I did not die. When I lay down at night, worn out and half frozen, someone wrapped blankets about me and built a fire by me. In the mornings I found food beside me. And so it was for many sleeps until at last I came to the village of my people, broken, caring for nothing. And I was thin, my face was sharp, my eyes were sunken, my step was slow.

"And the people looked upon me with wonder, saying: 'Half-a-Day has come back from killing Black Dog.'

"But the truth was different."

When Half-a-Day had finished, he stared long into the fire without speaking.

"Do you think Black Dog was a coward?" I asked at length. "Perhaps he only loved too much."

"I do not know," said Half-a-Day; "I only know sometimes I wish I had not looked upon his face."

THE WHITE WAKUNDA

H E was the son of Sky-Walker's oldest squaw and he was born in the time when the lone goose flies (February). It was a very bitter winter, so that many years after the old men spoke of it as "the winter of the big snows."

Sky-Walker, his father, was a seer of great visions, and he had a power that was more than the power of strong arms. He was a thunder man, and he could make rain.

And when Sky-Walker's oldest squaw bore a son there was much wonder in the village, for she was far past her summer and the frost had already fallen on her hair. Also, she was lean and wrinkled.

So the old men and women came to the lodge of Sky-Walker and looked upon the newborn child. They looked and they shook their heads, for the child was not as a child should be. He was no bigger than a baby coyote littered in a terrible winter after a summer of famine. He was not fat.

"He can never be a *waschuscha* [brave]," said one old man; "I have seen many *zhinga zhingas* [babies] who grew strong, but they were not like this one. He will carry wood and water."

And Sky-Walker's old squaw arose from the blankets where she lay with the child, and sat up, fixing eyes of bitterness upon those who came to pity, and she said:

"He will be more than a killer of men or a hunter of bison. Wakunda sent him to me, for I am old and past my time. See, I am lean and wrinkled, and it is already winter in my hair. Also I had visions. Let my man tell you; he knows."

And Sky-Walker, sitting beside the old mother, gave words to the old men and women, who knew his little words to be bigger than the big words of most men.

"The woman speaks true. She is past her time, and she has seen things that made me wonder, and I am wise. She had visions, but in them there was no singing of arrows, nor drumming of pony hoofs, nor dancing of braves in war paint, nor cries of conquered enemies; neither was there any thunder or lightning.

"There was only the soft speaking of quiet things —the sound of the growing of green things under the sun. And before the last moon died, once she wakened me from sleeping, for she had had a dream. She saw her son walking a mighty man among the tribes, yet he had no weapons.

"And a great light, greater than sunlight, was about him. This she told me. Many times have we seen together the drifting of the snows, and always her words were true words.

The White Wakunda

"And see, it is a boy, even as she dreamed. Also he has come in the time when the lone goose flies. I see much in this. He shall be alone, but high in loneliness, and he shall go far, far! Look where he gazes upon you with man-eyes! Are they the eyes of a *zhinga zhinga?*"

The old folks looked and pitied no more, for the eyes were not as other eyes. They had a strange light, making the old ones wonder.

So the word passed around and around the circle of lodges that Sky-Walker's oldest squaw had a son who was not a common *zhinga zhinga*. And as the talk grew, the name of the child grew with it. So he was called Wa-choo-bay, "the Holy One."

And as Wa-choo-bay grew, so grew the wonder of the people, for he never cried, and he talked soon. Also from the first he appeared as one over whom many winters had passed.

When he reached that age when he should have played with the other boys, he did not play, but was much alone upon the prairie outside the village. He never took part in the game of Pawnee *zhay-day,* the game of spear and hoop, which made the other boys laugh and shout.

One evening in his fifth year, his father, Sky-Walker, said to him:

"It is the time for the coming of the dreams to Wa-choo-bay. Let him go afar into a lonesome place without food and lift his hands and his voice

[31]

to Wakunda. Four sleeps let him stay in the lonesome place, that his dream may come."

So his mother smeared his forehead with mud
and muttered to the spirits:

"Thus shall you know Wa-choo-bay, who goes
forth to have his first dream. Send him a good
dream."

And Wa-choo-bay went forth into a lonesome
place without food.

And on the morning of the fifth day, when the
squaws were making fires, he returned, and as he
entered the village and went to the lodge of his
father the squaws gazed upon his face, seeing that
which was very strange.

They wakened the sleepers in the lodges, saying:

"Wa-choo-bay is come back with a strange medi-
cine-look upon his face! He has had a great dream;
come and see."

And the village awoke and crowded about the
lodge of Sky-Walker, who came forth and said:

"Go away! Something great has happened to
my *nu-zhinga* [boy], and he is about to tell me his
dream."

And the people went away, awed and silent.

In the stillness of his lodge Sky-Walker gazed
upon the boy's face and said:

"What has Wa-choo-bay seen?"

And Wa-choo-bay said:

The White Wakunda

"I went far into a lonesome place; there was nothing but the crows and the prairie and the sky. I lifted my hands and my voice as you told me. I said the words you told me. Then I slept, and when I awoke this is what I remembered; the rest was like big things moving in the mist.

"I was on the shore of the Ne Shoda [Missouri], and a little canoe came up to me, and I got in, for a voice told me to get in. Then the canoe swam out into the water and went fast. I went toward the place of summer. I rode far, many sleeps, and then as I was about to come to the end of my long riding, I awoke. Four times I saw this, and then I came here. What does it mean?"

"I do not know," said Sky-Walker. "I must think hard, and then maybe I shall know."

And Sky-Walker shut himself in his lodge and thought hard for four sleeps. And when the fifth morning came he said to Wa-choo-bay:

"I have thought hard, and now I know that it is the big things moving in the mist that you must see. Go forth and dream again in the lonesome place."

And so Wa-choo-bay went forth with the mud on his brow, crying to the spirits that he might see the big things that moved in the mist. He slept and dreamed. Again he was in the canoe and he rode far.

Then at last the river tossed him upon the sand,

and lo! there was a big, big village before him, and the lodges of it were strange and very big. Then the big village wavered like the picture of something in a pool that is disturbed, and vanished. And the sun was on the hills.

So Wa-choo-bay went back to his father and told him what he had seen, and Sky-Walker said:

"This is very strange. After many sunlights of flowing, the big muddy water comes to a place where the white men have a very big village. Let the sunlights pass, and then we shall know the meaning of this dream."

The days grew into years, and Wa-choo-bay sat at the feet of the old men, learning much.

He learned the names of the thunder spirits that are never spoken aloud. He learned the songs that the thunder spirits love. He learned to call the rain. He learned the manner of the rite of *Wa-zhin-a-dee*, by which one may kill a man without the use of weapons. And when he had grown to be a tall youth, he was taken into the sacred lodge where the holy relics are kept. For it seemed plain that Wakunda meant him for a great medicine-man.

But it was in the summer when he had reached the height of a man that Wa-choo-bay did that which marked him for the lonesome way.

It happened that the summer had been one of peace and plenty; so the Omahas called in the Pawnees and the Poncas for a powwow, which is a great feast and a talking.

And the two neighboring tribes had taken the peace trail and come to the Omaha village. Then there was much painting in the colors of peace, and the village that the three tribes made was more than one could see with a look.

In a great circle it lay in the flat lands of Ne Shoda, with an opening to the place of morning. And in the centre there was built a large semi-circular shade of the willow boughs, in which the braves would dance and sing, giving away presents of ponies, furs, hides, and trinkets that please the eye.

One day there was a great dancing and a great giving away. Many ponies had been led into the sunny centre of the semi-circular shade, and given away to those whom the criers called.

And Wa-choo-bay was there, standing tall and thin, alone amid all the revelers, for more and more as the sunlights passed he thought deep thoughts.

Among the Poncas sat a young squaw who was good to see, for she was slender and taller than a common brave. And upon her forehead was the tattooed sunspot that marked her for the daughter of the owner of many ponies. She was called Umba (Sunlight), and she was the best to see of all the daughters of the assembled tribes.

To-day she sat amid the reveling and saw none

of it. She saw only the tall youth, standing alone like a beech tree among a cluster of scrub oaks. And her eyes grew soft as she looked.

And when the centre of the place of shade had cleared, she arose and walked into the centre. There she stood, with soft eyes fixed upon Wa-choo-bay.

At length she raised her arms toward him and sang a low, droning song, like that a mother sings to her child in the evening when the fires burn blue.

And all the people listened, breathless, for she was fair, and the song, which was a song of love, was sung to Wa-choo-bay alone, standing thin and tall and deep in thought.

Then when her song had ceased, she took off her blanket of dyed buckskin, and, holding it at arm's length toward Wa-choo-bay, she said:

"I give my blanket to the tall and lonesome one. Let him come and take it, and I will follow him on all his trails, even if they be hard trails that lead to death!"

And Wa-choo-bay raised his eyes and gazed with a sad look upon the Ponca woman. His voice came strong, but soft:

"I cannot take the blanket; neither shall I ever take a squaw. For I am a dreamer of dreams. I shall never hear *zhinga zhingas* laughing about my lodge. I am going on a long trail, for I follow a dream. Yet have I never seen a woman so good to see. There is an ache in my breast as I speak.

The White Wakunda

Let this woman follow one who kills enemies and hunts bison. I dream dreams, and a long trail is before me, and its end is in the mist."

Then Umba moaned and walked out of the circle with her head bowed.

And Sky-Walker, seeing this, said:

"It is even as I said. He was born in the time of the lone goose. He shall be alone, but high in loneliness; and he shall go far, far."

And the time came when the tribes took the homeward trail. Then one day Wa-choo-bay raised his voice among the people and said:

"My time is come to go. I take a long, lonesome trail, for a dream dreamed many times is leading me."

Then he went down to the great river where a canoe lay, and the people followed.

They said no word as he pushed the canoe into the current and shot downstream, for a white light was upon his face, and the dream rode with him.

Then Sky-Walker and his old squaw climbed a high bluff and watched the speck that was Wa-choo-bay fading in the mist.

"This is the last I shall see," said the old woman, "for I am old and the winter is in my hair. But great things will happen when I am gone."

And under the shade of a lean hand raised browward she saw the black speck vanish in the blue.

Indian Tales and Others

Summers and winters passed. Sky-Walker and his old squaw died; the name of Wa-choo-bay became a dim and mystic thing. Yet often about the fires of winter, when the wind moaned about the lodges, the old men talked of the going away of the Holy One, making the eyes of the youths grow big with wonder.

And often the old men and women gazed from the high bluff down the dim stretches of the muddy river, wondering when Wa-choo-bay would come back, for it was said that great things would happen at his coming.

It happened many years after the going away of Wa-choo-bay that the Omaha tribe had its village in the valley on a creek near the big muddy water.

It was the time when the sunflowers made sunlight in the valleys and when the women were busy pulling weeds from the gardens.

One evening a band of youths, who had been playing on the bluffs overlooking the far reaches of the river, came with breathless speed and terror-stricken faces into the village.

"*Monda geeung* [devil boat]!" they cried, pointing to the river. "A big canoe breathing out smoke and fire is swimming up Ne Shoda."

The whole village scrambled up the bluffs, and what they saw was not forgotten for many moons. It was a boat, but it was not as other boats. It

The White Wakunda

breathed smoke and fire. It grunted and puffed like a swimmer in a heavy current.

It had a great arm that reached before it. Also it had two noses, where the smoke and fire came out. It had eyes along its side that sparkled in the evening sunlight. There was none to paddle it, yet it moved steadily against the current.

The people stood bunched closely together and shivering with fear as the monster approached. With a chugging and a swishing and a coughing, it swam, turning its head toward the bluff where the people watched and reaching out its one big arm toward them.

"It sees us! It wishes to eat us!" cried the people, and like a herd of frightened bison they ran to their village.

But the devil-swimmer did not come. The people listened. At length the sound of the mighty breathing stopped, then it began again and grew dimmer and dimmer until it died away far up the stream.

And when the people came forth cautiously from their hiding, a man, tall, thin, with a strange look upon his bronze face, stood in the center of the village.

Awed by the mien of the stranger, the people stared in silence. The sun had fallen and the shadows of the evening were about him. Also he wore garments that were not as Wakunda meant garments should be.

The stranger cast a long gaze about him, then raised his arms and said in a voice that was strong but soft:

"I breathe peace upon my people."

The words were Omaha words, yet they sounded strange.

Again the voice was raised in the shadows and passed like a wind among the people, shaking them.

"I am Wa-choo-bay—he who followed the long dream-trail—and I am come back with a great wisdom for the tribes."

But the people only trembled, and the old men whispered:

"It is not Wa-choo-bay, but his spirit. Well is the face remembered, but the words are not man-words."

Then the stranger passed about the circle of the wondering people, touching them as he went, for he had heard the whispering of the old men. And the people shrank from him.

"I am Wa-choo-bay," cried the stranger again. "I am the son of Sky-Walker. I am a man, and not a spirit. Give me meat, for I am hungry."

And they gave him meat, and he ate. Then only did the people know him for a man.

In the days that followed, Wa-choo-bay told many strange things of the white-faced race whose camp fires were kindled ever nearer and nearer the people of the prairie. Also he said words that were not common words. They were medicine-words.

And before many moons had grown and died these things traveled far and wide across the prairie, until in many tribes the wonder grew. Around many camp fires was told the tale of how an Omaha had come back after being many years in the lands that lay toward the place of summer; also of the devil-boat in which he came, and of the new wisdom he was talking.

So there was a great moving of the tribes toward the village of the Omahas. The Poncas, the Pawnees, the Osages, the Missouris, the Otoes—all heard the strange tale and took the trail that led to the village lying in the flat lands of Ne Shoda.

And in the time when the prairie was brown there was a great gathering of the prairie peoples in the flat lands.

The cluster of villages that they made was so broad that a strong man walked from morning until the sun was high before he reached the other side. Then one morning when the tribes had gathered Wa-choo-bay went to the top of a bluff that stood bleak against the sky, and the people followed, sitting below him upon the hillside, for they wished to hear the strange words that would be spoken that day.

Wa-choo-bay, standing thin and tall against the sky, raised his arms and his face to the heavens, breathing strange words above the people, upon whom a great hush fell.

And it happened that in the hush a tamed wolf among the people near the summit of the bluff raised its snout and mourned into the stillness.

And its master beat it for the noise it made until it cried with pain.

Then a strange thing happened. Wa-choo-bay walked in among the gazers and laid soft hands upon the wolf, calling it by gentle names until it licked his hands.

And when he returned to the summit, the wolf followed, licking the feet of Wa-choo-bay as it went.

Then Wa-choo-bay raised his voice, and it went even to the farthest listener, though it seemed a soft voice.

"This is the first I shall teach you: be kind to everything that lives."

And the people wondered much. This was a new teaching.

In the hush of awe that fell, Wa-choo-bay spoke again, while the wolf sat by him, licking his feet. He told of his being in the lands that lay toward the summer; of the great white-faced race that lived there; of the great villages that they built, having lodges bigger than half a prairie village.

He told of the strength of this great white-faced race; of how they were moving steadily toward the people of the prairie. And then he told in quaint phrases the story of Jesus and His teachings of kindness.

"These things I learned from the great medicine-men of the white-faced race, and they are wise men," said Wa-choo-bay. "It is this that has made their people great. So I have come to say: Have no more fighting on the prairie; be one great tribe, even like the white-faces; build great villages like them, for I have learned that only they who build great villages and do not wander shall live. The others must flee like the bison when hunters follow.

"And I will teach you the wise words of the great white Wakunda's Son, who died because he loved all the tribes. It is a teaching of peace—a teaching that we be kind to our enemies."

Then there arose one among the Osages, an old man, and he said:

"These are big words. Let Wa-choo-bay call down rain upon us if this big white God loves him."

Then arose one among the Pawnees, and he cried in broken Omaha:

"I say with my Osage brother, let Wa-choo-bay do some medicine-deed, that we may know him for a holy one."

And still another among the Poncas arose and said:

"If this be true that we have heard, how Wa-choo-bay came back in a holy boat, and that his big white Wakunda is so strong and loves Wa-choo-bay, let him send the rain, and we will fall upon our faces."

Then the whole concourse of tribes sent up a shout:

"Give us some medicine-deed!"

And when the shout had died, Wa-choo-bay smiled a smile of pity and said:

"I am not the big white Wakunda; I am only one who talks for Him and loves Him, for I have seen a new light. I can do no medicine-deeds. Neither can anyone among you do medicine-deeds. It is all a dreaming—and we must awaken."

Then there was a great crying, an angry storm of voices about the hill. It beat upon the bleak summit where Wa-choo-bay stood with face and hands raised to the heavens, breathing a prayer of the white-faces.

There was a breaking up of the crowd and a walking away. But one among the people hurled a stone with sure aim and struck Wa-choo-bay upon the side of the face. He staggered, and the blood came. But he showed no anger.

Turning the other side of his face, he said:

"Let him who threw the stone throw again and strike me here. Even so the great white Wakunda's Son suffered."

But the second stone was not cast, and Wa-choo-bay was left alone with the wolf upon the summit, kneeling and muttering words of kindness.

The White Wakunda

The day passed, and still he knelt upon the summit. But when the dark had fallen, he became aware of someone near him. He raised his head and saw in the starlight a woman lying upon her face before him, and she was moaning.

Wa-choo-bay lifted her and looked into her face. It was a face that he had known of old, only the winters had changed it.

"I am Umba, the Ponca woman," she said. "Many summers ago I spoke to you. Do you remember?"

And Wa-choo-bay said: "I have not forgotten."

Then said Umba, the Ponca woman: "Even now it is the same as then. I have come to take the hard trail with you, even the trail that leads to death, for in all these winters and summers I have taken no man."

And she wiped the blood from his face with her blanket of buckskin.

There was sorrow in the breast of Wa-choo-bay as he said these words, which the Ponca woman could not understand, though her tongue was one with his:

"From now through all the summers and winters that follow, your name shall be Mary.

"Have you heard my words?" he said after a long silence.

"I have heard," said the woman, "and I believe. I alone among all the people believe."

"Then shall you follow me on my lonesome trail. I see not its end, for it is in the mist."

The days when the prairie was brown passed, and the snows came. And there was one who followed a winter trail.

From village to village he went, speaking words of kindness and doing good deeds. But everywhere he was driven from the villages. And there were two who followed him, the woman, whose name was changed to Mary, and the wolf.

And ever the tall thin man gave kind words to those who offered blows.

It happened in the time of *Hunga-Mubli*—the time when the snows drift against the north sides of the lodges, that a rumor ran across the prairie —a rumor that a strange sickness had come to the village of the Poncas. It was the sickness called *Ghatunga,* the sickness of the big, red sores.

Then Wa-choo-bay and his two followers turned weary feet toward the stricken village of the Poncas. It was a hard trail, with little food and much cold.

And when the three entered the stricken village there was a rejoicing among the Poncas, for they said:

"Might it not be that this one whom we have spurned is stronger than we thought?"

But Wa-choo-bay sang no medicine songs; he performed no magic rites. With tender hands he nursed the sick. Also he knelt beside them and said soft words that were not the words of the prairie.

And it happened that the invisible arrows of the Terror fell thicker and thicker among the Poncas. The sickness spread, and the village was filled with the delirious shrieks of the dying.

So a great, angry wail went up against Wa-choo-bay.

"The sickness grows greater, not less," said those who were still strong. "This Wa-choo-bay's words are not true words. There is a black spirit in him."

So it happened that arms that were still strong seized Wa-choo-bay and bound him with thongs of buckskin. Then he was led afar from the village to the summit of a hill.

There they planted a post and bound Wa-choo-bay to it.

And the woman, whose name was changed to Mary, begged for him, and the wolf, with its four feet huddled together in the snow, mourned with an upward thrusting of the snout.

But Wa-choo-bay said:

"Do not wail for me. This is the place where my trail ends. This is what was in the mist. Let these whom I love do as they will do."

And when they had bound him to the post they whipped him with elkhorn whips.

"Where is your white Wakunda?" they cried, and it was a hate cry.

"Here beside us stands the white Wakunda and His Son!" said Wa-choo-bay; and his brow was wet with the sweat of pain. But the whippers did not see, and the whips fell harder.

And after some time Wa-choo-bay raised his head weakly to the darkening heavens, for the sun had fallen, and moaned soft words that were not prairie words.

Then his head fell forward upon his breast.

The whips fell no more. The whippers departed.

The sky was like a sheet of frosty metal and the stars were like broken ice.

Against the sky hung the thin figure of Wa-choo-bay lashed to the post, and beneath him in the shadow huddled two whose mourning was like a song.

THE MARK OF SHAME

IN the old times there were two brothers, Seha and Ishneda; and because of hate for him, they did many acts of unkindness to a man whose name was Shonga Saba.

And one night a man was killed and the man was Ishneda. So with the coming of the light, a whisper ran about the village, saying "Shonga Saba has killed." And the whisper was true; for Shonga Saba sat in his lodge all day, speaking no word. And when any came to speak, he lifted his lip in a bad way and snarled. A sick wolf does so.

It happened that morning that some hunters went forth, for it was the time for the hunting of bison and the tribe was resting on the trail. And when the hunters returned, their eyes were like the eyes of a scared deer. They told a story that frightened the people. They had shot at three elk and their aim was true; but the arrows came out on the other side—bloodless. And the elk changed into wolves, running away very swiftly.

So they who were wise saw famine coming. They recalled old times; how the game had often failed after a murder. For the spirit of the dead man makes it so. And the wise old men told these things, and the old women said it had been so; they remembered.

So there was a space of little speaking, for Fear sat upon tongues.

When the sun was going down, the people gathered about the big chief's tepee where the fathers were sitting with great thoughts. They did not smoke nor talk. They shivered as the long shadows crept out of the hills—yet it was the brown hot time.

And when it was dusk a chief made words which were whispers: "Let a *wachoobay* [holy man] take strong weapons and travel the back trail till the middle of the night, that he may meet the spirit that comes and kill it: for Famine walks with the spirit that comes, and there shall be the wailing of children and many flat bellies."

And the wachoobay went forth with strong weapons. He took the back trail; he looked straight ahead. And the people stared after him until the dark came between, as he walked to meet the two comers.

Then the chief's voice went over the people in the darkness, for the fires were not lit; an enemy was coming, and there is safety in darkness: "Let him who killled come among us." So one went and brought the man.

He stood among the people, felt but not seen;

and with him came a sobbing that grew into words:
"I, Shonga Saba, am here; and I have killed. Have
my people seen a bison bull stung with a fly until
he tore the earth with his horns? It was so. After
a long time of heat the storm comes out of the
night; it does angry deeds, and in the morning it
is past. It was so. My breast hurts. I struck
my enemy, but myself I struck also. Something has
died within me. So I go to do as the others have
done. I will take the punishment."

And though the people did not hear nor see him
go, they knew that he was gone. That night only
the children slept.

When Shonga Saba reached his tepee, he did that
which was the custom. He cut his hair, he took off
his garments, he smeared his forehead with mud.
Of tears and dust he made the mud. Upon his forehead he put the mark of his shame.

From the peak of his tepee, where the smoke
comes out, he tore the rawhide flap. It was blackened with the smoke of many fires. About his
shoulders he bound it; and it was the garment of
his shame.

And then he went forth from the camp. He
pitched a lonesome tepee outside the circle of his
people; for thus he should live four summers and
four winters. It was the custom.

And in the first light his woman came to him with
water and cooked meat. Also, she brought moan-

ing. Shonga Saba spoke no word nor looked up. The mud of tears and dust was upon his forehead, and the blackened garment of shame was upon his shoulders. There was a lump in his throat; but the water did not wash it away. There was an emptiness in him; but the meat did not fill it. And when he cut the meat, which was well cooked, the man groaned, for blood ran forth and made the food look like a wound.

Again the tribe took up the trail; they wanted to find the bison, for there was little meat. And the man followed at the distance of an arrow's flight behind his moving people, for such was the custom. But no thunder of bison came from the brown valleys where the trail went; neither was there any dust cloud of pawing hoofs. And the old women remembered old-time famines, and their hands trembled as they pitched the tepees in the dusk that ended the day's toil.

And in the mornings the old men gazed into the shining distance, looking from under their hands with eyes that glared as in battle. And all day, sweating and toiling on the trail, the people ate the distance with hungry eyes.

Round bellies flattened; for the evil days had come.

And the man who had killed saw all this. He too walked with hunger and something bigger than the food-wish. Also lonesomeness was ever by his side. In the nights he felt the mark upon his forehead like the sting of an angry knife; and the smoke-flap was as a fire upon his shoulders.

And one night he said: "I have brought these days of toiling without food upon my people. It was for this that my mother groaned at my coming. I should have been the food of wolves on that day when my eyes were not yet open. I will go away, for evil walks with me, and my feet scatter trouble in the trail. My woman is as one who has no man, and my children are as a stranger's children. I will walk far and seek peace among other peoples, among strange hills and valleys."

And he went in the night.

He was far into the lonesome places—and it was morning. He was weak with the night walking, for famine had made him thin. So he lifted his face and his hands to the sun. His palms he turned to the young light and he spoke earnest words to the Spirit: "Wakunda, trouble have I met, and trouble have my people met through me. Help me to walk in the good trail!"

And as he said the words, a cloud passed across the sun; it was like a smutch of mud across a shining forehead. The man who had killed, groaned. He hid his face in the grass that he might not see the mark of his shame. But as the day grew older the hunger pinched more, and the man got up, set his face away from the sun, and went on farther into the lonesome places. And in the evening he killed a rabbit with his bow and arrows. And as the rabbit leaped up at the sting of the arrow, it made a pitiful sound like that of a man struck deep with a knife in his sleep.

And the man fled, for a strange sickness had gripped him. The mark upon his forehead burned, and the smoke-flap was as a heavy burden upon his shoulders.

In the last light he found wild turnips and ate. They could not cry out; they could not bleed. And then sleep came, but not rest. While his body slept, his spirit killed Ishneda over and over again. And he saw the first light with haggard eyes.

And when he had eaten again of the wild turnips he said: "I will go to the village of the Poncas; they will take me in, for I will speak soft words." That day he traveled, and the next and the next. But two others had traveled faster than he—Famine and the Story of his bad deed; for none travels so fast as these. And these two had traveled across the prairie together.

And after much walking, Shonga Saba came to the top of a hill and turned hungry eyes upon the Ponca village in the valley. It was the time when the old day throws big shadows. He stood thin, bent against the sky. The smoke-flap at his shoulders lifted in the wind that the eyes in the valley might see.

The Mark of Shame

And a dead hush crept over the village; the sound of children died; the people disappeared. Full of wonder and fear, the lean, lonesome one walked with halting step down the dry hillside. He entered the village, and it was as a place where all are dead.

He came to the center of the village. He lifted his palms and made a piteous cry, which was like a dry wind moving in a wilderness. And then the head of an old man was thrust forth from a tent-flap, and from it came a husky voice: "Begone, O Bringer of Famine!"

And the man went forth. His head was bent, his shoulders stooped as with a weight. He walked far and met the Night. He lay down in its shadow. His forehead ached, and the smoke-flap was as a burning brand. And in the darkness he made a cry: "Wakunda, very far have I walked seeking peace; but it has fled before me. Help me to find the good trail!"

He was very tired, and on a sudden it was day again, and the dew was upon him. He found wild turnips and ate. He drank at a little creek that ran very thin among dying reeds. Then he walked, he knew not where. But now and then he whispered bitter words into the lonesome air: "In the land of the spirits is peace; there I would walk, but I cannot find the trail."

The day was very hot. The prairie wavered in the heat; the bugs droned; the light wind sighed in the dry grasses like a thirsty thing. The far hills seemed floating in a lake of thin fat. They looked lean and hungry, yellow as with a fever; and upon their sides the dry earth was broken like old sores.

Into the heat-drone the man sent his sighing. His feet were heavy; he wished to die, he wished to die.

And when the day was past the highest place, a rumbling grew below the rim of the earth, like the galloping of many bison—a sound of anger. And a cloud arose, black and flashing with fires across its front. The sky was an eye of fever and the cloud closed slowly over it like a big eyelid.

Then a hush fell. There was no moving of air, no droning of bugs. The prairie held its breath; and the cloud came on. It moved in silence. It threw long, ragged arms ahead of it, long, eager arms. And out of it leaped flames, like the spurt and sputter of a wind-blown camp fire in the night.

And in the hush the man heard strange sounds on a sudden. There was a crying and a shouting of battle cries. He reached the bald top of a hill and saw below him a fighting of many warriors. Bitterly they fought, as wolves fight in hunger. There was the lifting and falling of war clubs, the shrieking of arrows. Sounds of horror cut the big stillness like many knives.

And the man's heart leaped with joy—for here was death; this was the beginning of the trail that led to peace.

The Mark of Shame

With a cry he rushed from the summit. He ran with very young legs to meet Death, for he wished to die.

But on a sudden the warring bands ceased crying. The war clubs were not lifted. The arrows flew no more. On rushed the thin, bent runner from the hilltop, and the smoke-flap flaunted itself behind him. As in a dream the warriors stared upon the wild runner. Then a hoarse shout went up: "The Famine Bringer! The Famine Bringer!" Stricken with a common fear, they fled. And the storm broke upon the valley. It poured down water and fire upon one who lay there upon his face. It roared, it shrieked, it flamed about him; but he moved not.

So Death had fled him. And when the storm had passed, the stillness came back like a new pain. The drenched man arose and saw the blood-red sun slip down a ridge of steaming hills.

And near him lay one who had been killed with an arrow. The feathers stood forth from his breast. His face had the look of much pain; his hands gripped at the wet grass. And the lonesome one looked long upon the dead man, thinking deep thoughts. "Even the dead have pain," he said, "and they seek to hold to the good earth. See how he clutches it! I shall live and follow my trail, for on all trails there is pain; and Wakunda wishes me to live."

Indian Tales and Others

So he dressed himself in the garments of the dead warrior who needed them no more. He threw away the smoke-flap, and in a gully that roared with rapid waters, he washed the smutch from his forehead— the mud of dust and tears. And he said: "Now will I walk straight again, for the marks of my shame are gone. I will seek the Otoes, and they will take me in."

Is it not the way of a man to seek better things?

And it happened that in the village of the Otoes was much joy and much feasting. For the bison had come back; the famine was ended.

And it was dark. The lonesome one sighted the feast fires from far off and caught the far-blown scent of boiling kettles. They had the home-smell. His heart was glad as he entered the village and went in among the feast fires. And they about the fires said: "Who walks in from the night?" And Shonga Saba said: "A lonesome man, one with many stories to tell."

They sat him down, for stories are good with feasting. And he told a story while the meat went round and the kettles simmered and the embers crackled and went blue. And as he told, the people gathered close about to hear. They leaned forward, they breathed heavily, they stared. For his story was of a brave one who suffered much; it sounded true; there was trouble in his words. Also it had in it the muttering of war drums, the wails of women

The Mark of Shame

in the night, the snarl of bow thongs, the beat of hoofs.

But as the teller raised his face, glowing with the noble deeds of which he told, he saw the circled mass of staring faces, molded with the terrors of the tale and lit blue with falling embers.

What did they see that they stared so? *The mark!*

The story-teller leaped to his feet. As a wounded man he cried out: "It is not washed away!" He threw his arms across his forehead and fled through the parting throng into the night.

And when he had run far from something that followed yet made no sound, he cast himself down on the prairie and cried to the Spirit: "Wakunda, with water I washed it away, but it is not gone! Am I a wolf to howl always in the wilderness? I am sick for my home. I wish to hear laughter and be clean. Help me to find the trail!"

All night his words felt about in the dark for Wakunda.

The next day his wanderings began anew. And after many sunlights the first frost gripped the prairie, and the snows came. More and more the lonesome one thought of the fires of his people.

So his weary feet followed his longing, and the trail led home. But there was no greeting. In an empty lodge outside the village he made a fire that held the winter off but left him shivering. And once

again his woman came with sobbing and a downcast
face, bringing water and meat. He ate and drank,
yet thirst and hunger stayed. In the nights he
looked wistfully upon the fires of his people burning little days out of the darkness. He wished to
be beside them and hear the laughter, for the famine
had passed, and there was joy.

And often by day, Seha, the brother of the man
who was killed, came with taunting and words that
wounded as a whip-thong. But the lonesome one
made no answer, for having suffered much, he was
wise. And this was against the law of the fathers;
so it happened one day that Seha was bound to a
post in the center of the village, and the whippers
were there with elkhorn whips to punish Seha.

Then was a strange deed done, which even yet the
old men tell of to the youths. From the lodge ran
the lonesome one and stood before the whippers.
The long silence he broke with words: "Spare Seha
and bind me to the post, for mine was the bad deed.
I have suffered much and now I can see."

And the old fathers, who were wise, said: "Let
it be as the man says." And it was done. The lonesome one was bound to the post and took the lashes
on his back. He made no cry, nor was there any
wincing of his face. And it happened that in his
pain he sought out the face of Seha in the throng.
It was no longer hard with hate.

And then, suddenly, as the whips hissed about

The Mark of Shame

him, a light went across the face of the lonesome one
—a strange, bright light. And seeing this, the
arms of the whippers faltered, for it was very
strange.

Then in the silence that fell, the man raised a soft
voice: "At last the mark has left me! Bring my
children to look upon me, and let my woman sing!
I have found peace; for the mark of tears and dust
is gone—I know not how."

DREAMS ARE WISER THAN MEN

RAIN WALKER lay upon the brown grass without the circle of the village; and it was the time when the maize is gathered—the brown, drear time. He lay with ear pressed to the earth.

"What are you doing?" asked one who walked there.

"I?" said Rain Walker; and his eyes and face were not good to see as he raised his head. The dying time seemed also in his face. "The growers are coming up, and I am listening to their breathing," he said.

And the questioner walked on with a strange smile; for it was not the time of the coming of the growers.

Rain Walker stood in the center of the village and held his face to the sky.

"What are you doing?" said one who walked there.

"I?" and there was twilight in Rain Walker's eyes as he looked upon the questioner. "I shot an arrow into the air. It did not come back, so I am always looking for it."

Dreams Are Wiser Than Men

And the questioner smiled and went on walking; for no arrow rises that does not fall. A child knows that.

And the people said: "It is all because Mad Buffalo, the Ponca, took his squaw. He took her, and she went. It was after the summer's feasting and talking together that she went. Rain Walker is not forgetting."

And Rain Walker sat much alone; he sat much alone making strange songs not pleasant to hear. And as he made songs he made weapons. He fashioned him a *man-de-hi,* which is a long spear, tipped with sharp flint; and he sang. He wrought a *za-zi-man-di,* which is a great bow; and sang all the time. They were hate songs that he sang; they snarled.

He shaped many arrows; he headed them with sharp flints and tipped them with the feathers of the hawk; and all the time he sang. He made a *we-ak-ga-di,* which is an ugly club. He sang to himself and to the weapons that he made. To the harsh, snarling airs he wrought the weapons. The songs went into them, and they looked like things that might hate much.

And one drew near who was walking. "Why do you make war things?" said he.

"I?" and Rain Walker threw himself upon his stomach, writhing toward the questioner like a big snake. "I am a rattlesnake," he said, *"hiss-ss-ss-s!* go away! I sting!"

[63]

And the man went, for it is not good to see a man act like a snake.

And one night the weapons were finished. All that night the people heard the voice of Rain Walker singing. They said: "Those are the songs of one who wishes to go on the warpath!"

And in the morning Rain Walker came out of his lodge. The squaws trembled to see him; and the men wondered. For he had wept and his eyes were wild.

And Rain Walker raised a hoarse voice into the morning stillness before all the people: "Where is my woman—she who cooked for me and made my lodge pleasant? Tell me; for I walk there that the crows may eat me!"

The people shivered as though his voice were the breath of the first frost.

"You need not make words, my kinsmen; I know. I walk there and the crows shall eat me."

He went forth from the door of his lodge and came to the place where the head chief lived among the Hungas. He raised the door flap. "A-ho!" said he, for the chief was within eating. "I, Rain Walker, stand before you. I have words to say."

"Speak," said the chief.

"I am wronged. I wish war! I wish to see the Poncas destroyed!"

The head chief gazed long into the tear-washed

Dreams Are Wiser Than Men

eyes of Rain Walker, and he said: "It is a big thing to take that trail. It makes the wailing of women; it makes hunger; it makes the crying of *zhinga zhingas* for fathers that lie in lonesome places and never ride back. It is a hard path to take. I will think."

And it happened after the thinking of the big chief that a council was called—a coming-together of the leaders of the bands.

And the leaders came together, and sat with big thoughts. It was evening, and among the assembled leaders sat Rain Walker. His face was thin and cruel as a stone axe stained with blood.

Then the big chief raised his voice, and words to be heard grew there in the big lodge. "This man who sits with us has been wronged. When our brothers, the Poncas, were among us for the feasting and the talking together, Mad Buffalo was among them.

"A woman is a thing not to be understood. Now she dies on long winter trails for a man, or grows old and wrinkled suckling his *zhinga zhingas;* and now she leaves him for another; yet it is the same woman. I knew a wise man once; but he shook his head about these things; and so do I.

"You know of whom I speak. It was Sun Eyes; and she was this man's woman. Mad Buffalo smiled, and she went with him.

"And this man has come to me crying for war,"

continued the head chief. "Think hard, and let us talk together."

And he of the Big Elk band said: "Let the Poncas come down in the night and drive away our ponies, and I will gather my band about me. But it has not been so."

And he of the Hawk band said: "Let the Poncas destroy our gardens, and I will think of my weapons."

And he of the No-Teeth band said: "Let the Poncas speak ill of us, and my band will put on the war paint."

Then a silence grew and the head chief filled it with few words. "Let us pass the pipe; and all who smoke it smoke for war."

And there were ten chiefs in the council, sitting in a circle. The first touched the pipe lightly and passed it on as though it burned his fingers; and so the second and third, even to the tenth. And next to him sat Rain Walker. His breath came dryly through his teeth, like a hot wind in a parched gulch. With hands that trembled he grasped his pipe from the tenth, who had not placed it to his lips. Rain Walker placed it to his lips nervously, eagerly, as one who touches a cool water bowl after a long thirst. He struck a flint and lit it. Then he arose to his feet, tall, straight, trembling—a rage grown into a man!

"*I smoke!*" he cried; "I smoke, and through all

the sunlights that come I will walk alone and kill! The lonesome walker—I am he!

"I shall speak to the snake, and he shall teach me his creeping and his stinging. I shall speak to the elk, and he shall teach me his fleetness, his strength that lasts, his fury when he turns to fight. And I shall speak to the hawk and learn the keenness of his eyes!"

Rain Walker puffed blue streamers of smoke into the still twilight of the lodge, seeming something more than man in the fog he made.

"I smoke!" he cried; and his cry had changed into a song of snarling sounds and sounds that wailed. "I smoke, and I smoke alone; my brothers will not take the pipe with me. In lonesome places shall I walk with my hate, and not even the lone hawk in the farthest hills shall hear me make aught but a hate cry. I have no longer any people! I am a tribe—the tribe that walks alone! The *zhinga zhingas* of the women that are not yet born shall hear my name, and it shall be like a nightwind wailing when the spirits walk and the fires are blue! I will forget that I am the son of a woman; I will think myself the son of a snake, that bore me on a hot rock in a lonesome place. I will think that I never tasted woman's milk, but only venom stewed by the hot sun. And now I walk alone."

His cry had fallen to a low wail that made the flesh of the hearers creep, although they were leaders and brave. And with eyes that peered far ahead as into impenetrable distances Rain Walker strode out of the lodge. The night was coming; he went forth to meet it, walking.

As he walked toward the night his thoughts were of *choobay* (holy) things. He thought much of the spirits, and he reached a high hill as he walked. It was high; therefore it was a *choobay* place. And he climbed to the summit, bare of grass and white with flaked rocks against the sky, that darkened fast as the Night walked.

Then he lit his pipe and made *choobay* smoke. He wished to have the good *wakundas* with him, even though he walked alone. For well he knew that no man can walk quite alone. So he extended the pipe stem to the west, the south, the east, the north, and he cried, "O you who cause the four winds to reach a place, help me! I stand needy!" Then he extended the pipe stem toward the earth, and he said, "O Venerable Man who lives at the bottom, here I stand needy!" And to the heavens he held the stem and cried, "O Grandfather who lives above, I stand needy; I, Rain Walker! Though my brothers treat me badly, yet I think you will help me!"

And he felt much stronger.

Then, with his weapons about him, he set his face to the south, for there in the flat lands of Nebraska lay the village of the Poncas.

Dreams Are Wiser Than Men

And he walked in lonesome places all night. A coyote trotted past him and sat at some distance. "O brother Coyote," said Rain Walker, "I am on the warpath; teach me your long running and your snapping!" The coyote whined and went into a gulch.

"I walk alone, and none relieves my sorrow!"

So sang Rain Walker; and singing thus he walked into the morning. And the prairie was gray with frost and very big, and the skies were filled with a quiet, so that a far crow cawing faintly made a shout. Having nothing to eat he sang, and hunger went away. His song filled the world, for he walked alone where it was very silent.

To the hawk he cried for keenness of eyes; but the hawk circled on and was only a speck. Nothing heard the man who walked alone.

He killed a rabbit and ate; he found a stream and drank. Then he met the Night walking again, and they walked together until they met the Day; and the man saw below him in the flat lands of Nebraska the jumbled mud village of the Poncas.

And it happened that the people in the village were moving very early. There was a neighing of ponies and a shouting of men and a scolding and laughing of women. It was the time of the bison hunt, and they were going forth that day.

Rain Walker lay in the brown grass at the hilltop and watched with wistful eyes the merry ones as the long, thin file left the village, the riders and the walkers and the drags. It is pleasant to go on the hunt. Rain Walker felt that he would never go again.

His face softened; then suddenly it changed and became again as a barbed war arrow. Mad Buffalo rode, and after him went Sun Eyes walking! Her head hung low like a thing wilted by the frost. She laughed not; she, too, seemed as one who walked alone.

When the long, thin line, like a huge snake writhing westward into the hills, had disappeared, Rain Walker got up and walked fast. He walked fast, for he wished to be near the place of camping when the night came. And it was so.

He lay at a distance, watching the fires flare into the night and feeling very hungry, for he caught the scent of the boiling kettles. They smelled like home. And when the people had eaten and the fires had fallen, Rain Walker said, "Now I will begin my war. I need a pony, the Poncas have them."

He crawled upon his hands and knees to where the herd grazed. There had been no watch set, for all the tribes were at peace, except the tribe that walked alone.

And Rain Walker rode away into the night. He had big thoughts as he rode.

The hunting was poor that year; it happened so,

Dreams Are Wiser Than Men

they say. Still toward the place where the evening goes went the tribe, peering into far places for the bison; and ever there was one who crept near the tepees at night and heard the words of the Poncas, which are the same as the Omahas speak.

And they wandered, hunting, in the places where the sandhills are—the dreary places.

And one day it happened, they say, that a coyote and a hawk and some crows saw two men in a very lonesome place among the sand hills. They alone saw. And the two met, riding. One was a Ponca gone forth to seek the unappearing herd. He was tall and well made, and his pony was spotted. The other was also even as the first, although not a Ponca; but his pony was not spotted.

And when they met a great cry went up from the one whose pony was not spotted. The coyote and the hawk and the crows heard and saw. It seemed a strange cry in the silence that lived there. Then he who rode the spotted pony turned and fled; but an arrow is swifter than a pony, though it be wind-footed; and he who fled fell upon the sand and the pony ran at some distance and stopped. He looked on also.

And the two men met. He with the arrow in his back arose with a groan from the sand and growled as the other approached and dismounted. They seemed as two who had met and parted enemies.

They seized each other and rolled upon the sand. The coyote whined, the crows cawed, but the hawk only watched. But all the while the ponies neighed.

And the sting of the arrow weakened one, but he fought like a bear. He made a good fight. But the other fixed his hands upon his enemy's throat until the silent places were filled with a gurgling and a rasping of breath that came hard. Then there was only silence. The coyote ran away, the crows and the hawk flew. The ponies alone watched now.

And the man whose pony was not spotted arose and laughed very loud—only it was not the laugh of a glad man. Then the man who laughed stripped off the garments of the other and put them upon himself. Then he built a fire and lit his pipe and made *choobay* smoke. Then he spoke to the various *wakundas* that were somewhere there in the silence.

"I have killed my enemy. I will burn his heart and give you the ashes, O Grandfathers!"

The crows heard this, for they had come back looking for their feast.

And the man burned the heart of his enemy and scattered the ashes, singing a brave song all the while. He had learned to do this.from the Kansas; it is their custom.

Then the man got on the spotted pony and rode away, bearing with him the weapons of the man who stayed. And when he was gone the crows and the coyote came and made harsh noises at each other, for each was hungry, and there was a feast spread there upon the sand.

And it happened that evening, they say, that one rode into the Ponca camp and went to the tepee where Sun Eyes, the Omaha woman, waited for someone.

The man who came had his whole face hidden with a piece of buckskin, having eye and mouth holes in it. And Sun Eyes was cooking over a fire before her tepee.

"Ho, Mad Buffalo!" she said; "you have not found the bison. Why have you hidden your face?"

"I found no bison," said the man, "but I saw something in the hills which caused me to hide my face."

And Sun Eyes looked keenly at the man, for she thought it was some *wakunda* he had seen.

"Why do you speak in a strange voice?" said she; and she trembled as she said it.

"He who has seen something is never the same again!" said he.

And while the woman wondered the two ate together. And as the man ate he laughed very pleasantly at times like a man who is very glad.

"Why do you laugh, Mad Buffalo?" said the woman.

"Because I was very hungry for something, and I have it now," said the man.

And when he had ceased eating he sang glad songs, and again the woman questioned.

"I sing because of what I saw in the hills," said he.

And this seemed very strange to the woman. But it is not allowed that one should question a man who has seen a *wakunda*.

And it happened that the man was pleased to speak evil words of Rain Walker, and Sun Eyes hung her head; her eyes were wet.

Then said the man, having seen: "Why do you act so? Do you want him? Behold! Am I not as good to see as Rain Walker?"

And he acted as one who is almost angry and a little sad. But the woman only sobbed a very little sob, for as the chief said in the council, a very wise man does not know the ways of a woman.

And it happened that night, they say, that, as the two slept, Sun Eyes dreamed a strange dream that made her cry out. And the two sat up startled.

"What is it?" said the man.

"A dream!" sobbed Sun Eyes.

"What dream?" said the man, and his voice seemed kind.

"I cannot tell; I do not wish to be beaten."

"Tell it, Sun Eyes. Was it about Rain Walker?" She did not answer.

"Do not be afraid," he said. And she spoke.

"I dreamed that I saw my *zhinga zhinga* that I

am carrying. And it was Rain Walker's. It had his face, and it looked upon me with hate. It pushed me away when I offered my breast. It would take no milk from me. And it seemed that its look pierced me like a barbed arrow. Thus I awoke, and cried out."

The woman was weeping, and a tremor ran through the man. She felt it as he leaned against her, and she thought it anger.

"Take me there where I came from—to the village of my people!" she cried. "You are big and good to see, and many women will follow you! Take me to my people; Dreams are wiser than men; the *wakundas* send them. I wish to go back, that my child may smile and take my breast."

And the man rose and began dressing for the trail.

"I will take you back," said he. "Dreams are wiser than men."

And before the day walked the two went forth on the long trail, back to the village of the woman's people.

The man went before and the woman followed, bearing the burdens of the trail. But when the dawn came the man did a strange thing. He took the burdens upon his own shoulders, saying nothing. It seemed his heart had been softened; but his face being hidden, the woman could not see what was there.

And the trail was long; but the man was kind.

Indian Tales and Others

He seemed no longer the Mad Buffalo. He made fires and pitched the tepee like a squaw. He spoke soft words.

And after many days of traveling the two came, as the Night was beginning to walk, to the brown brow of the hill beneath which lay the village of the Omahas.

And the man said: "There are your people. Go!"

And the woman moaned, saying: "He will not take me, and the dream will be true. Never on the long trail did my heart fail; but now I am weak."

But the man said: "Sun Eyes, had not Rain Walker ever a soft heart? He will take you back. Look!"

And the woman, who had been gazing through tears upon the village of her people, turned and saw that the man had torn the buckskin from his face She gave a cry and shrank from what she saw.

But the man took her gently by the hand.

"He will take you back," he said; "dreams are wiser than men!"

VYLIN

THE council of the fathers sat in the Big Lodge with very grave faces, for they had come together to pass judgment upon the deed of a woman. As they passed the pipe about the circle, there were no words; for in the silence the good spirits may speak, and well they knew that it is a big thing to sit in judgment.

And after a time of silence and deep thought, the door-flap of the lodge was pushed aside by two who came—an old man bent with many loads, and a woman in whose eyes the spring still lived. And when the two had sat down outside the circle, the head chief spoke: "Let the man speak first." Then the old man, who had brought the woman, arose.

"Fathers, you see a man with a sad heart, for I have brought my daughter before you for judgment. The things which she has told me I could have buried very deep in my breast; but I am old, and the wisdom of the old is mine. Who can bury a bad thing deeper than the spirits see?

"And so I am here to make sharp words against myself, for the father and the child are one.

"You remember that the season of singing frogs

[April] has passed three times since one of the pale-faces came among us. He was a paleface, but he was not like his brothers who find gladness in doing deeds that are bad. You have not forgotten how his words and deeds were kind, his voice very good to hear, nor how his face had the beauty of a woman's, though it was not a woman's face. Also his hands were white as the first snow fallen on a green place; and his hair was long like the hair of our people, but it clung about his head like a brown cloud when the evening is old.

"He was hungry and lean when he came among us. His pony was hungry and lean. And we took him in with glad hearts; we lit the feast fires for him; his pony we staked in our greenest places; for he was not like his brothers.

"And we called him 'the man with the singing box,' for he brought with him a thing of wood and sinews; and over this, while we feasted, he drew a stick of wood with the hair of a pony's tail fastened to it, making songs sweeter than those of our best women singers, and deeper than the voices of men who are glad.

"Much we wondered at this, for the magic of the paleface is a great magic. And as he made the wood and sinews sing together, we forgot to eat and the feast fires fell blue; for never before had such a singing been heard in our lands. And once he made it sing a battle song that snarled like a wounded rattlesnake in a dry place, and cried like an angry warrior, and shrieked like arrows, and thundered like many pony hoofs, and wailed like the women when the band comes back with dead braves across the backs of ponies. And as he made it sing this song, even we who were wise leaped to our feet and drew forth our weapons and shouted the war cry of our people—so great was the song. And when our shouting ceased, the man made the medicine box sing low and sweet and thin like a woman crying over a sick *zhinga zhinga* in the night. And we forgot the battle cries; we gave tears like old women.

"Do you remember? This is the man of whom I speak.

"Many young moons grew old and passed away, and still he lived among us, until, lo! he was even as our kinsman, for he learned the tongue of our people, being great of wit.

"And he told us of a wanderer whose own people were unkind to him; a tale of one who was not of the people of whom he was born, because he loved the spirits that sing, more than a very rich man loves his herds of ponies blackening many hills where they graze. And it was of himself he told; he was the wanderer. So we loved him because of this and because of his kind words and because of the song which he made in his medicine box.

"And all the while my girl here was growing

taller—very good to see. Many times I said to my woman, 'There is something growing between these two.' And we both saw it with glad hearts, for he was a great man.

"And one night in my first sleep I was awakened by a crying of sorrows better to hear than laughter —a moan that grew loud and fell again into softness like a night wind wailing in a lonesome place where thickets grow. And my woman beside me whispered, 'It is the spirits singing.' But the girl here only breathed very hard. I could hear her breathing in the darkness.

"And I got up; I pushed the skin flap aside; I stood as though I were in a dream. For there by the tepee stood the man with the singing box at his neck. His long, white fingers worked upon the sinews; his arm drew the hair-stick up and down. His face looked to the sky and the white fires of the night were upon it. Never had I seen such a face; for it was not a man's face nor yet a woman's. It was the face of a good man's spirit come back from the star-paths. I looked at his lips, for it seemed that the singing grew up from his mouth; but his lips were very still.

"And my eyes made tears; for many forgotten sorrows came back to me at once, and I felt a great kindness for all things, which I could not understand.

"And when he dropped his arm and looked at

Vylin

me, his eyes threw soft, white fire into my breast,
and then I knew the singing was not for me. Once
when my woman was young and still in the lodge of
her father, I looked upon her with such a look.

"So I gave the girl to the paleface; and for a
time the singing box was still; for they made a
singing between them. And before the first frosts
made the trees shiver, the palefaces who trade for
furs came to our village, and the man went with
them; and with him went the woman. No man can
be deaf to the call of his kind; so he went. And now
the woman shall speak, and you shall judge her
deed."

The old man sat down and rested his face in his
hands. The young woman arose to her feet. With
lips parted the chiefs bent forward to catch the
words which should fall from her mouth. Tall and
thin she was, and shapely. But the shadows of a
great toil and a great sorrow clung about her lean
cheeks and under her black eyes, grown too big with
much weeping.

"Fathers," she began, "I will tell you how my
bad deed grew upon me; and you shall judge. I will
take the punishment, for I have felt much sorrow
and I can stand yet a little more.

"Three summers ago I followed the man of the
singing box into the North. This you know—but
the rest you do not know. It is the way of the paleface to toil for the white metal. They showed my

man the white metal, and it led him into the North among strange peoples, where there is much gathering of furs. And I went with him, for a woman must follow the man.

"Far into the North we went where the Smoky Water runs thin so that a very little man can throw a stone across it. And the singing box went with us.

"And we built a lodge of logs, after the manner of his people, near to a great log lodge where the big pale chief lived and said words that should be obeyed. And for a time our hearts sang together. But when the snows had come, it happened that the big pale chief spoke a word, and my man went with his brothers, driving many dogs farther into the North where there are furs of much worth.

"And when my man left he said, 'Take good care of Vylin while I am gone, for she is dearer to me than my life.' And I stared at him because I did not understand. It was the singing box of which he spoke; as though it were a person he spoke of it; he called it Vylin; and much I wondered.

"But because my heart was warm toward the man, I did acts of kindness to the singing box, which he called Vylin; for I had not yet learned that it was no box of wood, but the spirit of a dead woman of the palefaces.

"Through the long cold nights 1 held it close to me under the blankets. And often in the night I

Vylin

was awakened by its crying when in my sleep I touched it strongly. Like a *zhinga zhinga* it cried; and my heart was softened toward it, for I had no child then. Through the days I talked to Vylin. I washed it much that it might be clean and of a good smell. And often it made soft sounds like a *zhinga zhinga* that is glad. Then would I hold it to my dry breasts and sing to it.

"But more and more I learned that it was no box of wood, but a living thing. For I began to see that it had the shape of a woman. Its neck was very slender; its head was small; and its hair fell in four little braids across its neck and breast down to its hips. And the more I learned, the more my breast hurt; for he loved Vylin, and her voice was sweeter for singing than my voice. And I said, 'She does not sing for me—only for him does she sing, therefore she loves him well.'

"When the grass came again and the ice broke up, my man came back with the furs and the dogs and the men. They came floating down the river on big canoes. And I sang when he came again into his lodge, for the winter had been long. Also, I showed him how kind I had been to Vylin; I thought he would be very glad. But he frowned and spoke sharp words. He said it was wrong to wash Vylin. I was very sad; I could not understand. Does not a good mother wash her *zhinga zhinga,* that it may be clean and of a good smell? I had no

[83]

zhinga zhinga then, and so I had been a mother to Vylin.

"And when I told him this, he laughed a very harsh laugh, and said it was Vylin, not a *zhinga zhinga;* so that I was sad until he spoke a very soft word, then I forgot for many days.

"But as the grass grew taller and the scent of green things blew in every wind, my man grew strange toward me. Like a man with the ache for home he was. And more and more it became his way to be very silent while he made Vylin sing to him—O such strange, soft songs, like spirits weeping!

"And more and more my heart grew sore toward Vylin, for when I sang that he might forget her to look upon me, he frowned and spoke sharp words.

"So one day as he sat in a shady place, making songs with his fingers, I said to him: 'If so softly you should lay your fingers upon *my* neck, I too could sing as sweetly!' And he smiled, and it was like the sun breaking through a cloud that has hung long over the day. And he drew me close to him and said: 'Do you see the leaves upon this tree, and do you know how many?' And I laughed, for I was glad, and in the old days it had often been his wish to joke so. But he said: 'So many of the palefaces have listened to me making Vylin sing; and they wept to hear. But now am I far away and strange peoples are about me.'

Vylin

"And that was the last of my gladness for many moons; for more and more he wished to be silent. And when the snows came again he went away. And I was very lonesome and sad until I knew that I would be a mother. Then my heart sang, for I said: 'Now, my man will look upon me again and speak soft words as in the old times. Does Vylin bring him *zhinga zhingas?*"

"And all through the cold days I was glad; my heart was soft. I took good care of Vylin; I was kind to her, for at last I thought that she would be second in his heart. I pitied her as I thought this. I washed her no more, but ever through the frosty nights I kept her warm with many blankets, even though I shivered.

"And when the grass came my man came also. And another came, a *nu zhinga*. But my man looked with cold eyes upon my *zhinga zhinga;* so I wept many nights, many, many nights. And much weeping made me not good to see. So the man looked upon me no more; only upon Vylin did he look. With very soft eyes did he look upon her; with such eyes did he look upon me in the old days.

"My heart grew very bitter. Often I heard him talking soft talk to her—such as he talked to me in the old times. And I wished to tear her hair, her yellow hair from her head! I wished to kill her, to walk upon her, to hear her groan, to see her die!"

The woman's eyes flashed a battle light. Her

[85]

hands were clenched, her face was sharp and cruel. Very tall she grew in her anger—a mother of fighting men.

"And that night," she said, "I threw angry words at the man. I spoke bad things of Vylin. I called great curses down upon her. And I said: 'She sings, but does she bring you sons to feed you when you are old?' And he laughed with a harsh sound.

"So that night when the man slept I got up very stealthily from the blankets. My breast hurt, and many black spirits pressed their fingers into my heart. I took a knife—a very sharp knife. I uncovered Vylin where she lay sleeping in her blankets. I felt for the place where her heart should be. Then I struck, struck, struck! Very deep I sent the sharp knife, and I laughed to hear the great groan that Vylin made as she died.

"And also the man heard. He leaped from his blankets. He struck me with his fist; he beat me. He called down all the big curses of his people upon me. He gave me the *nu zhinga*. He pushed me from the door into the darkness.

"'Begone!' he said, 'for you have killed Vylin!'

"And I went into the darkness with my *nu zhinga*. Many days have I walked with much hunger; and always the *nu zhinga* was a heavy burden. And now I am thin; my feet are weary."

A deep sighing shook the young woman as she

Vylin

sat down.   The old man arose, and there was a sound of heavy breathing as he spoke to the chiefs who sat to judge: "My girl has spoken of her bad deed.   She has killed the singing spirit that the white man loved.   How shall she be punished?"

And after a long stillness the head chief spoke: "The heart of a woman is a strange thing; who shall judge it?"

And one by one they who sat to judge arose and left the big lodge.

MIGNON

"**B**UT, Yellow Fox," I protested, "no one understands them; they do not understand themselves!"

Yellow Fox grunted and smiled, showing a very white set of wolfish teeth. We two were sitting together outside the lodge, and, male-like, we had hit upon the topic of woman. The locust-like cadences of the songs and the shuffle of dancing feet came muffled to us. The scent of boiling beef and the sharp smell of wood fires permeated the sultry night air. The full moon lifted a Rabelaisian face of lusty red above the hills, and I saw by its light the eager spirit of the story-teller bright in the eyes of Yellow Fox.

"What they understand I do not know," he began; "I only know I do not understand. And I have travelled far. When I was a young man, many strange valleys knew my feet, and from many hill-tops my eyes looked forth. For from my first moccasins my feet caught the itch for going. And in many villages of strange peoples I have lived for little spaces, until the feasts were tasteless and the

Mignon

maidens ugly. Then did my moccasins itch my feet again, so that I went forth and sought new feasts, other maidens.

"And I have known many maidens. None of them did I understand; and least of all—Mignon.

"Even to-night something of the soft summer smell of her is in my nose; and if I were not old I would walk far, walk far; for that smell is like a voice calling over big waters and many valleys—a voice so far away that the ear does not catch it—so thin that it is no sound, but a feeling.

"Have I told you the way a white man came to our lands once and led me on a long, strange trail? It happened so. He was a keeper of many strange men and many horses and many strange animals, and for money he showed these to many peoples, and so grew rich.

"And the man showed me much money; he told me of new lands and new peoples; he spoke of feasts, of women that were as dreams. Therefore, I felt the itch in my feet again, and I went with the man. And we came at last to many big tepees, where the man kept the strange things that he showed to the people for money. One of his tepees was as big as the village of a tribe—and he had many.

"I had my place among all these strange things; for the white man said: 'You are the wild man that growls like a bear and eats babies. I give you money and you must look very wild and growl much when the boys stick at you with straws.' And this was good fun.

"So I stood twice every day fastened to a post by a thong of metal. The people stood about me and stared. I growled, I pulled at the fastenings, I ate raw meat; I was very wild. Many came to see, and when I would have gone back to the lands of my people, the white man showed me more money, so that I stayed.

"We traveled very far with the big tepees. We came to the Big Salty Water, but we did not stop there; we crossed it—and were in another land.

"And then there was a big village—a very big village. There we stopped, and the people came to see.

"You know that vill'ge—Par's—Par's?" asked Yellow Fox, falling momentarily into English.

"Yes, Paris," I corrected, "and you were with Barnum."

"Ah," he assented, speaking his own tongue again; "and it is a village of women that make the eyes glad and the blood quick! I stood many days, growling for the people and eating raw meat. And one day Mignon came. A young man of her own people was with her. They stared and talked much together. Some of their talk I knew, for it was the talk that the fur traders used, and my father's father was a trader for furs.

Mignon

"And Mignon made the eyes glad. She was tall for a woman and not thick. The women of my people are short and thick. Her face was very white, and her eyes were big and deep—like waters in a shadow.

"And the man made jokes at me that stung like elkhorn whips, for he was thin and looked as one whose blood is half water. I could have choked him with two fingers like a worm. *So!*"

Yellow Fox snapped his fingers viciously.

"And it pleased the young man to shove his finger into my ribs and laugh. So I grasped his arm very hard. I put his finger to my mouth; I bit it and the blood came. He cried *ow ow;* then I said to the woman, using what speech of hers I knew: 'Take this baby man of yours away or I will eat him, for I am hungry. But you are good to see; I like you; touch me.'

"And she, wondering that I spoke her speech, touched me!

"Ah—everything was changed!"

Yellow Fox suddenly passed into a dreamy mood. The moon, grown pale with its ascent, illumined his masterful countenance, over which I could see the dream of old days flitting like a ghost. The song of the women dancing about the feast fires within arose into a high and tenuous minor of yearning, filling up the momentary gap in the story like a chorus. In the wake of the passing gust of song, the voice of Yellow Fox arose, soft, low, musical—the voice of memory.

"Her hands she laid upon me—soft and white and thin, they were. She passed them over the muscles of my breast; she stroked my arms. Soft as a mother's touch was hers; like a mother's touch —but I felt a fire burning at her finger tips, that made me wish to fight big men for her, and make them bleed and make them groan and make them die, slobbering blood in the dust! Then afterward to take her far away, thrown across my back like a dead fawn; to build a lodge for her in a lonesome place where man's face never was!

"Much hair she had—much hair that hung above her face like a dark cloud upon a white sky at evening. And it brushed across my breast! I shivered as in a wind that drives the snow before it—and yet I was not cold.

"And then she was gone—swallowed up in the river of people. But not all of her was gone. A smell sweeter than the earth-smell when the spring rains fall was in my nostrils! A smell that gnawed within me like a hunger—yet I did not wish to eat! A smell of soft, white flesh—oh, very soft and white! And now in my old age I call that smell Mignon.

"And the people, like a noisy, muddy stream, flowed round me, past me. But I growled no more; for I did not wish for fun. I hated them—they stank!

Mignon

"Two sunlights passed—and in the evening I stood under many lights, bound with the iron thongs; and the noisy, stinking stream of people was about me. Their staring eyes were as many bugs that swarmed about and stung me. I strained at the iron thongs; I hurled the black curses of my people in among them—and they were pleased. But this was no play; I wished to rush among them and walk upon them; for I had seen, and now no longer did I see.

"But suddenly the smell came back! It grew up like the smell of spring when the ice makes thunder in the rivers and the flowers come out! And she was there beside me.

"I forgot the people; I was no longer angry. I was in a big lonesome prairie with the sunlight and the singing winds, and she was with me, and all the air seemed soft and cool as when a black-winged raincloud shuts out a day of heat.

"I can feel her hands upon me yet."

Yellow Fox sighed. A passionate outburst of song from the dancers within filled the quiet night with sounds of longing, through which the cowhide drums throbbed.

"And the words she spoke were soft. They made me wish to shout the mating songs of my people. They made me very strong. And then I learned her name—Mignon.

"Mignon! Mignon! Such a sound the spring winds make among the first leaves; and yet—it is not all a sound; it is part a smell!

"And after that she came often; every evening she came, like a south wind blowing over prairies sweet with rain at sunset. Many things she asked me and I told her many things. I made with my mouth a picture of my own lands; and some of it she put in a little book, and some she only drank with all her face, as though thirsty.

"And they who had traveled far with us, the pitchers of the tepees and the tenders of the animals, laughed softly in passing, showing their teeth in mirth—for were they not jealous?

"One night she did not come. And it happened on that night that the big tepees were folded up for another trail; and in the morning we were far away. My breast cried out for her; my nose longed for the smell which was Mignon.

"So I spoke of her to the pitchers of the tepees, and they laughed very loud and long, sending forth breaths that stank as they laughed. They said bad things of Mignon. They said, 'Can you not understand? She is of those that her people have cast out.' And this made my breast cry out for her again; for was I not also alone? Were not my own people far away? But the rest of it I knew to be another white man's lie! One liar I struck very hard in the teeth; and when he got up from the

Mignon

dust, slobbering blood and toddling like a baby, he laughed no more and said no more bad things of Mignon. And was this not proof that he had lied?

"Is the first earth-smell of the spring bad? Had not many maidens of the prairies longed for me; and were they not good? Was I not big and of heavy muscles? Was I not young and good for the eyes of women?

"Since I am old and much withered, I can say this; for I have become another man."

The song of the women-singers within had ceased, but the sullen drums kept up a throbbing snarl. At length the voice of Yellow Fox continued in a low monotone:

"We stopped in many big villages; and my breast was sick. More and more I wished for the prairies. At night I heard the dry winds talking in the grasses. I spoke no more of Mignon, for I was afraid to hear again the laughter of the pitchers of the teepees. One more laugh would have made my eyes blind with blood, and I would have killed.

"I lost the wish to eat; I grew shadow-thin. So the owner of the tepees said: 'This wild man is dying for a sight of his prairies; I will send him back.'

"I traveled far, and again I was in my own land. I saw the hills; I smelled the smoke of the fires of my people. But this no longer filled me. I had seen, and now no longer could I see.

"And the winter came. I sat alone much, and as I sat alone, I had big thoughts. I said: 'This that I have seen was a dream thing. It is gone; and I cannot find the sleep trail that leads to it again. Therefore, I will do as others. I will take a woman of my own people. I will eat again; for this dream has only made me thin.'

"So I made a young woman of my people glad. I took her into my lodge. But even through the time of driving snows, I smelled the smell of spring. Mignon! Mignon! I heard the rain winds singing in the first leaves! Mignon! Mignon! I heard the sighing of summer waters! Mignon! Mignon! It was half a sound and half a smell—dream sound, dream smell—so thin, so thin!

"And the time came when the big swift arrows of the geese flew northward, spreading softness as of many camp fires in all the air; and the River wakened and shook itself, shouting with a hoarse voice into the south. The green things came, and there was a singing of frogs where the early rains made pools. The smell, which was Mignon, breathed up out of the earth; the sound, which was Mignon, lived in the trees and grasses.

"And then the time came when it is no longer the spring, and not yet quite the summer. One evening I sat before my lodge, smoking and thinking big thoughts. And the sun was low. A dust cloud grew far down the road that twisted like a yellow snake toward the village of the white men. It was a wagon coming. It grew bigger; a white man was driving it. It came near; there was a woman in it. I stared very hard; I rubbed my eyes, for what I saw was as though it had all grown up out of my pipe smoke.

The woman was tall and not thick. Much hair she had—much hair that hung above her face like a black cloud upon a white sky in the evening. And in all the air about, there grew a smell sweeter than the earth-smell when the spring rains fall. I sat very still; I did not wish to frighten the dream away. And the woman came toward me with much rustling of garments, like the speaking of green leaves in the wind or the thin, small drumming of raindrops.

"Then, between the puffing of two smoke rings, the Spring had grown big—and was the Summer! It was Mignon! It was Mignon!"

Yellow Fox lifted his face to the full moon, and his voice was raised to a poignant cry as he uttered the word that was half sound, half smell. Then for some time he brooded with his chin resting in his hands, while the women-singers within filled the heavy air with wailings. At length he sat up and leisurely filled his pipe. His face had become a wrinkled mask again. He smoked a while, then passing the pipe to me, he continued, and his voice was thick as though he still breathed smoke:

"After the snows have run away, the earth-smell rises and all things grow drunk with it. The he-wolf sniffs it; he forgets his last year's mate; he takes another and forgets. The air and the earth and the water are full of new loves, and nothing is ashamed.

"It was so.

"When the next sunlight came I made ready for the trail. I rolled up my tepee. All the while my woman stared upon the woman who had come, with eyes made sharp with hate. I called in my ponies from the grazing places. I hitched a pony to the drag. I put upon the drag the tepee and the food and the little box that Mignon had brought with her —a box of many garments—garments that made songs when she walked, like the songs of rain in the leaves. I lifted Mignon upon the drag-pony's back, and we rode away on the summer trail.

"I heard my woman wailing and crying out bitterly in my lodge, but a spirit led me on—the spirit that calls the green things out in the spring—the spirit that whispers into the ear of the sleeping River and makes it leap up and shout and tear the thongs that bind it—the spirit that makes the wolves cry out in the lonesome places that the mate may hear.

"And we came to a place by the river where the hills were high and many leaves made coolness.

Mignon

There I pitched the tepee; and the days were as little flashes of light, and the nights were as little shadows passing.

"Never before had I found it so good to live. Mignon made songs that laughed and cried; and when she did not sing, the rustle of her garments was a song. I became as a squaw; I brought the wood and water; I made the fires; I cooked. I was bowed before her. Never before had I bowed before any one, for I was strong. I could not understand. She was so soft and white and of so sweet a smell!

"But the time came when she no longer sang. She grew silent, and each day gazed long upon the river. Her hands touched me no more with the touch of soft fires. So I grew kinder still. I spoke soft words. I made sweet sounds to call her. But she frowned and pushed me away.

"Fires burned in me, so I said: "You think always of that baby man whose finger I bit. I could choke him with my fingers—*so!*' But she laughed in my face, making sharp jokes to fling at me. I was stung as with whips when the whippers are angry. I said: 'Go back to your baby man!'

"I did not wish her to go; they were the words of my anger. But she got up very straight and tall. There was lightning in her eyes. Thunder slept in her face. And her hair seemed as a black cloud that blows up angrily out of the hot south!

"She went to the tepee; she made ready to go; and all the while I watched with fires in my breast. Then suddenly she turned upon me—her face was a flame. She flung words at me: 'You are all the same!' She spit in my face! I have been struck in the teeth by strong men, but never have I felt so hard a blow. I sat as a man in a dream. I heard the angry song of her skirts as she fled up the back-trail. And then I was as one who wakens with a great hunger, and smells raw meat! I leaped up; I ran after her; I meant to kill her!

"I caught her; I struck her with my fist, even as I struck the man who lied. I put my fingers at her throat and pressed very hard. I carried her back to the tepee. I thought I had killed her.

"Oh, the smell of her flesh as she lay very still— as though I had stepped upon a flower!

"And then after a long time, when my heart was growing sick, she opened her eyes and looked upon me. O tender, tender were her eyes and full of soft fires! It was the old look, only it was stronger. She raised herself to her knees; she put her arms around my neck; she put her lips on my lips; she called me soft names!

"I thought this was some woman's trick. I pushed her from me. I said: 'I am hungry; you are my squaw; cook my food!' And she brought wood and water; she made a fire; she worked for me. All the

Mignon

while her eyes were soft, and often she touched me with finger tips that burned as of old with soft fires. I could not understand. When I was kind, then was she not kind."

Yellow Fox took the pipe from my hands and smoked long in silence. He sighed deeply, breathing in great breaths of smoke. At length, growing impatient, I ventured a question: "And what became of Mignon?"

He laid down his pipe and said in a low voice: "The woman who wailed in the lodge had not forgotten!

"The plums ripened," he continued, "and the flowers that bloomed upon our summer trail were heavy with seed. The hills grew brown. A grayness like smoke was in all the air. The grapes hung thick and purple.

"And it happened one night when the first small pinch of frost was in the air, that Mignon would sing soft baby songs, such as the mothers of her people sang, she said. Oh, such soft, low songs! I hear them yet. A kindness was in her face, like that in the face of a young mother. I saw it by the light of the wood fire that held the frost away. And when she had sung much, as to a child, she put her hands upon my shoulders and she said a strange thing. This is what she said, I remember: 'Some time, Yellow Fox, I will sing to your *zhinga zhinga;* will you be glad?'

"And I wondered much, for her eyes were wet when she said it.

"And that night she fell to sleep with her soft hands clutching my arm. And something made me wish to sing. And then I slept.

"But in that time when the night is deepest and sleep is like a weight upon the eyes, a sharp cry woke me. I leaped up. The fire was almost dead. I heard feet flying through the dead leaves into the darkness. One hand felt warm and wet; I raised it to my nose and it was blood. And then I heard a gasping for breath and a sound of gurgling. I put my hand upon the breast of Mignon—and it was wet with blood!

"I scraped the embers together and made a little flame. I looked into her face and it had the look of death. Eyes that ached she turned upon me. I stopped the blood with torn garments. I called her soft names and she clutched my fingers. Then she was very quiet. I could hear leaves dropping out in the night."

Yellow Fox lapsed into another prolonged silence. The dancers and singers in the lodge had ceased. A heavy, sultry silence filled the night. When he spoke again his voice came low and muffled:

"I buried her after the manner of my people. I sang the songs of the dead. Above her grave I killed the pony that she rode. And then I went

away upon the trail that was no more the trail of
summer. But the winds in the grasses sang her
name. Mignon! Mignon! I heard the rain winds
singing in the first leaves. Mignon! Mignon! I
heard the sighing of summer waters. Mignon!
Mignon! I smelled the smell of spring. Everywhere it was—Mignon!—half sound, half smell—
dream-sound, dream-smell—so thin—so thin."

THE LAST THUNDER SONG

THE summer of 1900 debilitated all thermal adjectives. It was not hot; it was *Saharical!* It would hardly have been hyperbole to have said that the Old Century lay dying of a fever. The untilled hills of the reservation thrust themselves up in the August sunshine like the emaciated joints of one bedridden. The land lay as yellow as the skin of a fever patient, except in those rare spots where the melancholy corn struggled heartlessly up a hillside, making a blotch like a bedsore!

The blood of the prairie was impoverished, and the sky would give no drink with which to fill the dwindling veins. When one wished to search the horizon for the cloud that was not there, he did it from beneath an arched hand. The small whirlwinds that awoke like sudden fits of madness in the sultry air, rearing yellow columns of dust into the sky—these alone relieved the monotony of dazzle.

Every evening the clouds rolled flashing about the horizon and thundered back into the night. They were merely taunts, like the holding of a cool cup just out of reach of a fevered mouth; and the clear

The Last Thunder Song

nights passed, bringing dewless dawns, until the ground cracked like a parched lip!

The annual Indian powwow was to be ended prematurely that year, for the sun beat uninvitingly upon the flat bottom where the dances were held, and the Indians found much comfort in the shade of their summer tepees. But when it was noised about that, upon the next day, the old medicine-man Mahowari (Passing Cloud) would dance potent dances and sing a thunder song with which to awaken the lazy thunder spirits to their neglected duty of rain-making, then the argument of the heat became feeble.

So the next morning, the bronze head of every Indian tepeehold took his pony, his dogs, his squaw, and his papooses of indefinite number to the pow-wow ground. In addition to these, the old men carried with them long memories and an implicit faith.

The young men, who had been away to Indian school, and had succeeded to some extent in stuffing their brown skins with white souls, carried with them curiosity and doubt, which, if properly united, beget derision.

The old men went to a shrine; the young men went to a show. When a shrine becomes a show, they say the world advances a step.

About the open space in which the dances were held, an oval covering had been built with willow boughs, beneath which the Indians lounged in sweating groups. Slowly about the various small circles went the cumbersome stone pipes.

To one listening, drowsed with the intense sunshine, the *buzzle* and mutter and snarl of the gossiping Omahas seemed the grotesque echoes from a vanished age. Between the fierce dazzle of the sun and the sharply contrasting blue shade, there was but a line of division; yet a thousand years lay between one gazing in the sun and those dozing in the shadow. It was as if God had flung down a bit of the young world's twilight into the midst of the old world's noon. Here lounged the masterpiece of the toiling centuries—a Yankee! There sat the remnant of a race as primitive as Israel. And the white man looked on with contempt of superiority.

Before ten o'clock everybody had arrived and his family with him. A little group, composed of the Indian Agent, the Agency Physician the Mission Preacher, and a newspaper man, down from the city for reportorial purposes, waited and chatted, sitting upon a ragged patch of available shadow.

"These Omahas are an exceptional race," the preacher was saying in his ministerial tone of voice; "an exceptional race!"

The newspaper man mopped his face, lit a cigarette and nodded assent with a hidden meaning twinkling in his eye.

"Quite exceptional!" he said, tossing his head

The Last Thunder Song

in the direction of an unusually corpulent bunch of steaming, sweating, bronze men and women. "God, like some lesser master-musicians, has not confined himself to grand opera, it seems!"

With severe unconcern the preacher mended the broken thread of his discourse. "Quite an exceptional race in many ways. The Omaha is quite as honest as the white man."

"That is a truism!" The pencil-pusher drove this observation between the minister's words like a wedge.

"In his natural state he was much more so," uninterruptedly continued the preacher; he was used to continuous discourse. "I have been told by many of the old men that in the olden times an Indian could leave his tepee for months at a time, and on his return would find his most valuable possessions untouched. I tell you, gentlemen, the Indian is like a prairie flower that has been transplanted from the blue sky and the summer sun and the pure winds into the steaming, artificial atmosphere of the hothouse! A glass roof is not the blue sky! Man's talent is not God's genius! That is why you are looking at a perverted growth.

"Look into an Indian's face and observe the ruins of what was once manly dignity, indomitable energy, masterful prowess! When I look upon one of these faces, I have the same thoughts as, when traveling in Europe, I looked upon the ruins of Rome.

"Everywhere broken arches, fallen columns, tumbled walls! Yet through these as through a mist one can discern the magnificence of the living city. So in looking upon one of these faces, which are merely ruins in another sense. They were once as noble, as beautiful as———"

In his momentary search for an eloquent simile, the minister paused.

"As pumpkin pies!" added the newspaper man with a chuckle; and he whipped out his notebook and pencil to jot down this brilliant thought, for he had conceived a very witty "story" which he would pound out for the Sunday edition.

"Well," said the Agency Physician, finally sucked into the whirlpool of discussion, "it seems to me that there is no room for crowing on either side. Indians are pretty much like white men; livers and kidneys and lungs, and that sort of thing; slight difference in the pigment under the skin. I've looked into the machinery of both species and find just as much room in one as the other for a soul!"

"And both will go upward," added the minister.

"Like different grades of tobacco," observed the Indian Agent, "the smoke of each goes up in the same way."

"Just so," said the reporter; "but let us cut out the metaphysics. I wonder when this magical *cuggie* is going to begin his humid evolutions. Lamentable, isn't it, that such institutions as rain prayers should exist on the very threshold of the twentieth century?"

"I think," returned the minister, "that the twentieth century has no intention of eliminating God! This medicine-man's prayer, in my belief, is as sacred as the prayer of any churchman. The difference between Wakunda and God is merely orthographical."

"But," insisted the cynical young man from the city, "I had not been taught to think of God as of one who forgets! Do you know what I would do if I had no confidence in the executive ability of my God?"

Taking the subsequent silence as a question, the young man answered: "Why, I would take a day off and whittle one out of wood!"

"A youth's way is the wind's way," quoted the preacher, with a paternal air.

"And the thoughts of youth are long, long thoughts; but what is all this noise about?" returned the reporter.

A buzz of expectant voices had grown at one end of the oval, and had spread contagiously throughout the elliptical strip of shade. For with slow, majestic step the medicine-man, Mahowari, entered the enclosure and walked toward the center. The fierce sun emphasized the brilliancy of the old man's garments and glittered upon the profusion of trinkets, the magic heirlooms of the medicine-man. It was not the robe nor the dazzling trinkets that caught the eye of one acquainted with Mahowari. It was the erectness of his figure, for he had been bowed with years, and many vertical suns had shone upon the old man's back since his face had been turned toward the ground. But now with firm step and form rigidly erect he walked.

Any sympathetic eye could easily read the thoughts that passed through the old man's being like an elixir infusing youth. Now in his feeble years would come his greatest triumph! To-day he would sing with greater power than ever he had sung. Wakunda would hear the cry. The rains would come! Then the white men would be stricken with belief!

Already his heart sang before his lips. In spite of the hideous painting of his face, the light of triumph shone there like the reflection of a great fire.

Slowly he approached the circle of drummers who sat in the glaring center of the ellipse of sunlight. It was all as though the first century had awakened like a ghost and stood in the very doorway of the twentieth!

When Mahowari had approached within a yard of the drums, he stopped, and raising his arms and his eyes to the cloudless sky, uttered a low cry like a wail of supplication. Then the drums began to throb.

The Last Thunder Song

With a slow, majestic bending of the knees and an alternate lifting of his feet, the medicine-man danced in a circle about the snarling drums. Then like a faint wail of winds toiling up a wooded bluff, his thunder song began.

The drone and whine of the mysterious, untranslatable words pierced the drowse of the day, lived for a moment with the echoes of the drums among the surrounding hills, and languished from a whisper into silence. At intervals the old man raised his face, radiant with fanatic ecstasy, to the meridian glare of the sun, and the song swelled to a supplicating shout.

Faster and faster the old man moved about the circle; louder and wilder grew the song. Those who watched from the shade were absorbed in an intense silence, which, with the drowse of the sultry day, made every sound a paradox! The old men forgot their pipes and sat motionless.

Suddenly, at one end of the covering, arose the sound of laughter! At first an indefinite sound like the spirit of merriment entering a capricious dream of sacred things; then it grew and spread until it was no longer merriment, but a loud jeer of derision! It startled the old men from the intenseness of their watching. They looked up and were stricken with awe. The young men were jeering this, the holiest rite of their fathers!

Slower and slower the medicine-man danced;

fainter and fainter grew the song and ceased abruptly. With one quick glance, Mahowari saw the shattering of his hopes. He glanced at the sky; but saw no swarm of black spirits to avenge such sacrilege. Only the blaze of the sun, the glitter of the arid zenith!

In that one moment, the temporary youth of the old man died out. His shoulders drooped to their wonted position. His limbs tottered. He was old again.

It was the Night stricken heart-sick with the laughter of the Dawn. It was the audacious Present jeering at the Past, tottering with years. At that moment, the impudent, cruel, brilliant youth called Civilization snatched the halo from the gray hairs of patriarchal Ignorance. Light flouted the rags of Night. A clarion challenge shrilled across the years.

Never before in all the myriad moons had such a thing occurred. It was too great a cause to produce an effect of grief or anger. It stupefied. The old men and women sat motionless. They could not understand.

With uneven step and with eyes that saw nothing, Mahowari passed from among his kinsmen and tottered up the valley toward his lonesome shack and tepee upon the hillside. It was far past noon when the last of the older Omahas left the scene of the dance.

The Last Thunder Song

The greater number of the white men who had witnessed the last thunder dance of the Omahas went homeward much pleased. The show had turned out quite funny indeed. "Ha, ha, ha! Did you see how surprised the old *cuggie* looked? He, he, he!"

But as the minister rode slowly toward his home there was no laughter in his heart. He was saying to himself: "If the whole fabric of my belief should suddenly be wrenched from me, what then?" Even this question was born of selfishness, but it brought pity.

In the cool of the evening the minister mounted his horse and rode to the home of Mahowari, which was a shack in the winter and a tepee in the summer. Dismounting, he threw the bridle reins upon the ground, and raised the door flap of the tepee. Mahowari sat cross-legged upon the ground, staring steadily before him with unseeing eyes.

"How!" said the minister.

The old Indian did not answer. There was no expression of grief or anger or despair upon his face. He sat like a statue. Yet, the irregularity of his breathing showed where the pain lay. An Indian suffers in his breast. His face is a mask.

The minister sat down in front of the silent old man and, after the immemorial manner of ministers, talked of a better world, of a pitying Christ, and of God, the Great Father. For the first time the Indian raised his face and spoke briefly in English:

"God? He dead, guess!"

Then he was silent again for some time.

Suddenly his eyes lit up with a light that was not the light of age. The heart of his youth had awakened. The old memories came back and he spoke fluently in his own tongue, which the minister understood.

"These times are not like the old times. The young men have caught some of the wisdom of the white man. Nothing is sure. It is not good. I cannot understand. Everything is young and new. All old things are dead. Many moons ago, the wisdom of Mahowari was great. I can remember how my father said to me one day when I was yet young and all things lay new before me: 'Let my son go to a high hill and dream a great dream'; and I went up in the evening and cried out to Wakunda and I slept and dreamed.

"I saw a great cloud sweeping up from under the earth, and it was terrible with lightning and loud with thunder. Then it passed over and disappeared. And when I awoke and told my people of my dream, they rejoiced and said: 'Great things shall come to this youth. We shall call him Passing Cloud, and he shall be a thunder man, keen and quick to know, with the keenness and quickness of the lightning; and his name shall be as thunder for men to hear.' And

The Last Thunder Song

I grew and believed in these sayings and I was strong. But now I can see the meaning of the dream—a great light and a great noise and a passing."

The old man sighed and the light passed out of his eyes. Then he looked searchingly into the face of the minister, speaking in English:

"You white medicine man. You pray?"

The minister nodded.

Mahowari turned his gaze to the ground and said wearily:

"White god dead too, guess."

THE ALIEN

THROUGH the quiet night, crystalline with the pervading spirit of the frost, under prairie skies of mystic purple pierced with the glass-like glinting of the stars, fled Antoine.

Huge and hollow-sounding with the clatter of the pinto's hoofs hung the night above and about—lonesome, empty, bitter as the soul of him who fled.

A weary age of flight since sunset; and now the midnight saw the thin-limbed, long-haired pony slowly losing his nerve, tottering, rasping in the throat. With spike-spurred heels the rider hurled the beast into the empty night.

"Gwan! you blasted cayuse! you overgrown wolf-dog! Keep up that tune; I'm goin' somewheres. What'd I steal you fer? Pleasure? I reckon; pleasure for the half-breed! Gwan!"

Suddenly rounding a bank of sand, the pinto sighted the broad, ice-bound river, a stream of glinting silver under the stars. Sniffing and crouching upon its haunches at the sudden glow that dwindled a gleaming thread into the further dusk, the jaded beast received a series of vicious jabs from the spike-spurred heels. It groaned and lunged forward

The Alien

again, taking with uncertain feet the glaring path ahead, and awakening dull, snarling thunder in the under regions of the ice. Slipping, struggling, doing its brute best to overcome fatigue and the uncertainty of its path, the pinto covered the ice.

"Doin' a war dance, eh?" growled the man with bitter mirth, gouging the foaming bloody flanks of the animal. "Gwan! Set up that tune; I want fast music, 'cause I'm goin' somewheres—don't know where—somewheres out there in the shadders! Come here, will you? Take that and that and *that!* By the——!"

The brutal cries of the man were cut short as he shot far over the pommel, lunging headlong over the pinto's head, and striking with head and shoulders upon the glare ice. When he stopped sliding he lay very still for a few moments. Then he groaned, sat up, and found that the bluffs and the river and the stars and the universe in general were whirling giddily, with himself for the dizzy center.

With uncertain arms he reached out, endeavoring to check the sickening motion of things with the sheer force of his powerful hands. He was thrown down like a weakling wrestling with a giant. He lay still, cursing in a whisper, trying to steady the universe, until the motion passed, leaving in his nerves the sickening sensation incident to the sudden ending of a rapid flight.

With great care Antoine raised himself upon his

elbows and gazed about with an imbecile leer. Then he began to remember; remembered that he was hunted; that he was an outcast, a man of no race; remembered dimly, and with a malignant grin, a portion of a long series of crimes; remembered that the last was horse-stealing and that some of the others concerned blood. And as he remembered, he felt with horrible distinctness the lariat tightening about his neck—the lariat that the men of Cabanne's trading post were bringing on fleet horses, nearer, nearer through the silent night.

Antoine shuddered and got to his feet, looming huge against the star-spent surface of the ice, as he turned a face of bestial malevolence down trail and listened for the beat of hoofs. There was only the dim, hollow murmur that dwells at the heart of silence.

"Got a long start," he observed, with the chuckle of a man whom desperation has made careless. "Hel-*lo!*"

A pale, semicircular glow, like the flare of a burning straw stack a half day's journey over the hills, had grown up at the horizon of the east; and as the man stared, still in a maze from his recent fall, the moon heaved a tarnished silver arc above the rim of sky, flooding with new light the river and the bluffs. The man stood illumined—a big brute of a man, heavy-limbed, massive-shouldered, with the slouching stoop and the alert air of an habitual

The Alien

skulker. He moved uneasily, as though he had suddenly become visible to some lurking foe. He glanced nervously about him, fumbled at the butt of a six-shooter at his belt, then catching sight of the blotch of huddled dusk that was the fallen pinto, the meaning of the situation flashed upon him.

"That cussed cayuse! Gone and done hisself like as not! Damn me! the whole creation's agin me!"

He made for the pony, snarling viciously as though its exhausted, lacerated self were the visible body of the inimical universe. He grasped the reins and jerked them violently. The brute only groaned and let its weary head fall heavily upon the ice.

"Get up!"

Antoine began kicking the pony in the ribs, bringing forth great hollow bellowings of pain.

"O, you won't get up, eh? Agin me too, eh? Take that, and that and *that!* I wished you was everybody in the whole world and hell to oncet! I'd make you beller now I got you down! Take *that!*"

The man with a roar of anger fell upon the pony, snarling, striking, kicking, but the pony only groaned. Its limbs could no longer support its body. When Antoine had exhausted his rage, he got up, gave the pony a parting kick on the nose, and started off at a dogtrot across the glinting ice toward the bluffs beyond.

Ever and anon he stopped and whirled about with hand at ear. He heard only the murmur of the silence, broken occasionally by the whine and pop of the ice and the plaintive wail of the coyotes somewhere in the hills, like the heartbroken cry of the prairie, yearning for the summer.

"O, I wouldn't howl if I was you," muttered the man to the coyotes; "I wished I was a coyote or a gray wolf, knowin' what I do. I'd be a man-killer and a cattle-killer, I would. And then I'd have people of my own. Wouldn't be no cur of a half-breed runnin' from his kind. O, I wouldn't howl if I was you!"

He proceeded at a swinging trot across the half mile of ice and halted under the bluffs. He listened intently. A far sound had grown up in the hollow night—vague, but unmistakable. It was the clatter of hoofs far away, but clear in faintness, for the cold snap had made the prairie one vast sounding-board. A light snow had fallen the night before, and the trail of the refugee was traced in the moon-light, distinct as a wagon track.

Antoine felt the pitiless pinch of the approaching lariat as he listened. Then his accustomed bitter weariness of life came upon the pariah.

"What's the use of me runnin'? What am I runnin' to? Nothin'—only more of the same thing I'm runnin' from; lonesomeness and hunger and the like of that. Gettin' awake stiff and cold and half starved and cussin' the daylight 'cause it's agin me like everything else, and gives me away. Sneakin'

The Alien

around in the brush till dark, eatin' when I can like a damned wolf, then goin' to sleep hopin' it'll never get day. But it always does. It's all night some-wheres, I guess, spite of what the missionaries says. That's fer me—night always! No comin' day, no gettin' up, somewhere to hide snug in always!"

He walked on with head dropped forward upon his breast, skirting the base of the bluffs, now seem-ingly oblivious of the sound of hoofs that grew momently more distinct.

As he walked, he was dimly conscious of passing the dark mouth of a hole running back into the clay of a bluff. He proceeded until he found himself again at the edge of the river, staring down into a broad, black fissure in the ice, caused, doubtless, by the dash of the current crossing from the other side.

A terrible, dark, but alluring thought seized him. Here was the place—the doorway to that place where it was always night! Why not go in? There would be no more running away, no more hiding, no more hatred of men, no more lonesomeness! Here was the place at last.

He stepped forward and stooped to gaze down into the door of night. The rushing waters made a dismal, moaning sound.

He stared transfixed. Yes, he would go!

Suddenly a shudder ran through his limbs. He gave a quick exclamation of terror! He leaped back and raised his face to the skies.

How kind and soft and gentle and good to look upon was the sky! He gazed about—it was so fair a world! How good it was to breathe! He longed to throw his great, brute arms about creation and clutch it to him, and hold it! He wished to live.

The hoofs!

The distant muffled confusion of sound had grown into distinct, staccato notes. The pursuers were now less than a mile away. Soon they would reach the river.

With the quick instinct of the hunted beast, Antoine knew the means of safety. His footprints led to the ice-fissure. He decided that none should lead away. He could not be pursued under ice. Stooping so that he could look between his legs, he began retracing his steps, walking backward, placing his feet with great care where they had fallen before. Thus he came again to the hole in the clay bluff, and disappeared. His trail had passed within a foot of the hole, which was overhung by a jutting point of sandstone. No snow had fallen at the entrance; he left no trail as he entered.

Stopping upon his hands and knees, he listened and could hear distinctly the sharp crack of hoofs upon the ice and the pop and thunder of the frozen surface.

"Here's *some* luck," muttered Antoine. He crawled on into the nether darkness of the hole that grew more spacious as he proceeded. As he crawled, the sound of pursuing hoofs grew dimmer. Antoine half forgot them. His keen sense had caught the peculiar musty odor of animal life. He felt a stuffy warmth in his nostrils as he breathed.

Suddenly out of the dark ahead grew up two points of phosphorescent light. Antoine fell back upon his haunches with a little growl of surprise. Years of wild lonesome life had made him more beast than man.

The lights slowly came closer, growing more brilliant. Then there was a harsh, rasping growl and a sound of sniffing. Antoine waited until the expanding pupils of his eyes could grasp the situation with more distinctness. "Can't run," he mused. "Lariat behind, somethin' growlin' in front. It's one more fight. Here goes fer my damnedest. Rather die mad and fightin' than jump into cold water or stick my head through a rawhide necktie!"

He crawled on carefully. The lights approached with a strange swaying motion. Then of a sudden came a whine, a sharp, savage yelp, and Antoine felt his cheek ripped open with a stroke of gnashing teeth!

He felt for an instant the hot breath of the beast, the trickle of hot blood on his cheek; and then all that was human in him passed. He growled and hurled the sinewy body of his unseen foe from him with a blow of his bear-like paw.

The dark hole echoed a muffled howl of anger, and

in an instant man and beast rolled together in the darkness.

At last the man knew that it was a gray wolf he fought. He reached for its throat, but felt his hand caught in a hot, wet, powerful trap of teeth. He grasped the under jaw with a grip that made his antagonist howl with pain. Then with his other hand he felt about in the darkness, groping for the throat.

He found it, seized it with a vise-like clutch, shut his teeth together, and threw all of the power of his massive frame into the struggle.

Slowly the struggles of the wolf became weaker. The lean, hairy form fell limp, and the man laughed with a sobbing, guttural mirth—for he was master.

Then again he felt the trickle of blood upon his cheek, the ache of his bitten hand. His anger returned with double fury. He kicked the limp body as he lay beside it, never releasing his grip.

Suddenly he forgot to kick. There were sounds! He heard the *thump thump* of hoofs passing his place of refuge. Then they ceased. There were sounds of voices coming dimly; then after a while the hoofs passed again, and there was a voice that said "saved hangin' anyway."

The hoof beats grew dimmer, and Antoine knew by their hollow sound that his pursuers had begun to cross the ice on the back trail. He again gave his attention to the wolf. It lay still. A feeling of supreme comfort came over Antoine. It was sweet to be a master. He laid his head upon the wolf's motionless body. He was very weary, he had conquered, and he would sleep upon his prey.

He awoke feeling a warm, rasping something upon his wounded cheek. A faint light came in at the entrance of the place. It was morning. In his sleep Antoine had moved his head close to the muzzle of the wolf. Now, utterly conquered, bruised, unable to arise, the brute was feebly licking the blood from the man's wound.

Antoine's sense of mastery after his sound sleep made him kind for once. He was safe and something had caressed him, although it was only a soundly beaten wolf.

"You pore devil!" said Antoine with a sudden softness in his voice; "I done you up, didn't I? You hain't so bad, I guess; but if I hadn't done you, I'd got done myself. Hurt much, you pore devil, eh?"

He stroked the side of the animal, whereupon it cried out with pain.

"Pretty sore, eh? Well, as long as I'm bigger'n you, I'll be good to you. I ain't so bad, am I? You treat me square and you won't never get no bad deals from the half-breed; mind that. Hel-*lo!* you're a *Miss* Wolf, ain't you? Well, for the present, I'm a Mister Wolf, and I'm a good un! Let me hunt you up a name; somethin' soft like a woman, 'cause you did touch me kind of tender like. *Susette!*

—that's it—*Susette*. You're Susette now. I hain't got no people, so I'm a wolf from now on, and my name's Antoine. Susette and Antoine—sounds pretty good, don't it? Say, I know as much about bein' a wolf as you do. Can't teach me nothin' about sneakin' and hidin' and fightin'! Say, old girl, *hain't* I a tol'able good fighter now? O, I know I am, and when you need it again, you're goin' to get it good and hard, Susette; mind that. Hain't got nothin' to eat about the house, have you, old girl? Then, bein' head of the family with a sick woman about, I'm goin' huntin'. Don't you let no other wolf come skulkin' around! You know me! I'll wear his skin when I come back, if you don't mind!"

And he went out.

Before noon he returned bringing three jack rabbits, having shot them with his six-shooter. "Well, Susette," said he, "got any appetite?"

He passed his hand over the wolf's snout caressingly. The wolf flinched in fear, but the man continued his caresses until she licked his hand.

"Now, we're friends and we can live together peaceable, can't we? Took a big family row, though. Families needs stirrin' up now and then, I reckon."

He skinned a rabbit and cut off morsels of meat.

"Here, Susette, I'm goin' to fill your hide first, 'cause you've been so good since the row that I'm half beginnin' to love you a little. There, that's it

The Alien

—eat. Does me good to see you eat, pore, sick
Susette!"

The wolf took the morsels from his hand and a
look almost tame came into her eyes. When she
had eaten a rabbit, Antoine had a meal of raw flesh.
Then he sat down beside her and stroked her nose
and neck and flanks. There was an air of home
about the place. He was safe and sheltered, had a
full stomach, and there was a fellow creature near
him that showed kindness, although it had been won
with a beating. But this man had long been accustomed to possessing by violence, and he was satisfied.

"Susette," he said in a soft voice; "don't get mean
again when you get well. I want to live quiet and
like somethin' that likes me oncet. If you'll be good,
I'll get you rabbits and antelope and birds, and you
won't need to hunt no more nor go about with your
belly flappin' together. And I know how to make
fire—somethin' you don't know, wise as you be; and
I'll keep you warm and pet you.

"Is it a bargain? All you need to do is just be
good, keepin' your teeth out'n my cheek. I've been
lonesome always. I hain't got no people. Do you
know who your dad was, Susette? Neither do I.
Some French trader was mine, I guess. We're in
the same boat there. My mother was an Omaha.
O Susette, I know what it means to set a stranger
in my mother's lodge. *'Wagah peazzha!'* [no good
white man], that's what the Omahas called me ever

since I was a little feller. And the white men said 'damn Injun.' And where am I? O, hangin' onto the edge of things, gettin' ornry and nasty and bad! I've stole horses and killed people and cussed fer days, Susette. And I want to rest; I want to love somethin'. Cabanne's men down at the post would laugh to hear me sayin' that. But I do. I want to love somethin'. Tried to oncet; her name was Susette, jest like your'n. She was a trader's daughter—a pretty French girl. That was before I got bad. I talked sweet to her like I'm a talkin' to you, and she kind of liked it. But the old man Lecroix —that was her dad—he showed me the trail and he says: 'Go that way and go fast, you damn Injun!'

"I went, Susette, but I made him pay, I did. I seen him on his back a-grinnin' straight up at the stars; and since then I hain't cared much. I killed several after that, and I called 'em all Lecroix!

"Be a good girl, Susette, and I'll stick to you. I'm a good fighter, you know, and I'm a good grub-hunter, too. I learned all that easy."

He continued caressing the wolf, and she licked his hand when he stroked her muzzle.

Days passed; the heavy snows came. Antoine nursed his bruised companion back to health. Through the bitter nights he kept a fire burning at the entrance of the hole. The depth of the snow made it improbable that any should learn his where-

The Alien

abouts; and by that time the news must have spread from post to post that Antoine, the outlaw half-breed, had drowned himself in the ice-fissure.

The man had used all his ammunition, and his six-shooter had thus become useless. With the skill of an Indian he wrought a bow and arrows. He made snowshoes and continued to hunt, keeping the wolf in meat until she grew strong and fat with the unaccustomed luxurious life.

Also she became very tame. During her weakness the man had subdued her, and through the long nights she lay nestled within the man's great arms and slept.

When the snow became crusted, Antoine and Susette went hunting together, she trotting at his heels like a dog. To her he had come to be only an unusually large wolf—a good fighter.

One evening in late December, when the low moon threw a shaft of cold silver into the mouth of the lair, Antoine lay huddled in his furs, listening to the long, dirge-like calls of the wolves wandering inward from the vast pitiless night. Susette also listened, sitting upon her haunches beside the man with her ears pricked forward. When the far away cries of her kinspeople arose into a compelling major sound, dying away into the merest shadow of a pitiful minor, she switched her tail uneasily, shuffled about nervously, sniffing and whining.

Then she began pacing with an eager swing up

and down the place to the opening and back to the man, sending forth the cry of kinship whenever she reached the moonlit entrance.

"Night's cold, Susette," said Antoine; " 'tain't no time fer huntin'. Hain't I give you enough to eat? Come here and snuggle up and let's sleep."

He caught the wolf and with main force held her down beside him. She snarled savagely and snapped her jaws together, struggling out of his arms and going to the opening where she cried out into the frozen stillness. The answer of her kind floated back in doleful chorus.

"Don't go!" begged the man. "Susette, my pretty Susette! I'll be so lonesome."

As the chorus died, the wolf gave a loud yelp and rushed out into the night. A terrible rage seized Antoine. He leaped from his furs and ran out after the wolf. She fled with a rapid, swinging trot over the scintillating snow toward the concourse of her people. The man fled after, slipping, falling, getting up, running, and ever the wolf widened the glittering stretch of snow between them. To Antoine, the ever-widening space of glinting coldness vaguely symbolized the barrier that seemed growing between him and his last companion.

"Susette, O, Susette!" he cried at last, breathless and exhausted. His cry was dirgelike, even as the wolves'.

She had disappeared in the dusk of a ravine.

The Alien

Antoine, huddled in the snows with his face upon his knees, sobbed in the winter stillness. At last, with slow and faltering step, he returned to his lair; and for the first time in months he felt the throat-pang of the alien.

He threw himself down upon the floor of the cave and cursed the world. Then he cursed Susette.

"It's some other wolf!" he hissed. "Some other gray dog that she's gone to see. O, damn him! damn his gray hide! I'll kill her when she comes back!"

He took out his knife and began whetting it viciously upon his boot.

"I'll cut her into strips and eat 'em! Wasn't I good to her? O, I'll cut her into strips!"

He whetted his knife for an hour, cursing the while through his set teeth. At last anger grew into a foolish madness. He hurled himself upon the bunch of furs beside him and imagined that they were Susette. He set his teeth into the furs, he crushed them with his hands, he tore at them with his nails. Then in the impotence of his anger, he fell upon his face and sobbed himself to sleep.

Strange visions passed before him. Again he killed Lecroix, and saw the dead face grinning at the stars. Again he sat in his mother's lodge and wept because he was a stranger. Again he was fleeing from a leather noose that hung above him like a black cloud, and circled and lowered and

raised and lowered until it swooped down upon him
and closed about his neck.

With a yell of fright he awoke from his nightmare. His head throbbed, his mouth was parched.
At last day came in sneakingly through the opening—a dull, melancholy light; and with it came
Susette, sniffling, with the bristles of her neck
erect.

"Susette! Susette!" cried the man joyfully.

He no longer thought of killing her. He seized
her in his arms; he kissed her frost-whitened muzzle; he caressed her; he called her a woman. She
received his caresses with disdain. Whereat the man
redoubled his acts of fondness. He fed her and
petted her as she ate; whereas the bristles on her
neck fell. She nosed him half fondly.

And Antoine, man-like, was glad again.

He ate none that day. He said to himself, "I
won't hunt till it's all gone; she can have it all." He
was afraid to leave Susette. He was afraid to take
her with him again into the land of her own people.

All day he was kind to her with the pitiful kindness of a doting lover for his unfaithful mistress.

That night she consented to lie within his arms,
and Antoine cried softly as he whispered into her
ear: "Susette, I hain't a goin' to be jealous no more.
You've been a bad girl, Susette. Don't do it again.
I won't be mean less'n you let *him* come skulkin'
round here, damn his gray hide! But O, Susette"—

his voice was like a spoken pang—"I wisht—I wisht I was that other wolf!"

The next morning Antoine did not get up. He felt sore and exhausted. By evening his heart was beating like a hammer. His head ached and swam; his burning eyes saw strange, uncertain visions.

"Susette," he called, "I hain't quite right; come here and let me touch you again."

Night was falling and Susette sat sullenly apart, listening for the call of her people. She did not go to him. All night the man tossed and raved. After a lingering age of delirious wanderings, dizzy flights from huge pitiless pursuers, he became conscious of the daylight. He raised his head feebly and looked about the den. Susette was gone. A fury of jealousy again seized Antoine. She had gone to that other wolf—he felt certain of that. He tried to arise, but the fever had weakened him so that he lay impotent, torn alternately with anger and longing.

Suddenly a frost-whitened snout was thrust in at the opening. It was Susette. The man was too weak to cry out his joy, but his eyes filled with a soft light.

Susette entered sniffing strangely, whining and switching her tail as she came. At her heels followed another gray wolf—a male, larger-boned, lanker, with a more powerful snout. He whined and moved his tail nervously at sight of the man.

Antoine lay staring upon the intruder. "So that's him," thought the man; "I wisht I could get up."

A delirious anger shook him; he struggled to arise, but could not. "O God," he moaned; it was an unusual thing for this man to say the word so; "O God, please le' me get up and fight!"

A harsh growl stopped him. The gray intruder approached him with a rapid, sinuous movement of the tail. His jaws grinned with long sharp teeth displayed. The rage of hunger was in his eyes fixed steadily upon the sick man.

Antoine stared steadily into the glaring eyes of his wolfish rival, already crouching for the spring.

On a sudden, a strange exhilaration came over the man. He seemed drinking in the essence of life from the pitiless stare of his adversary. His great limbs, seeming devitalised but a moment before, now tingled to their extremities with a sudden surging of the wine of life. His eyes, which the fever had burned into the dullness of ashes, flamed suddenly again with the eager lust of fight.

He raised himself upon his haunches, beast-like, and with the lifting of a sneering lip that disclosed his grinding teeth, he gave a cry that was both a snarl and a sob.

Antoine met the impetuous spring of the wolf with the downward blow of a fist, and sprang whining upon his momentarily worsted foe. Never before had he fought in all his bitter pariah life as

The Alien

now he fought for the possession of his last companion.

His antagonist was larger than Susette, the survivor of many moonlit battles in the frozen wilderness of hills.

Lacerated with the snapping of powerful jaws, bleeding from his face and hands, the man felt that he was winning. With a whining cry, less than half human, he succeeded in fixing his left hand upon the hairy throat, crushed the wolf down upon its back, and with prodigious strength, began pressing the fingers of his right hand in between the protruding lower ribs. He would tear them out! He would thrust his hand in among the vitals of his foe!

All the while Susette, whining and switching her tail, watched with glowing eyes the struggle of the males.

At this juncture she arose with a nervous, threatening swaying of the head, approached the two cautiously, then hurled herself into the encounter. She leaped with a savage yelp upon him who had long been her master.

The man's grip relaxed. He fell back and threw out his arms in which once more the weakness of the fever came.

"Susette!" he gasped; "I was good to you; I—"

His voice was choked into a wheeze. Susette had gripped him by the throat, and the two were upon him.

THE PARABLE OF THE SACK

"A MAN'S chief business in this world," remarked my friend, who is something of a philosopher in his way, "is to break his heart under some load. Only the worthless ones fail to do it."

I smiled, for I am rather a cheerful person.

"It's a fact, and you can't smile it away," he continued. "We are all bearers of sacks filled with God knows what; and little does it matter so they be heavy enough for the purpose. But thrice happy is he who does not look into his sack too soon. All of which reminds me of a story."

Whereat he told his story in substantially the following manner:

One July day during the gold excitement of the '70s the Deadwood stage thundered down the hill into Bear Gulch, swung round sharp in a cloud of sand from the heels of the reined-in leaders, and drew up in front of the King Nugget saloon. A tenderfoot stepped out. By way of impedimenta he had with him an old-fashioned valise and some preconceived ideas of the West.

His whole story, so far, could have been read

merely by opening the valise; for it contained, as I happen to know, many (shall I say it?) unnecessary articles which could have been placed there only by the hands of woman in accordance with feminine notions of masculine comfort.

His mother had packed the valise, you see, and very well was it packed, though her hands had trembled with dreadful misgivings and her tears dampened some of the unnecessary articles, perhaps.

As to the preconceived ideas, they were plainly evidenced to the loungers about the saloon by the stranger's general appearance. He wore leather breeches of a very wicked Western cut, slashed into fringes at the bottom; a pair of exaggerated plainsman's boots and a buckskin coat, though the day was hot. About his middle hung a heavy belt supporting many rounds of cartridges and two very bright and shiny revolvers. No doubt he had his new rôle well thought out, and so he made his entrance in the costume of the part.

But all these trappings were so obstreperously *new!* You felt that a little careful scrutiny would reward you with a sight of the penciled selling price and the cabalistic cost mark of some Omaha outfitter!

Yes, the stranger was young—a fault which, however, with the aid of good health and fair luck may be corrected.

You could easily find a description of him from

his neck down in almost any of those dime novels that deal with the Wild Bill type. But for a description of him from his neck *up*—well, you would have to read pastoral poetry and that sort of thing. The spirit of the country—with all that it means—was in his face.

His eyes were clear and guileless—like a June sky over green wheatfields—and his cheeks made you think of Rambo apples tinting slowly in the sun. At first glance you would have said, "Here is one who has listened much to the tinkle of cowbells floating up green draws, and dreamed big dreams in the hush of harvest nights." You looked twice, and then you saw, in spite of the heroic effort of a swagger, that he had not yet outgrown his mother.

A ridiculous sort of hero, you say? Perhaps. But are not all heroes a bit ridiculous in the last analysis?

Be sure there was a stout, honest heart beating regularly under that buckskin coat; a heart that had not yet learned how to break under the strain of impossible ventures. And behind those clear eyes the rich virgin soil of an unsophisticated brain awaited the seed of big luxuriant beliefs.

Indeed, an ideal hero for the bearing of a sack!

He smiled boyishly as he pushed through the bevy of loungers and entered the bar-room of the King Nugget. One who smiles in his particular way has

The Parable of the Sack

never known suspicion. Somehow, his smile makes me think of sweet cider and heaped-up apples and simple folk sitting about open fireplaces when the first nip of frost is abroad in the night.

He passed among the gamblers at the tables with a forced nonchalant air, as though he had not looked upon such for the first time in his life. When he ordered whisky at the bar his voice was quite gruff. The horses down on the little Indiana farm would have pricked up curious ears at the sound of it, and the cows would have mistaken it for the voice of a stranger.

A guttural mirth grew up in the bar-room, and the loungers and gamblers crowded about the bar to have a look at this latest type of the greenhorn. But the stranger was too busy getting his first drink of whisky down his throat to notice the nudges and grimaces that went around at his expense. The unaccustomed drink gagged him a bit, and he was thinking, with a little twinge of shame, of a certain promise made to his mother. But mothers can never really understand the ways of men. Still, warm, fresh milk and the water from the spring that bubbled out under the old oak back home were really better drinks.

A rough miner shouldered his way through the mob, winking sidewise as he went, and resting his elbows on the bar, turned a mock-serious and wolfish face upon the greenhorn.

"How was crops when you left?" he inquired, carefully picking an imaginary hayseed out of the stranger's hair. "Pumpkins big this year?"

This warmed the heart of the greenhorn. Although he could not quite confess it to himself, he felt a strange sense of gnawing in his breast when he thought of home. The world was really so much broader than he had dreamed. Crops? Here was a subject for talk! Oh, he knew all about crops. Corn didn't promise very well this year. He thought, however, that wheat would go twelve bushels. Rye was poor because of dry weather during heading time. That is, he was speaking about the crops around Johnson Corners—Johnson Corners, Indiany, you know.

"Give Mr. Johnson Corners a drink on me!" said the inquiring one to the grinning bartender; "and make it whisky. Mr. Johnson Corners don't drink nothing but whisky! How was all the folks down on the old farm?" he went on for the benefit of the audience that leaned far over the bar, the better to view the greenhorn's beaming face.

Oh, the folks? Why, the folks had moved to town, you know. The folks were his mother and Nellie. Nellie was his sister. The old man (he used the word with an effort at worldliness) had been dead five years come that Fall. You see, the old farm had been sold that Spring. A man couldn't

The Parable of the Sack

be tied down to a plow all his life. There wasn't money enough in it, you know. A man had to get out into the world and do things!

The liquor and the great good-nature of his audience warmed him up. He became effusive. He held forth concerning his mother and his sister and his plans for the future. You saw the mother very plainly, for youth is naturally eloquent on some themes. You saw her patient face, becoming a little seamed with worries, yet kind and wistfully hopeful. You saw Nellie also—a plain but winsome country lass, wearing her first long dresses. And as he warmed up to his theme, it all came out: how he had conceived the idea of selling the old farm and using the remainder of the money—after the mortgage was paid—to go West and get immensely rich, and then go back and do ever so many delightful things for the mother and Nellie.

Nellie was to have music lessons—you just ought to hear her play on the organ! And he would see that his mother had silk dresses like Mrs. Jones, the banker's wife down at the Corners.

To be sure, the neighbors shook their heads dismally at his plans, and the men down at the grocery store—Deacon Brown in particular—said home was a pretty good place and farming not such a bad business. But what was a man to do? Hang onto a plow all his life when there was gold to be picked up? Not he! By jing, he knew a thing or two; and so there he was! Would the gentlemen have a drink on him?

The greenhorn proudly produced a roll of bills from an inside pocket and was offering to pay, when he felt a hand on his shoulder and turned about. He found himself looking into a most suave and friendly face, belonging to a man who wore a flashy suit of plaids.

"By God!" cried the man of plaids, thrusting forth a friendly hand to the greenhorn, "but ain't I glad to meet a man from Indiany! Shake! I came from there myself! Barkeep, this treat's on me. It ain't often I meet a man from my own State!"

The man of plaids held forth expansively concerning the essential brotherhood of Indiana's sons. It developed that he came from Coal City, and that was only twenty miles from the Corners! Why, he knew the country thereabouts like he knew the wart on his hand! How the greenhorn's heart warmed toward the man of plaids as they walked out of the bar-room arm in arm!

When the two were outside, the man of plaids cast a cautious eye about him, drew very close to the greenhorn and continued: "Of course, my friend, you're looking for a claim, and right now let me put a flea in your ear. Don't you trust none of them in there!" He pointed a deprecatory thumb over his shoulder at the bar-room now filled with noisy laugh-

The Parable of the Sack

ter. "You're what they call a tenderfoot, you know; though I can see with one eye that it won't take you long to get your feet tough! Eh?" He poked a jovial finger into the young man's ribs. "Now I happen to own the real bonanza claim of these diggin's, and I can't work it 'cause I got to start back home. Yep, back to Indiany—Coal City. Mother's sick. Guess that's why I have such a feeling for you. Can't explain it no other way. Mothers and sisters and all that—sort of touching, you know. So when I heard you talking in there I said to myself, 'Here's a chance to do a good turn for somebody that'll appreciate it.' And so what am I going to do? Give you a claim where you can pick out all the damned gold dust you can pack away in a sack!"

The man of plaids lapsed into an eloquent silence and watched the effect of his words bloom like a flower in the face of his auditor. The greenhorn's eyes dilated, his breathing deepened; there was a perceptible stiffening of his spine and a slight, haughty curving of his lip. He saw gold! Gold! Great yellow floods of it! Already he was standing before his critics at the Corners grocery store. Already he had placed a heavy sack upon the counter. He stood with folded arms, calmly awaiting the dramatic moment of his crushing triumph. Now old Deacon Brown opens the sack—there is a gasp —an exclamation of wonder—

"But let me put another flea in your ear," broke in the man of plaids. "Don't mention this to a soul—not a soul! They'll steal it! Like as not——" Here the man of plaids lifted a sinister right hand, imitating the act of firing a revolver and simulated the facial spasm of a man who has recently taken an ounce of hot lead into his system. "Not a word, mind you!" he went on. "Not a word to a soul! And when you get a sackful—all you can carry—cut loose, vanish, go up in smoke! I mean, take to the woods and go fast!"

The greenhorn was ecstatic. What could he ever do in payment for this? As for getting away with the gold, once he had it—well, he would look after that! He was green, he knew, but he knew a thing or two all the same!

He rhapsodized on the theme of his heart, developing it with brilliant luxury of detail up to the glorious golden climax. Nellie and his mother ran through it like the recurring dominant chords of a melody. And, little by little, a tremulous bashful new note crept in. He spoke of Bessie.

Bessie? Oh, the man of plaids guessed who *that* was! And he was so good-natured about it that he inspired confidence, and the faint, tremulous, tentative note grew rich and full, until your heart would have leaped to hear the name. And oh, how charmingly the man of plaids played second to this music of youth!

The Parable of the Sack

That night the brothers slept together, talking long about the dear old State. And with the peep of day, carrying a sack and a pick, they were off into the woods. They walked rapidly down gulches, up hills, through dense jackpine thickets. Ever now and then the man of plaids stopped short and put a questioning hand to his ear. "Hist!" he whispered. "No, it's only the echo of our footsteps. Thought somebody was following. We can't be too careful, you know!"

On they plunged into the wilderness. "Are we almost there?" gasped the greenhorn. "Yes," answered the man of plaids at length, "here we are at last. *Look!*" He pointed to the bank of a dry gully. The greenhorn looked and his eyes dilated; he gasped for breath.

A thin yellow streak was visible in the bank before him. "Take your pick and dig there," said the man of plaids. The greenhorn grasped the pick with trembling hands and dug. A thin glittering stream of yellow dust flowed down the bank and made a dazzling mass at his feet. He shrank back with a feeling of awe that was half terror.

A stream of gold dust flowing at his feet! At one knock the doors of happiness had swung wide! Tears of joy sprang in his eyes and trickled down his cheeks, grown suddenly livid with the awfulness of it. In that breathless moment he repurchased the old farm, built a costly palace upon it, bought silk dresses without number, heard wonderful melodies played by the trained fingers of Nellie, married Bessie—struck the whole countryside dumb with wonder and admiration!

"My friend," broke in the man of plaids, "the stage starts in an hour, and I must go. Unfortunately, I haven't enough money, and mother may be dying. Now five hundred dollars——"

Mechanically, still staring at the thin, glittering stream before him, the dreamer reached into his inside pocket, drew out the roll of bills and cast it on the ground. Many minutes passed; minutes in which days, months, years flew like the notes of a song through the brain of the dreamer.

At length he fell forward upon the beautiful stuff, gathered it in his arms, put his hot face close to it and laughed deliriously. Suddenly he straightened up with terror in his face. Had anyone heard? Oh, the beautiful yellow stuff! What if someone had heard and it should be taken from him!

He heard only the dawn wind moaning in the pines and the chirp of a hidden bird. He was alone —the man of plaids had gone.

With the nervousness of dread he began gathering up this visible happiness that dazzled him. He scraped it up carefully and filled his sack so full that it would not tie. What should he do—throw away some of the precious stuff? He felt a pang of regret at the thought that he could not take it all.

The Parable of the Sack

He scooped out a double handful and looked wistfully upon it. How much was that—a hundred, a thousand, five thousand dollars? He faltered long in the act to throw it away—and ended by putting it in his pocket.

He now found that he could tie the sack. But could he carry it? The thought struck him cruelly. After many minutes of hesitation, he tried.

He could not even shoulder it! Ah, gold was very heavy; he remembered having heard that it was very heavy. With trembling hands he untied the knot and took out another double handful. Could he throw it away—a whole handful of glittering happiness? What joy might not this much bring to mother and Nellie? He put that also in the pocket of his coat.

But still he could not shoulder the sack. With a sudden spasmodic effort of the will, he closed his eyes and dipped repeatedly into his treasure and cast it away. After all, three-fourths of it was better than none. But every thrusting of the hand into the sack was like a stab.

Again he tied the sack. At last he could lift it to his shoulder. But the weight was crushing. Ah, the dear weight—how he loved it!

He tottered off into the dense timber to the East. East—that was toward Johnson Corners. He would go East. He remembered having a compass in his pocket, feeling a little proud at his forethought in buying it. But now through the dense pines filtered the glow of the dawn. He tottered on with his face to the glow, and every step took him nearer Johnson Corners.

The glow crept up the pines, and the bearer of the precious sack became aware that his breath was coming painfully, that his temples were throbbing as though they would burst. He set the sack down to rest. Certainly it was very heavy, but he was strong. He would not throw away another ounce— not even the smallest pinch!

He shouldered it again and tottered manfully on into the wilderness. Thus with frequent rests he forged slowly into the East. The sun rose high and sank and the stars peeped in through the rifts in the foliage. Then an overpowering weakness seized the toiler, and he lay down with his head on the sack.

How dreadfully quiet the night was! He had heard of bears and mountain lions. He shuddered at the thought of them. But it was not the mere thought of death that made him shudder. It was the fear that death might take this precious weight from his shoulders.

A spirit of dauntlessness nerved him. He drew his shiny revolvers and lay very still. He would fight—fight! Oh, how he would fight! Let anything stand between him and his treasure now! He was ready.

The Parable of the Sack

He swooned away, and was at last in Johnson Corners—in the old church down at the Corners. Bessie was there beside him, dressed like a queen. The preacher was saying something that made his heart leap wildly—and it was dawn! He blinked in the gray light for a moment, then leaped up, shouldered his sack and plunged on again into the glow. But his shoulders pained him a little—oh, just a very little! He had often been as sore as that after pitching hay all day! He would get over that.

Really, the sack was not so heavy, after all. But nevertheless he often set it down panting. And when the sun broke through the tops of the trees he remembered that he had not eaten. Why, he must eat—that was the reason he grew so tired under the load! He had not eaten! But what should he eat?

A squirrel frisked and chattered on a branch above his head. Could he kill it with a revolver? He would try. He drew one of his shiny guns and took good aim.

But what if someone should be near and hear the report of the shot? He put the gun back in its holster and shouldering his sack forged ahead. There were wild berries growing all about him. He would eat berries. Berries were really good food; and how delicious these berries were!

But at regularly decreasing intervals he was

obliged to set the sack down. That night his sleep was filled with wonderful organ melodies and all Johnson Corners was gathered together to hear Nellie play. And his mother was very conspicuous in that vast throng—such a shiny silk dress as she wore! It made Mrs. Jones, the banker's wife, look very dowdy indeed.

He got up this morning much stiffer than before, and when he tried to shoulder the sack he groaned.

Perhaps it *was* too heavy, after all. One shouldn't want too much. One might get nothing at all if one wanted too much. Wouldn't it be wise to—he recoiled from the thought—yes, to take out just a little?

For an hour a silent battle raged within him, and then, with a sense of choking, he untied the sack and dipped out a half-dozen handfuls. Hastily retying the sack, he summoned all his strength and hurried away from the spot. He dared not look upon all that wasted wealth. How much was it that he had thrown away? But then, was he not carrying untold wealth? Ah, that merely showed how very rich he was! Poor men cannot throw gold away like that! This thought exhilarated him, and he forged ahead with a lighter heart.

Five days passed. In this time he had eaten berries and drunk from occasional streams. But on the morning of the sixth day he struggled in vain to shoulder the load. He tried repeatedly, but his muscles refused to lift it to his shoulder.

He buried his face in the sack and sobbed unmanfully. Would it all go like that—little by little? And he had carried it so far already; it meant so much to him.

He lightened the load until he could get it to his shoulder and pushed on into the East. As he went he comforted himself with the determination not to sacrifice any more—not a pinch more! Not a pinch —no, not if he should die under it!

The sack was now less than half full.

Many days passed—he kept no count of them— and still his determination gave him strength for the load that seemed to increase with every step. And with the nights came dreams, as ever, only they began to take on gray, melancholy tones and sounds of moaning went through them. All through the weary days he turned these dreams over and over in his mind until they haunted him. And one night he saw his mother and Nellie very plainly. They were both weeping. And he thought feverishly: "It is because they have not heard from me!" Then the dream changed, and he was standing in the grocery store down at the Corners and all the old faces were there, turned expectantly upon the sack which he had just placed on the counter. He saw old Deacon Brown go up to the sack, untie it and thrust his hand in. *"Why, it's empty!"* said the deacon, and all the loungers roared with laughter.

Whereat the dreamer awoke, staring into a pale sky, and heard the multitudinous chatter of birds in the forest about him. Eagerly he untied the sack and thrust his hand into it that he might give the lie to the dream. It was all there—the beautiful, glittering, priceless stuff! He let it run slowly through his fingers the better to taste the unutterable joy of possession.

All that day he struggled under the load with a heart almost blithe. It was as though he had really lost his treasure and regained it, so vivid had been the dream. He seemed very much nearer home that day, although the load seemed heavier. But he felt stronger to bear it.

But in the weary fag-end of the long afternoon he topped the summit of the last hill, and there before him spread a vast and treeless plain rimmed with the gray mist of distance. His heart sank within him. He dropped the sack to the ground and stood staring blankly at the far horizon. Somewhere beyond that rim of mist, and then yet other rims of mist, lay home. Could he ever cross that long, lonesome stretch? For the first time he felt the terrible meaning of *distance*. Tears ran down the deepening hollows of his cheeks as he stared upon this motionless, pitiless, treeless waste. It had the calm, stern, inexorable look of death.

The Parable of the Sack

One can travel an endless trail and still hope, so long as he cannot see the way lengthening before him. Heretofore he had been constantly in the forest, traversing a continuous series of little spaces. But *this*——

Why should he go on, after all? It would be so much easier to die.

Die! His wan face flushed with a sudden anger at the treacherous thought!

Die?

And what would become of mother and Nellie and Bessie? *Die!* And the farm sold? And the money gone? And all the neighbors wagging their heads and saying they knew it would be so?

No! He would not die! But he would rest the balance of the day, and in the morning he would be strong as ever again.

But the next morning found him weak and stiff in the joints, though the dream was very strong in him again. And, haltingly, ever conscious that the weight at his back was cruelly heavy, he pushed on toward the sun that made a path of fire ahead of him. Somewhere down that interminable path of fire was Johnson Corners.

As the day advanced, he became conscious of sharper pangs of hunger than he had ever known before. This struck him with terror. In the forest there had been an abundance of wild berries; but *here?*

Indian Tales and Others

He remembered that it had once been his habit to pray. But that seemed years ago—when he was very, very young. He felt that he had grown very old. But now he remembered the teachings of his mother. He breathed prayers pleadingly into the waste about him. He prayed for food. *Meat!* His gnawing stomach cried out for red meat.

After hours he neared a scrubby clump of plum bushes that clung to the arid bank of a dry gully. Suddenly he was aroused from a morbid dream of starvation by a snorting in the thicket. A deer plunged out and raced across the plain before him. With a quick instinct that prompts a hungry beast to kill, he dropped the sack, snatched a revolver from his belt, and emptied it at the flying animal. The deer topped the barren summit of a little rise, and dropped out of sight. He snatched the other gun from his belt and fired frantically into the empty space before him. Then he flung the smoking weapon to the ground and cursed savagely.

When he lifted the sack he felt childishly angry with it for being so heavy. He would make it lighter. It *was* too heavy! What was the use in saying it wasn't! With a sort of fury he untied the knot and poured a fourth of the precious stuff on the ground. Then he shouldered the lessened weight and pushed on rapidly, trying to believe that he didn't care.

The Parable of the Sack

The sun rose high; the far undulations of the baked plain wavered feverishly in the heat, as though seen through fluttering gauze. He watched the blue-gray patch of shade at his feet slowly elongating into a shadowy finger that pointed East. And all the while feverish, snatchy visions of pumpkin pies and dumplings and corn-bread came and went in his head.

Suddenly his half-dream state was broken by a sound of snarling, snapping, yelping, as of many dogs fighting. He found himself near the brow of a little hill. The sun was a blotch of yellow flame on the jagged purple rim behind him, and his thin gray shadow stretched up the slope into the sky ahead.

He toiled on up the slope and saw in the green valley of a creek below him a pack of wolves fighting over a meal. Now again his hunger became an active passion, firing his will. He loaded a revolver and, shouting hoarsely, he emptied it in the direction of the fighting pack. The wolves scattered, whining, drooping their tails like whipped dogs.

He found the torn carcass of a fawn in the valley; its flesh was still warm. That night he sat by a fire and feasted. It was the first fire he had made, for he had no fear of men in this wide waste. And he was very happy. Here was food for days if taken sparingly. And how sweet the muddy water of the little creek was! It ran very thin among dying reeds, but he scooped out a little basin and thought of the spring that bubbled out under the old oak as he drank.

Often in the night he saw slinking dusky figures against the sky on the ridge above him. They howled dismally at the man in the valley who feasted on their kill and sang so merrily.

But in the gray dawn he awoke feeling sluggish and sore and depressed. Then a cruel perplexity confronted him. How could he carry the sack and the meat too?

Once he thought he would eat all he could and abandon the rest. But the memory of his hunger cried that down. What should he do? Lighten the sack again? It had already grown so lank that it set snugly about his shoulders without support. He argued long with himself.

No food—no gold!

Some food—some gold!

He ended by taking the meat and three-fourths of the remainder of the once plump sack.

The meat of the fawn lasted him five days, and during that time the contents of the sack remained untouched, for his hunger steadily lightened his load. During this time he had succeeded in finding water at least once a day.

But, with the last of the meat, water failed him. He now found himself in a perfectly flat tableland. His dragging feet stirred up a hot, acrid dust that

The Parable of the Sack

choked him. And for the first time he knew how thirst can dominate hunger.

The day passed, and still the arid flat stretched about him—unchanged. He seemed to have stood still all day. Only the dull aching of his back and limbs gave the lie to this featureless plain that taunted him with having remained motionless all day.

The night flitted past, leaving no sense of duration, and with the dawn he was up again, toiling under the sack. His thirst had grown upon him during the night. It tortured him cruelly. So he forced himself to think of that far hour of triumph that he might not think of his thirst.

All day he trudged along, painting the glorious mental picture; and when the cool of the evening came it had all grown up very plain before him; so plain, indeed, that he already stood in the grocery store, feeling a little light-headed, to be sure, but nevertheless victorious. He talked aloud, it was so real.

"Ha, ha!" he laughed hoarsely. "Thought I was a fool, eh? Thought farming was a pretty good business, did you? Just run your old bony fingers through *that*, Deacon Brown! Oh, you needn't wag your old goat's beard like that! It's gold! Just *feel* it! Walk up, gentlemen, and take a look into that sack! Ho, ho, ho! Where's the farm hereabouts that you can raise *that* on?"

The scene changed.

"Look, mother! Look, Nellie! Thousands and thousands of dollars! I got it myself! Oh, I had three times as much as that, but I got so tired and thirsty that I couldn't pack it. How'll the Joneses feel, do you reckon? We'll buy back the farm, and you won't ever have to work again, mother! And you can take lessons and lessons and lessons, Nellie!"

Exalted with his words, he had lifted his face to the Eastern sky. He stopped short, gasped! There in front of him, only a little way ahead, he saw a sparkling river flowing through green pastures!

All the ache and heaviness of the limbs left him. He felt light as a feather and powerful. He cried aloud with joy. At last, here was a river—*water! water!*

He set out at a trot, no longer feeling the weight at his back. At last he had won! He sang snatches of old songs he had learned at the singing bees.

Suddenly a thin, oily film passed over the river and pastures. Strange gaps opened here and there in the scene. Then the whole became agitated, indistinct, as though seen by a bleared eye.

He looked again. There was nothing ahead but the arid, featureless flat and the darkening sky.

That night was filled with the hideous laughter of a hundred grotesque deacons who stared into an empty sack. And somewhere in the burning hollow

The Parable of the Sack

of a strange world he could hear the moaning of women.

Suns set and rose, and day was scarcely distinguished from night. Every morning a little more was taken from the sack, until a child could have shouldered it.

The man no longer tried to get it to his shoulder. He carried it limply in his arms before him. And every morning as he lightened his load, he prayed the same prayer: "Oh, God, let me be stout enough to pack it!"

But one day, when he had grown too weak to feel joy, he came to a place where the tableland sloped abruptly into a river valley. He saw below him a cluster of rude houses. It was a trading post. Slowly, painfully, he made his way into the town. He found his way into the only store, and reaching a lean, trembling hand into his pocket, he cast a handful of the precious stuff on the counter.

"Eat—drink," he stammered.

The trader stared strangely upon the bent, haggard thing before him, that should have been twenty years old but, somehow, was sixty.

"Why, what is this?" said the trader, brushing the precious stuff about with careless fingers.

At last the dull embers of the old joy flared up into flame, and a light of triumph shot across the ashen face of the man who had borne the sack.

"It's gold!" he croaked. *"See! I've got almost a sack of it!"*

"You damn fool," said the trader, "that's nothing but yellow mica—powdered yellow mica!"

When my friend, the philosopher, had finished I mused for some time over his story. At length I said: "And did that really happen? Is it a true story?"

He gave me a pitying smile.

"Did it happen, you ask?" said he. "Perhaps; *I* don't know as to that. Is it true? Yes, certainly it is true. For you must know, my friend, Truth does not happen—it just *is!*"

THE SCARS

MY friend, the old frontiersman, poked an extra supply of sobs into the stove, meditatively watched the sudden flame lick about the husks, then began this monologue after his usual manner:

Yes, I've got a nice place here—nice ranch. Didn't work for it either—lied for it!

Now, I'm not given much to that sort of thing, as you will grant; but when I see a place where a good manly twisting of the truth can sweeten matters up a bit, I'm not so scrupulous.

Back in the late fifties I was living in St. Louis, pretty nigh broke, for all I'd lived a hard, industrious life up and down the river. One day I got a note bearing the postmark of some California mining town, and it informed me that I had a considerable credit with a certain St. Louis bank. I never heard directly where the money came from, but I thought I knew. I bought this place with some of that money, you see. And there's a little story attached to this.

For a number of years I was employed by the

American Fur Company as expressman. Every winter I made the trip from St. Louis to Fort Pierre, a distance of about a thousand miles. Carried messages from headquarters to the posts and from the posts back to headquarters. From St. Louis to Pierre the trip was made on horseback, and from there up, other expressmen carried the mail on dog sleds.

Great days, those! Sometimes when I get to thinking over old times, I wonder if the railroads haven't taken some of the iron out of the blood of men.

In the winter of '50—that was the year the gold fever was raging, you know—I got to Pierre about the middle of February. When I had delivered the mail and was making ready to start south again with the returns, old Choteau, the factor of the post, called me into the hut he called his office, and made an unusual request of me. "We've got a half-breed here," he said, "who's got to be elevated. Understand? Killed a man in the most atrocious manner. He's due at a necktie party down at St. Louis about next spring, and I'd rather not keep him at the post; can you take him down?"

I was somewhat younger in those days, and ready for most anything new. Also, I had found the trail a little lonesome at times. Riding a preoccupied broncho through hundreds of miles of white silence, hearing the coyotes yelp, dodging Indians, and bucking blizzards weren't ever calculated to be social functions, you know. So I was glad to have company on the trail, even if it had to be the company of a criminal. Anyway, I had been so taught in the great rough school of primitive men, that I had not that loathing for a killer of his kind that is felt by this generation.

"Certainly," said I to the factor. "Put him on a mule, and I'll see him into the government corral at St. Louis." So it was arranged that I should take the man to the authorities.

I did not hear his name spoken and I didn't take the trouble to ask. It seemed to me that a man who was being shipped out with a tag on him reading "Nowhere," had little use for a name. No one was apt to dispute his identity.

Well, they put him on a mule, handcuffed, with a chain to his ankles passed around the belly of the mule. He was, of course, unarmed, and I drove him on ahead of me to break trail. He was a powerfully built fellow, neither tall nor short, and close-knit. He had a face that was not so bad, showing the French and Indian strains in him plainly. When we had been riding along silently for several hours, I called to him to stop and rode up beside him.

I looked into his eyes, and that look satisfied me that I was safe in doing what I had thought of. His eyes were large and black and quiet.

"I am going to take the damned irons off your

legs and arms," I said; "you can't keep warm this way." He watched me taking them off and said nothing. I threw the irons away. "Go on," I said. And he went, giving me a look that thanked me more than words could have done.

He had the eyes of a brave man. I was never much afraid of a brave man; it's the cowards you have to watch, you know.

All day we rode, saying nothing. In the evening we made a shelter with our blankets in the bend of a creek where the plum bushes were thick. The man was a good hand at the business, and seemed anxious to please me.

We cooked and ate supper, then rolled up in our blankets. I put my two six-shooters under my head for fear that I might have somehow misread the man's eyes.

When I awoke in the morning, he had breakfast cooked and the nags saddled. When we were eating I said: "Why didn't you take my horse and run away? I could never have caught you with the mule."

He searched me for a moment with his eyes.

"Because I'm not a coward," he said.

And all day we rode again in silence, until, toward evening, he set up a wild sort of a song—a *chanson* of his fathers, I suppose—in a voice that was strong but sweet.

"You sing!" said I.

The Scars

Breaking off his song and turning about on his mule, he said quietly, as though he were discussing the best way to make biscuits when you haven't any soda: "Did you ever see a dead liar?"

"Perhaps," said I; "but none in particular."

"And that is why you never sing."

That was the last word that day. Up to this time the weather had been rather too warm for winter—an ominous sort of a warm, you know. A mist hung over the country, drifting with a light wind from the southeast. During the night the wind whipped into the northwest, and in the morning we had a genuine frank old blizzard howling around us; one of those fierce old boys that nobody cares to face. We had camped in a wooded nook on the south side of the river bluffs and were pretty well protected, so I decided to lay up there until things brightened up a bit.

The man, for I had not yet learned his name, which was not necessary, as the mail I carried attended to that, volunteered to gather wood; and so I lay in the tent near the fire that roared in front, smoking my pipe and swapping cusses with myself on account of the delay.

After a while the man came in with a big arm load of wood, whistling merrily. "Well, you beat 'em all," I said. "I say a man who can whistle like that on his last trip is a game one. What's your name and who are you? Here, want to smoke?"

Indian Tales and Others

I gave him my pipe. He took it and blew rings meditatively for a while. "Well," said he, "the name doesn't matter much, and I'm the fellow who's elected to be elevated!"

We both laughed strangely, and I began to open my stock of yarns, truthful and otherwise, to relieve the tedium of the day. I had told a number of stories when the man seemed to brighten up all at once. His eyes became on a sudden unusually brilliant.

"I know a story that's a fact," said he. "It's about a friend of mine—one of the best friends I ever had, I reckon. At least he never went back on me. Shall I tell it?"

"Go ahead," said I.

And this is the story he told me:

"My friend's name is Narcisse. I knew him when he was just a little shaver. I knew his mother and his father. In fact I was, at one time, just like one of the family.

"Narcisse was a wild sort of a boy always, though I do think his heart was in the right place, as they say. Never betrayed a friend, never stole, and never knuckled to an enemy. But he was a wild boy and didn't stay at home much after he was in his first 'teens. Knocked about the world considerable, Narcisse did, and wound up out here in this God-forsaken end of creation. Worked on a cordelle gang, handled mackinaws, hammered pack mules, fought Indians, starved and feasted, froze and

The Scars

toasted, like all the others who come out here. Entered the fur trade as *engagé* of the Company, and was sent to a post up river.

"Now if there was a weak spot in Narcisse, it was his leaning toward womenfolks. None of your fooling, though! Narcisse loved just like he'd fight—pretty serious, you know. When he said a thing, Narcisse he meant that; and when he wanted to do something real bad, he did that—O, spite of hell he did that! You know the breed? Well, that was Narcisse.

"There was an old French trader living at a post further up—old man Desjardins. He had a daughter—Paulette—by an Indian woman who died when the girl was just a baby, and the old man raised her somehow—God knows how—till she grew to be about the prettiest girl you'd see anywhere in a year's tramp, being a good walker. Old man doted on the girl, and until she was full-grown there wasn't anybody could come nigh enough to her to make a sweet grin effective. But once Narcisse and his friend, Jacques Baptiste, got snowed in there on one of their trips.

"Now them two, Jacques and Narcisse, was about the best friends you ever saw, I reckon. They never had any secrets from one another; and many's the time they had split the last bit of grub on long winter trails, and made a feast of that little.

"Now Paulette was a slender little creature with

black eyes and lots of black hair. Lots of hair! That makes a woman fetching, don't you think so? Well, Narcisse and Jacques sang old French songs during the blizzard, and kind of got into the old man's heart like. Nothing like old-time songs to fetch a man when he's got to that place where there isn't any way to look but back. So the old man made 'em welcome and said for 'em to come back when they could.

"On the trip from old man Desjardins' place to Pierre, them two friends talked pretty frank, like they always did. Both of 'em was in love, and neither of 'em was ashamed of it. Told each other so.

"When they camped the first night they talked it all over and Narcisse said: 'Jacques, we've always split even, but here's where we can't. It's for one of us all right, but one of us has to go without. How about this?'

"And Jacques puffed at his pipe a long time, and after a while he said: 'Let's agree that we'll always go up there together, and let her take her pick.' And Narcisse agreed; so that's the way they fixed it.

"Managed to drop in pretty often after that. But there wasn't any way of telling which was it. One visit she'd smile more at Jacques than at Narcisse, and they'd think it was settled; and then next time it was t'other way.

"It was a game, and both of 'em played it like

The Scars

a game. They were too good friends to slip a bower or ace up their sleeves. They let Paulette deal the hands and they played 'em the best they could, same as honest poker, you know. And all the time old man Desjardins looked on like the man that runs the game, a-raking in the ante, which was the singing and the laughing they did and the things they brought up with 'em, for they never came empty-handed.

"Well, the next fall came; the game was still on and neither of 'em had stole a hand nor a chip that wasn't his. And along about the first of September the factor of Pierre sent the two friends on a trip to Benton. They went up on the last boat and were to drop down again in a mackinaw before the winter set in, after doing a little business for the Company.

"On the trip up Narcisse and Jacques had a quiet little game, which was poker. They didn't play for money—played for Paulette. Sort of made a jack-pot out of the girl, and it took Jacks or better to open. One deal and a draw and the high hand could go to see the old man by himself and close the game that had hung on so long.

Narcisse insisted on having Jacques deal.

" 'Well,' said Jacques, after the draw, 'the jack-pot's mine!'

"Narcisse throws down three aces. Jacques gasps a little gasp and throws his cards face up on the table, turns white and walks away. He had two pairs—kings and queens!

"There wasn't anything more said about it; but Jacques wasn't the same man at all. Acted like he was thinking, thinking all the time. Face got that peaked look that comes of too much thinking; eyes always looking a long ways off.

"How do I know this? W'y, Narcisse told me.

"Hurt Narcisse like everything to see this; but hadn't he won fair? Friends can split even on grub and follow the same trail for years, but there comes a time when they must smoke their last pipe together at the forks. But it's all part of the game and a man oughtn't to grumble if he don't get a pat hand, as long as the deal's fair.

"Narcisse and Jacques got to Benton, and when they got ready to start back, the river had frozen up, because the winter came down early that year. So they had another winter trail to follow together before they reached the forks. The factor at Benton gave 'em a couple of good dogs to carry their bedding and they started out afoot.

"Jacques didn't have much to say. With that peaked, set look on his face he went a-trudging on in the snow from sunup to sundown. Narcisse couldn't help feeling a little happy, because Paulette was the prettiest girl that ever haunted these parts since the river was dug. It wasn't any more than human, and he'd won fair.

The Scars

"Well, they passed Union and they passed Les Mandanes and they passed Roubideaux', and then there was a long stretch of lonesome country ahead of 'em till they got to Brown's Landing, about two hundred miles above Pierre.

"One day it came on to blow and snow, and they made a camp in the bluff just like we did here. That's what reminded me of the story. Jacques made camp while Narcisse was chopping wood. He cut down a dead cottonwood and when it came down, he tripped up in the deep snow and the tree fell on him. Broke his leg above the ankle. Well, there he was a couple hundred miles toward Nowhere in November with one leg.

"Pretty hard on Narcisse, wasn't it? But Jacques all at once began to be his old self again. Set the leg as good as he could and tied it up so it would stay in place, and joked and was kind to Narcisse.

" 'Seems like old times, pard,' said Narcisse to Jacques. 'Danged if I wouldn't be glad it happened if we wasn't so far from somewheres; because we mustn't let the trail fork, old pard. I knew you'd be the same again when I was hard run.'

"And Jacques smiled and said there never was any hard feeling, he guessed. But the peaked look didn't go away, nor the far-away look in the eyes.

"When the weather cleared up, Jacques said he'd leave a plenty of wood and grub for Narcisse and he'd make a run for Brown's Landing and come back

with dogs and a sled. And that made Narcisse's
heart warm toward Jacques, because it was just like
he was before the girl came between 'em.

"And Jacques left before sunup one morning, and
when it came day Narcisse went to fix him some
breakfast, and there was only enough grub left for
five or six days. That scared him, because it was a
long trip to Brown's and back, and he couldn't walk.

"But he didn't cuss Jacques. He just said to himself: 'He didn't go to take so much, and it was
dark when he left.' And then he just took the hand
that was dealt him and began playing against a run
of hard luck. The grub lasted only about a week,
and close picking at that. Jacques had plenty of
wood chopped up, and Narcisse sat all day by the
fire with his leg aching and his stomach a-gnawing,
a-looking down the white waste toward Brown's.
And night 'd come and no dog sled. Then day 'd
come and he'd begin looking, looking. And when
the grub was all gone, he soaked up all the leather
there was about him and sucked that. And then he'd
begin looking, looking, looking into the white waste,
till he got so's he could see dozens of dog sleds coming and vanishing, coming and vanishing.

"But he didn't cuss Jacques. He said: 'The
poor devil's been killed like as not; he wouldn't go
back on his pard.' And one day he felt he was getting too weak to watch much more, and so he set a
pole in the snow with a strip of blanket tied to it;

The Scars

and that tuckered him out so's he couldn't hardly crawl back to shelter. And with the last strength he had, he dragged the wood that was left up close to him where he could reach it, because he knew that in another day he couldn't get up.

"And then he began forgetting everything 'most, and having bad dreams that scared him, all the time a-worrying about the fire like as if he was half asleep, and hearing dogs barking, and trying to get up.

"And then at last he didn't know anything, till he was on a dog sled with the feel of hot soup in his belly. And when he came to, he said: 'I knowed you'd come, Jacques; it was hard sledding without the grub, though.'

"And then he found out it wasn't Jacques at all; only some Jesuit missionaries traveling from the North. They'd seen his signal of distress a-flying, and had come and got him.

"And still Narcisse didn't cuss Jacques. He said: 'Poor devil's got killed or something.'

"And by and by the Jesuits got him to Brown's Landing, and he laid up there till the last of December, getting so he could walk. There wasn't anybody at Brown's who had seen Jacques; and Narcisse's heart ached; he thought sure Jacques was dead.

"And when Narcisse got well, he borrowed a horse from the factor at Brown's and went south to Pierre. It was night when he got to the post. He rode up to the cabin where he and Jacques bached together, and tied his horse. There was a cheery light coming out of the windows, and that seemed odd, seeing that Jacques was likely dead somewheres up the trail. And what seemed stranger, there was someone singing inside, and every now and then a woman 'd laugh. God! man, did you ever hear a woman laughing when your heart had been aching for weeks?

" 'Beats the devil!' Narcisse thought, 'how quick folks fill your place when you're dead!' Gave him a tight feeling in the throat to think how someone was laughing inside, and Jacques somewheres up trail with the coyotes sniffing at him and the snow blowing over him all day and all night!

"Then Narcisse slips up quiet as could be to the window and peeps in. He falls back like someone had hit him hard in the face. But nobody had. All he saw inside was Paulette and Jacques!

"Narcisse leans against the cabin, dazed like, for quite a spell. Seemed like he couldn't get it all through his head at once. Then he saw it all—the cards had been stacked on him. He should 've been dead and he wasn't. That was the trouble.

"Didn't cuss Jacques even then, Narcisse didn't. Wasn't mad—just ached in his chest like. And by and by he goes up to the window and taps on it with his fingers. And Jacques comes out into the starlight, whistling.

The Scars

"When he runs into Narcisse a-tottering around the corner like a drunken man, he gasps and leans against the cabin, a-holding on to it and staring.

" 'Good God!' he wheezes. 'Good God!'

" 'Old pard,' says Narcisse; and his voice was like it had smoke in it, 'you win; I pass; mine's a bob-tail flush; but you stacked the deck!'

" 'For Christ's sake, Narcisse,' whispers Jacques, 'don't let her see you! Don't let her hear you! Come on!'

"And he takes down toward the river, a-walking like the devil was after him; but it wasn't anybody but Narcisse, limping a little with a bad leg.

"And when they came to the river Jacques didn't seem to have anything to say but 'O, it's a devil of a mess! A hell of a mess!' Said it over and over like he was half crazy. And Narcisse said: 'Last fall I'd have killed the man who'd said this about you, Jacques. It isn't the girl so much, Jacques; but you and I have starved and frozen together many's the time, and we always split fair till now. It was hard sledding up there without the grub and with only one leg. You stole the cards on me this deal, Jacques; but I'm not going to call for a new deal. I'll play the hand.'

"Just that way Narcisse said it. And with Jacques muttering, 'O, it's a devil of a mess,' they came to an air hole where the black water was gurgling and chuckling.

"And all at once Jacques flared up and snarled: 'Why in hell didn't you die?' And slashing out with a long knife, he made a long gash in Narcisse's scalp, and gave him a shove toward the hole. But he didn't go in, Narcisse didn't. He's got that scar yet, but he's got a deeper one where nobody sees.

"And then Narcisse somehow forgot the long trails they'd tramped together and the starvings and the freezings together. Couldn't think of anything but the sting of the knife and the trickle of the blood. And the white starlight swam round him like water in a suck hole, and got red like blood, and buzzed and hummed. And he was a better man than Jacques—better fighter. And when the light quit swimming around and got white again and the stillness of the frozen night came back, Narcisse found himself sobbing and turning his heel round and round in somebody's mouth. And it was Jacques.

"And what does Narcisse get?"

The man, after finishing his tale, took a handkerchief from his pocket, carefully placed it about his throat like a halter, threw his head to one side and simulated strangulation.

We didn't tell any more stories after that. When night came we rolled up in our blankets, after having made a rousing fire. I did not sleep much that night. The man did, however. He was the coolest I ever saw. Went to sleep like a child, knowing full well that he too had a noose awaiting him.

When I was sure that he was sound asleep, I got up and carefully took off his bearskin cap, which he had not removed night or day since we had been together.

I saw by the blue glow of the falling embers that which I had expected to see—a long, ugly gash running across his scalp. It was not yet quite healed.

In the morning, as the storm had died in the night, we saddled up. "You take the mule and go on ahead," I said; "I'll probably catch up with you by noon."

The man obeyed. I did not expect to catch up with him, but along about noon I overtook him.

"You seem determined to travel my way," I said.

He stared at me for some time, and then said quietly: "I'm not a coward just because I'm going to hang."

And we rode on together.

The next morning when we had saddled up, I said: *"Narcisse,* here is one of my six-shooters and some ammunition. There is the grub. If you travel west far enough, you will come at last to the gold country. Ever think of going to the gold country?"

The man gasped and placed his hand to his head. "When did I have my cap off?" said he.

"You have a good mule there," continued I, evad-

ing his question. "You have grub, a gun and ammunition. Why don't you go west?"

"Why are you saying that?" he said.

"Because," I answered, "because I have seen
both scars!"

I pointed west. The man slowly fastened the
grub sack on his mule, mounted, gave me a look
which I have never forgotten, and rode west.

I have never seen him since. As for me, I got into
the next post that evening with a worn-out horse and
a tale of calamity.

THE RED ROAN MARE

IT'S all very well to laugh at what you can't understand, and there's no defense against laughter. I myself used to ridicule such things, for the life of a trooper in the Sioux campaign of the 70's was hardly calculated to make a healthy man believe in any phase of existence that could not be ventilated effectually by the slash of a saber or put out of business with a drop of hot lead.

But that was before Jim Dolan went out; and since then—well, it's just as though a man were walking in a night of drizzle through a strange country, conscious only of the ground under his feet and of the impenetrable darkness, when suddenly a flash of lightning lifts the gloom, revealing his unsuspected relation to a whole landscape. And after that he believes in considerably more than the ground under his feet, for he feels that world all about him silent in the shadow.

Mind you, I'm not saying that it all really happened. Part of it might be explained by the scalp-wound Jim got in Reno's fight on the Little Big Horn, and part may have been due to my own fatigue and hunger and to the drenching, melancholy

weather of those last days. Make what you can
of it; I tell it as it seemed to me.

I had known Jim only since early March of that
year, 1876, at which time he had been detailed for
scout duty to my regiment, the Second Cavalry, then
a part of General Gibbon's command stationed at
Fort Ellis. Nevertheless we were fast friends.

He was a big, handsome, magnetic fellow, such as
women love and men admire; and I never could
make out why he should have taken a liking to me,
for I was always a quiet man, morose, as some
thought, little given to pleasantries; and what
courage I ever displayed was not of the dashing sort
—rather a species of fear than genuine courage—
the master-fear of being afraid.

But Jim's was the true Celtic temperament. The
gloomiest circle of troopers that ever hugged a
grudging, smudgy bivouac fire of sage-brush grew
merry with his presence. He seemed to regard
danger as the acme of life, and life as rather a good
practical joke, the point of which was all but spoiled
by too many serious boneheads—like myself.

Humor and daring in him seemed somehow to be
the same thing, and I have often thought that he
really deserved little credit for his remarkable courage, which was attributable less to the driving will
and the sense of duty than to a superabundance of
animal spirits. Thus constituted, so fitted to make
Hard Luck the bumpkin of a farce, he should have

gone out like a brilliant light snuffed at full flare. Ah, how differently it happened!

As for William George, I knew him but slightly, and what I saw of him left an unpleasant impression. We of the "Montana Battalion" had marched down the left bank of the Yellowstone from Fort Ellis under orders to join with General Terry's forces pushing west from the Little Missouri, and had been in camp over a week opposite the mouth of the Rosebud, when the steamer *Far West* arrived with Terry and his staff.

About noon of the same day the long line of Custer's cavalry, the unforgetable Seventh, filed down from the table-land across the river and went into camp in the valley. When the boat was about to cast off, bearing Gibbon and Terry to the last council of war in which Custer would ever participate, Jim suggested that we cross with her.

"For," he said, "I've got a friend in H troop of the Seventh—haven't seen him since my last trip to Fort Lincoln. Want you to know him."

So I went along and met William George.

He was grooming a big, red roan mare when we found him, and it struck me that the manner in which he greeted his genuinely delighted friend was a trifle cold. He seemed less interested in the man than in the mare, of which he was evidently very fond, judging by the gentle care that he lavished upon her from ear-tip to fetlock.

Indian Tales and Others

A neat-built, wiry little chap he was, scarcely a
full inch to spare above the army height. His rest-
less, black eyes were set a mite too close to a thin,
sensitive nose, and his upper lip had a disagreeable
habit of curling at the corner. He seemed always
on the point of sneering, though when he spoke,
which was seldom, he was civil enough in his saturn-
ine way.

I felt sure no length of association could have
made us pals, and I expressed something of the kind
to Jim afterward. But he insisted that I was mistaken.

"Bill's a good sort," he said, "but you've got to
bore through his shell to know the heart of him.
Down at Fort Abe he beat me to the finest girl that
ever lived, and so I guess I'm no prejudiced party.
He's too serious; that's all that ails him. Why,
you'd think his life was being held for a ransom of
a hundred and seventeen dollars and no cash in sight
the way he takes things! You've got to have real
sand to think that way and still go ahead, and a
sandy man is sure to be a good sort when you get
past his burs."

Nevertheless, in spite of Jim's generous view, my
unpleasant impression persisted.

At the council it was decided that Custer should
proceed with the Seventh Cavalry up the Rosebud,
following the fresh Sioux trail discovered by Major
Reno a few days before. Should the trail be found

to turn toward the Little Horn—which proved to be the case—he was to continue southward as far as the headwaters of the Tongue, thence turning toward the Little Horn.

Our column under Gibbon was ordered to proceed up the Yellowstone to the mouth of the Big Horn, there to be ferried over by the *Far West*, and thence to march to the forks of the Big and Little Horns. Thus, if all worked well, the hostiles were to be enclosed by the two columns on the twenty-sixth of June, and Custer was advised by Terry not to attack before that date.

Among the white scouts transferred for service with the Seventh was Jim Dolan.

Well, our forces arrived in the early morning of the twenty-seventh. On the twenty-fifth Custer, with five troops, had attacked a village containing no less than seven thousand Sioux warriors. The whole world knows what we found strewn along the broken rise east of the river. I need not dwell upon that ghastly wreck of valor, for neither Jim nor his friend was found there, and such a tale may be left to the Xenophons of the past, or, better still, let us hope, to some not impossible Homer of the future.

Farther to the south we came upon a very different scene, where, upon a barren hilltop, surrounded by their slain and wounded, barricaded by their dead horses and pack-mules, sun-blistered, thirst-maddened, the remnant of the Seventh under Major Reno had held out for thirty-six hours against the whirlwind assaults of a body of cavalry that had not a superior in the annals of war-craft.

Upon learning of the approach of Terry's column the Sioux had retreated toward the Big Horn Mountains, burning the grass behind them to screen their movements; and, accordingly, the hour yielded us no sterner duty than that of relieving our plucky comrades.

Among the wounded were Jim Dolan and William George. When I came upon Jim he was leaning against the carcass of a pack-mule with a bloody bandage on his head and a pipe in his mouth. His eyes had a dazed look and his face was pinched; but he was making a heroic effort to smoke. A bullet had bitten the scalp evidently early in the engagement, for he remembered little after the retreat to the hilltop, and seemed to be of the impression that it was still the 25th of June.

When I asked him how he was getting on he smiled like a sick child, and remarked that he felt a good deal like the fag-end of a drunk without the memory of the fun; and when he grinned I saw how he had been chewing his pipe-stem.

"Did they get Bill?" he asked anxiously. I had not yet come upon Bill. "I hope he's all right—it means so much to the poor devil—the girl and all that, you know," said Jim. "Hunt him up and tell me. Don't mind me; I'll be fit as a fiddle in a day or two."

"I found Bill with a hole in his side huddled up behind a clutter of dead horses. He was bled white, and when I first saw him I thought he was dead. But he opened his eyes and the light of recognition came slowly into his vacant stare.

When he spoke, scarcely above a whisper, the sequence of his questions struck me as peculiar. Had I seen his mare—a red roan? And was Jim killed? I had not seen the mare, and Jim had a scalp wound. Would Jim die?

One should say nothing but good of the dead, and I may have been mistaken; but I thought my hopeful answer to that last question sent a fleeting expression of vexation across the white face as he closed his eyes and groaned. Then, too, he may have been thinking of the mare. Men have strange whimsies when the chill white wind begins, as it had begun for him.

We immediately set about the task of carrying the wounded down to the steamer *Far West*, which with great difficulty had succeeded in reaching the forks of the Big and Little Horns some fifty miles from the Yellowstone. My troop and one other of the second were detailed to carry the litters in relays, and about sundown we set out with our pitiable burdens upon a most melancholy and toilsome journey.

Indian Tales and Others

Our progress was painfully slow, for the rough trail was rendered more difficult by the darkness, and for many of the wounded the least jar was torture. At midnight, having covered less than five miles, we decided to wait for the day.

It was during that gruesome night-watch that I caught the first glimmering of the relation between Jim and Bill, though at the time it all seemed to me little more than the whim of a dying man. In my rounds through the camp during the dark hour before daybreak, I came upon William George, ghastly white in the blue glare of a smoldering brush-fire. He was evidently delirious, for he was muttering incoherently, and when he opened his eyes he called me Jim.

I thought to humor the poor fellow, and kneeling beside him stroked his head and spoke as I imagined Jim might speak to him in his tenderest mood. He stared long and searchingly upon me, and then he said: "Bring me the mare, Jim. I've got to start now—I've got to ride fast before it gets me. I must go to her before it gets too cold."

And I said "Yes; but it'll be daylight soon, and you'd better not start till then."

His eyes narrowed with a look that would have been murderous had there been any vitality behind it. "You're hiding the mare from me, so I can't go," he said; "and you'll ride there yourself—and it'll get me." He made a pitiful struggle to get up

[186]

The Red Roan Mare

and fell back exhausted. I once killed a wounded coyote with a club and it stared at me as Bill stared then. "But I'll be there too, damn you!" he whispered.

Then he was off to the fight on the barren hilltop, and by his broken muttering I knew that once more he heard the bickering of the carbines, the shrieking of wounded horses, the moaning of tortured comrades and the yells of the charging Sioux. I thought he would die before morning; but he clung to life as a man plunged into an air-hole clings to thin ice.

We did not set out again in the morning, but spent the day making mule-litters, and it was nearly sundown before we were ready to resume the march.

Between long saplings, hitched fore and aft to the pack-saddle of a mule, we slung blankets for the accommodation of the wounded. I see it now very vividly—the long train winding down the wild valley of the Little Horn through a flame-painted night —the shadowy bulks of the pack-animals lurching on the rough trail—huge, distorted shadows leaping along the banks like ghostly outriders of a ghostly cavalcade—the white faces lifted momentarily out of the gloom by the capricious flare of the wind-smeared torches. It is the wierdest picture in my memory, save one.

Well on toward morning we sighted the lights of the steamboat glimmering through the murk at the end of a long lane of bonfires that had been kindled by the crew for our guidance.

Early the next morning the *Far West*, with her cargo of suffering, started on her record-breaking voyage to Fort Lincoln, seven hundred miles away: and that was the last I saw of William George. Or was it? Nearly forty years have passed since then, and perhaps with age one's flesh wears thin and one sees through to the other side. However that be, the more I ponder the strange happenings of those last days, the more am I prone to believe that I saw him again.

When, in midsummer, offensive operations were resumed, we pushed eastward under General Crook in pursuit of Sitting Bull's band.

The Sioux, apparently content with one successful stroke, had broken up into small bodies, the scattered remnants trickling back to the reservations. It was a wild-goose chase; and when, early in September, we reached the headwaters of the Heart River, we were half whipped, though we had met no enemy.

We had traveled over four hundred miles since leaving our wagon-train, and our jaded animals were dropping out by the score; for the buffalo-grass had been burned before us by a dissolving foe. Ragged, half starved, we had little more than ammunition and nerve, and many of our men began to develop symptoms of scurvy.

The Red Roan Mare

One hundred and sixty miles to the east was Fort Lincoln. Two hundred miles to the south, across a desolate region, lay the Black Hills. To strike east for supplies meant a loss of two weeks, during which time the new mining settlements in the hills would be left defenseless. A ten days' march to Deadwood on the two days' rations remaining to us seemed impossible.

Nevertheless, we turned south.

There was no disguising the fact—we who had met no foe were in headlong retreat; and hunger, more terrible than the whole Sioux nation, harried us van and flank and rear, like invisible cavalry. It had come on to rain—a ceaseless leaking of low, gray skies that washed the salt out of our saddle-bags and chilled us to the bone.

Now and then, all day long, the crack of a pistol, dulled by the fog, told us that one more leg-weary horse had fallen and could not get up.

That evening we bivouacked in a desolate valley. There was no wood, and I, like all the rest of the column, even to Crook himself, was huddled up to a cheerless smudge of sage-brush, watching the stragglers hobble in with the water streaming from their hats, when, out of the twilit rain-blur that blanketed a rise to the east, appeared a horse and rider, bearing down upon us at an easy canter that certainly could not have been managed by any of our animals.

Indian Tales and Others

It was not that the sage-brush suddenly burned more brightly, or that the melancholy drench abated in the least; but the bivouac immediately became less cheerless for me: for better is a half-drowned smudge of sage-brush shared with a pal than the glow of oak logs alone.

It was Jim Dolan with despatches from Fort Lincoln.

Superficially he was the same old Jim; but I felt a difference: not in appearance—he looked well, and had evidently fully recovered from his wound; not in his talk—it was still warm-hearted and merry enough, considering the long ride and the diabolical weather. The difference was subtle, and may, in fact, have been in me.

Perhaps you will get my feeling when I say that there seemed to be a thin veil over his personality. I thought at the time that the vague change was fully explained when I asked about his friend, William George, and saw how his eyes took on a far look. Bill had died on the trip down the Yellowstone, and was buried at the mouth of the Powder.

That was all I got out of him then, and I did not push the subject, seeing the effect it produced. I attributed that effect to the warm Irish heart of him cherishing the memory of a vanished friend; and when next day, riding at his left through the pelting rain, I noted the gauntlet of his bridle-hand marked in ink, "W. G.—H 7C," I was deeply moved, for I had never experienced such devotion of man to man.

We were floundering through the mud at the crossing of the north fork of the Grand when a courier from our advance guard under Mills brought the news of a clash with an Indian village under Chief American Horse at Slim Buttes some seventeen miles to the south.

Re-enforcements were immediately ordered forward, including my troop of the Second, and Jim rode with us.

About noon, emerging at the mouth of a ravine, the whole arena of action was spread out before us. To the north, south, and west towered the grotesque, weather-carved heights of the Slim Buttes, swathed in trailing clouds of mist and smoke. It was like a Greek theater on a grander scale, the valley being the orchestra.

The first glance at the welter of men and horses that thronged the scene revealed to us the fact that we had at last met with some of the chief actors in the tragedy of the Little Big Horn; for, scattered about among the bands that still contested the victory with Mills, were tattered guidons and uniforms of Custer's regiment.

A few moments later our troop was charging a small body of Sioux who had taken up an advantageous position at the mouth of a coulée, when that befell which, as I am prone to believe, was the first of a series of strange happenings that ended as you shall hear. While we were pursuing the fleeing band at a stiff gallop up the gulch, Jim's horse struck a gopher hole and went down with a broken leg.

I drew rein and cantered back. Jim picked himself up, laughing, and, placing a pistol to the horse's head, put the poor beast out of its misery. The thudding reverberations of the shot had scarcely died away in the misty gulch, when a shrill whinny came from behind a clump of brush near by.

"There's luck," said Jim; "no walking for me to-day."

I dismounted, and we pushed through the brush, expecting to find the pony of some fallen Sioux. What we found was a big, raw-boned mare, bridled but barebacked. That she was a red roan in no way excited my imagination; for, as you know, I am a matter-of-fact sort of man, and I had seen many red roans in my time—a not uncommon color in a horse.

But what did strike me as odd was the look on Jim's face. He had been laughing a moment before, but now there came upon his countenance the blank expression of a sleep-walker. He had stopped stock-still, his cheeks were blanched; and he was staring wide-eyed, not at the mare—but across her back! He seemed not to breathe.

What time elapsed I do not know; but when the mare, with ears pricked forward, approached us, nickering, the strange look vanished.

The Red Roan Mare

"Well, I'll be damned!" Jim muttered, now advancing with a coaxing hand outheld.

"For what?" said I.

"Oh, nothing!" he replied; "just one of my fool notions. Speed in that nag—eh? And tough as whang-leather!"

Our comrades, returning from their scamper up the gulch, came upon us while Jim was cinching his saddle on the new mount. We rode back through the dripping ooze without a word. In fact, at the time the incident did not assume the importance which I am now persuaded to attach to it, and it passed easily out of my mind; for Crazy Horse had come up with the main body of the Sioux, and during the rest of the day there was little leisure for the entertainment of whimsies. We were too much occupied with the brutal business of maintaining our strategically weak position in the valley against the hostiles potting at us from the heights. I should probably have forgotten the matter entirely in the hardships of the ensuing days had it not been forced upon me again by Jim himself.

With the waning of daylight the enemy withdrew. The rain abated to a drizzle, and the night was pitch-black. Jim and I rolled up beside a smoky fire, and I, thoroughly fagged, must have fallen at once into a dead sleep.

I was startled by a hand laid heavily on my shoulder and a voice in my ear. Seizing my carbine,

I leaped to my feet, thinking in the first wild moments of waking that a night attack was being made upon us. Then I became aware of the silence of the camp, and knew that it was Jim who had aroused me.

He had stirred the fire to a mockery of cheeriness, and was sitting beside it wrapped in his blanket. "Sorry I had to wake you," he said; "but I had to do it—had to talk to somebody—can't sleep."

I sat down beside him, feeling more than a little bit surly. "What's wrong?" I asked. He did not answer at once, but stared into the fire, and I was on the point of anger when I noted that he had a frightened expression—like that of a child who has just escaped from something in the dark. Jim of all men!

"Why, Jim," I said, "are you sick?"

He gave me a searching look with something like an appeal in it, and said: "How can a man get out of six feet of clay?"

A hideous suspicion flashed coldly upon me as I thought of the scalp-wound. I had seen men horribly mutilated, and felt no sensation but that of pity. Such things happened in the business of a professional fighting man. But that one should suddenly discover his friend to be some one else—some strange dweller in a fanciful world—I felt prickly all over.

He must have felt my shudder. "For God's sake,

old pard," he said, "don't think I'm crazy! I'm simply puzzled, and I want to thresh the thing out with you. It's about Bill."

I nodded and waited.

"Bill and I were pals, as you know," he went on at length. "We campaigned together with the Seventh in 1868, and there wasn't ever anything between us until a year ago, though I always felt that I forced the friendship. Bill was peculiar—never seemed to give the whole man. Always I felt that just a shy bit of him stuck to its hole like a badger. It used to hurt me, because I was fond of him and never held anything back. But you can't have a friend made to order after your own specifications, so I got to taking him just as he was, and it worked better that way."

Here Jim's voice trailed away into the silence of a deep study. The fact that what he had said was rational enough somewhat calmed my first fear, and yet was it quite a normal proceeding to wake a man in the dead of night and insist upon his listening to ever so interesting a delineation of character?

"Well?" I urged with some impatience. Whereupon he began again, talking in a monotonous tone, as though he were only half there.

"Then the woman came in—it was at Fort Lincoln—and there was a change. Bill and I had always shared everything, and I did not look upon the acquaintanceship as serious; for marriage had not occurred to me as a possibility—and it was not necessary to look twice to know that the woman was good. As to her feeling for me, I thought her no more than gracious. I was slow in realizing the fact that it was otherwise with Bill, though I felt a growing coldness that puzzled me. But one day some long-suppressed hell boiled over, and that part of him which he had been with-holding from me came out in a flare of rage. It wasn't good to see.

"The woman had become a matter of life and death to him—and he was jealous. It struck me as ridiculous, and I laughed like a fool. Then I took him by the shoulders and I looked deep into his eyes that had a tangled light in them, and I said: 'Look here, Bill! I wouldn't swap a first-class he-friend for all the females that ever strutted. The nicker of my horse is sweeter to me than her laughter is to you.'

"Soon after that I got myself sent to Fort Ellis with despatches, and that was when I met you. And the more I thought about Bill on my lonesome rides the more tenderness I felt for him and the more I was sorry. As you know, I did not see him again until the Seventh camped at the mouth of the Rosebud last spring. You remarked a coldness in his greeting—and you were right. They were engaged. His term of enlistment expired this fall. It was going to happen then, and they were going back East."

The Red Roan Mare

Jim trailed off again and fussed absent-mindedly with the fire. I had fully awakened by that time, and felt reassured as to his sanity; for, though I was still groping after the point of his narrative, I began to catch at vague meanings, moving like shadows in a fog; and Bill's raving during that night watch on the Little Big Horn came back to me in a new light.

"It was the night he died," Jim continued, "a hell of a night. I'll see it to my last day—the whole afterdeck of the *Far West* cluttered with writhing men under the lamps that smoked in the river wind. And the engines pounded and the men groaned and the stern-wheel snored, kicking back the yellow miles, and the exhaust went on forever and ever—*swish, s-w-i-s-h.* My head was near splitting with it. And all at once, above the clatter and the moaning, I heard a wild cry with my name in it. It was Bill calling me from the other side of the boat, and he kept it up till I crawled over to where he was.

"He was right on the edge of things and slipping fast. It nigh tore the heart out of me to see the face of him, and God knows I would gladly have swapped wounds with him then. The old Bill that I knew had already gone, and he eyed me like a snake writhing under a boot-heel.

" 'You'll get there, and I won't,' he wheezed. Then he flopped around till he got up on one elbow, and he looked like a man who is yelling, though the voice he fetched was only a thin squawk, and he said: 'Leave her alone, Jim, I tell you; leave her alone!' Then he fell back all crumpled up and shivering. And I swore I wouldn't have anything to do with the girl; but he didn't seem to know me after that. He died that night, and next day we landed at the mouth of the Powder and buried him."

Once more Jim was silent. Then at length he said in a low voice, as though he were talking to himself: "I've broken my promise. I was Bill's friend, and I was wounded, and she was kind to me. It came on me too strong when I was too weak— and afterward I couldn't somehow shake it off. And, after all, Bill was dead, and the living have to take happiness where they can. She gave me his spurs and gauntlets that I brought to her and asked me to wear them. God knows I have worn them with a heart full of love for Bill."

Out of another silence Jim hurled strange words, turning upon me with the manner of a man who gives the lie to an accuser: "Bill was dead, I tell you! I saw him die! I saw him buried! I saw them shovel the clay on him! And yet I saw him —plainer than I see you now—sitting on his own mare this afternoon!"

Again the hideous suspicion, that Jim's seemingly rational narrative had all but allayed, flashed coldly upon me. This could not be sane, I thought, because it was not then within the limits of my experience. It gave me the feeling of a man trying to scramble up the crumbling walls of a sand-pit. I tried to laugh, feeling that bluff ridicule might shock him back to sanity, but my attempt was a fiasco. The wound had bitten too deep, and Jim was dying at the top.

"Laugh if you like, old pard," he said; "but I saw what I saw. Come with me."

He got up and started toward where our animals were tethered out in the dark. I followed, heard the soft nicker of the mare as Jim approached, saw his head and the dim bulk of a horse leap suddenly out of the dark in the sputtering flare of a sulphur match. "Look," he said as I came up and peered over his shoulder. The mare was branded high up on the rump, U. S.; and lower, near the flank, 7HC.

The match went out, and for a moment I was in the grip of a panic doubt as to all those fundamental preconceptions upon which my tight little world was built. It was like a sprawling tumble down a black hole. But immediately old habits of thought reasserted themselves, and my fear for Jim's sanity came back redoubled. I assumed the rôle of the worldly wise cynic, the man who knows all about existence and therefore can't be buncoed.

"Well, and what of it?" said I as we walked back to the fire. "There were horses in H troop of the Seventh, were there not? I believe, as a general rule, they are to be found in cavalry regiments; and some of Reno's were captured by the Sioux. You've got to take hold of yourself, Jim, and quit brooding about Bill. Where's your sense of humor? A dead man playing dog in the manger! As for what you saw—simple enough. Head full of Bill—red roan mare—Bill on the mare. Shake it off and let's get some sleep, for hell will be popping all over the place in the morning."

He made no reply, rolling up to the fire with his back to me. But he did not sleep. I know—for neither did I. But when the wretched camp became visible in the dirty light of a sodden, sunless dawn, I felt angry with myself for my ineffectual denial of Jim's vagary during the black hours of wakefulness. What a fool I had been to give even a second thought to the fantastic improbability of another life amid the brutal and still unmastered verities of this one!

Men were so many bellies. Let the sleek and pampered forget that fact, pule about souls, and all that. As for the girl—that sort of thing was all very well for an idle moment of moonlight amid safety and an unbroken sequence of square meals; but here was a sterner business. I would wipe the affair out of my consciousness and I would make it very plain to Jim what I thought of the matter if he forced it upon me again.

We buried our dead in a deep ravine, and a thousand horses in columns of twos trampled over the new graves, obliterating all traces of the spade, that the last resting-place of our fallen comrades might not be violated by the skulking Sioux. Then, though technically we were victorious, having captured and destroyed a village of the enemy, we resumed our flight—a gaunt, ragged multitude of men and horses fleeing from our own want.

Either piqued at my apparent lack of sympathy or ashamed of his own unmanly whimsy, Jim did not ride with me that day, but chose to accompany Up-ham's battalion of the Fifth, upon which fell the duty of covering our retreat.

The fog soon engulfed the rear guard; but all morning we could hear the dull popping of the cav-alry carbines and the deeper drawling of the Indian rifles. The trail now led steadily upward amid gro-tesque peaks fringed with jack-pines, looming ghost-like about us.

At dawn the drizzle had again increased to a downpour, and unseen gulches boomed around us. When, for a moment, the capricious wind drew back the curtain of the fog ahead, the detailed picture of our utter wretchedness fetched many a groan— the infantry, a shivering rabble of vagabonds, floundering through the sticky mud; the cavalry, mostly afoot, dragging their exhausted mounts be-hind them, disheartened, footsore crow-baits with drooping heads and tucked-in tails streaming with the drench.

And when, toward noon, my troop came upon a bevy of hollow-eyed stragglers who were skinning a horse, the fact of our condition was driven home with a new force. Henceforth we would eat our four-footed companions. It seemed almost like cannibalism.

It may well be that my breakfast of sage-brush smoke and drizzle after a bad night had left me weak, or that the ultrahuman character of the rain-washed landscape got on my nerves—or both—but in spite of my sane determination of the morning I could not drive Jim's absurd fancy out of my head.

There it stuck despite my efforts to oust it; and, strangely enough, I often caught myself slipping away in a semi-dream state in which the whole absurd business undeniably took on the character of a foursquare actuality; and before I was aware of the change I would be seriously considering what might be the intent and procedure of William George. Then it would come to me that William George was dead, and once more the fear for Jim Dolan's sanity would fasten upon me.

Early that afternoon we went into bivouac along the brushy bank of a creek flowing northward out of towering bluffs that appeared to bar our retreat like a wall. Somehow we succeeded in kindling fires, and the whole camp was soon steaming from the improvised shelters made by flinging soppy blankets over sticks thrust into the mud.

The Red Roan Mare

Toward nightfall Upham's battalion joined us, and Jim rode up to where I happened to be sitting alone, huddled under my dripping blanket over a little brush fire that struggled valiantly against the downpour.

The excitement of the rear-guard fight had apparently done him good, for as he flung a leg across the mare and dismounted, he essayed a joke. "Ham and eggs for six, chef!" he commanded with playful bruskness; "and be quick about it."

His tone cheered me. It was the old Jim come back again. No doubt he had merely given way to a passing fancy, and God knows there was in our circumstances sufficient justification for an occasional lapse from the strictly rational.

When we had finished with a chunk of roasted horse-flesh, and Jim had ended his animated narrative of the rear-guard fight, so reassuring had been his manner that I ventured on a sally, intended to be witty, regarding his vagary of the previous day and night; for it seemed to me an opportune moment had arrived for ending the incident with a gust of wholesome laughter.

But no sooner had my ill-conceived joke passed my lips than a sickening sense of its utter failure smote me. Far from laughing, as I had expected, Jim suddenly grew grave, and a troubled look came into his eyes. Night had fallen now, and the rain-smeared splotches of light from the bivouac fires

strung along the ravine served to intensify the out-
lying darkness.

"I hoped you wouldn't say anything more about
it," said Jim. "It's getting on my nerves. I've
fought it all day." Here he handed me his gauntlets. "Put them on," he said.

I obeyed, feeling a necessity to humor my poor
friend; for I had heard that in certain forms of
mania there may be intervals of complete freedom
from the characteristic obsession, which the least
suggestion may suffice to recall. The horse-flesh,
though stringy and tough, had banished the peevish-
ness which accompanies a certain stage of hunger,
and now I felt nothing but pity for the man. It was
the scalp-wound, after all.

"Do you notice anything queer?" he asked.

"They are well soaked, aren't they?" I replied
casually, feigning not to have noticed the initials on
the left one. He eyed me with the same appealing
stare that I had noted the night before, and said:
"How could there be four hands in one pair of
gauntlets? Tell me that! I've felt it all day; and
the mare knew it. Often when I felt it strongest
she would turn her head back, nicker caressingly,
and nip at the toe of my boot."

Seeing that neither cajolery nor humoring would
do any good, and yet feeling the necessity for doing
something, I assumed a stern air which I was far
from feeling, and expressed myself rather pointedly.

The Red Roan Mare

"Now look here, Jim," I began; "I'm going to be open with you, knowing that I can trust to that solid foundation of horse-sense which I have never found lacking in you." Then I set forth quite frankly my theory of the scalp-wound, made it plain that I considered him a sick man, ventured the conviction that he was in dire need of a friend to guide him, and offered my services in that capacity. "And if the mare and the gauntlets have that effect upon you," I ended, "for God's sake shoot the nag and burn the gauntlets!"

I thought to shake him out of his morbid condition by appealing to the instinct of self-preservation; and you may imagine my despair when, far from appearing alarmed at my prognosis of his alleged ailment, he smiled calmly, a little sadly, and resting a hand on my shoulder, said: "It's good of you, old pard; but there's something bigger than you and I in it. I'll not mention it again. As for the mare and the gauntlets—would I shoot Bill, would I burn him?"

I fell to sleep that night with the melancholy conviction that sooner or later my poor friend would lapse into idiocy, and I got only slight comfort from the determination to speak to the surgeon about his case.

Some time during the night I awoke suddenly, feeling certain that I had heard bugles sounding the charge. I leaped to my feet, only to note how silent the night was, save for the whisper of the rain out in the darkness. Most of the bivouac fires had succumbed to the drench and the remainder sent up columns of faintly glowing steam and smoke soon swallowed in the murk.

I was preparing to roll up again when I noted that Jim was missing.

At the same time there came from the outer gloom a low whinny—coaxing and caressing as of a much petted horse welcoming its master. The sound explained to me not only the fancied blare of bugles, but the absence of Jim as well. Doubtless he had gone to the mare for some fantastic reason sufficient to his poor, addled mind.

It was plainly my duty to look after him, so, having heaped the charred ends of the brush upon the dying coals, I went to where the mare was staked out; and what I saw by the groping glow of the replenished fire made my heart ache with pity. Jim was grooming the mare.

Approaching, I addressed him as though he were doing something quite usual. "About through with the mare, Jim?" I asked. "Better hurry up and come back to the fire."

He wheeled about and—*it wasn't Jim at all!*

The face there turned upon me was the one I had seen during the gruesome night-watch on the Little Big Horn. It was the face of a dying man,

The Red Roan Mare

and before I could catch my breath it had shuddered into nothing like a face in a pool struck by a sudden gust of wind, and only the mare remained.

When at length I regained control of my limbs I hastened back to the fire, shivering violently. As I came up, Jim appeared, wrapped closely in his blanket and walking rapidly from the opposite direction. Neither of us spoke as we curled up beside the fire. Was I, too, going off my head?

That question made the long night hideous for me.

We broke camp at the first light and pushed on toward the Black Hills. Still the rain came down; in fact, it did not cease during those terrible eleven days of the retreat from the headwaters of the Heart to the Belle Fourche.

And now began the long, last stage of a march which for severity and hardship, as an authority has remarked, has but few parallels in the history of the army. I need not dwell upon the details. It is enough to say that no wood was to be found, that grass was scarce, and that the soil through which we floundered was gumbo. No fires at night; no coffee in the morning. Only the endless muck and the ceaseless autumn rain, and the weariness and the hunger. And all the while skulking bands of Sioux hung upon our flanks and rear like wolves lusting after the stragglers of a bison herd.

Hour after hour Jim and I trudged along together, leading our leg-weary horses, or rode knee to knee when the going was better; and never a word passed regarding that which neither of us could forget. A strange fear tied my tongue; fear not only for my friend's sanity, but for my own. As for Jim, he had promised silence, and he kept his promise to the end.

The end!

It came suddenly and in a manner far other than any I had groped after in my wildest imaginings. It was the third day of the march across the God-forsaken plain, and my troop had been detailed to guard the rear and to pick up the stragglers; for many of our men were falling exhausted by the way, and the scattered bands of Crazy Horse still harried us. Evening was coming on—a slow, imperceptible deepening of the general grayness.

Fagged, gaunt, shivering, we rode in silence, save for the low murmur of the rain and the dull, sucking pop of the gumbo clinging to the hoofs of our staggering horses.

A band of Sioux appeared at the mouth of a shallow *arroyo*, some three hundred yards to our left, and opened fire. Mechanically, almost listlessly, we wheeled about and returned the compliment, though the mark was little more than a clutter of dark blotches against a background of muddy gray.

The Red Roan Mare

Suddenly amid the snarling of the carbines a wild cry came from Jim on my right—a shuddering cry like that of a man who flees some horror of a nightmare. My first thought was that he had been hit. I turned to him and saw—

Shall I say that I saw it? Or had the strain of those terrible days reduced my vitality to the point where hallucination was only a matter of suggestion? Explain it as you wish, and be content with your thumb-rule measurement of a preconceived cosmos, as you must.

I saw it in that flash of timelessness—the red roan rearing with the sting of plunged-in spurs, Jim staring upon me with a face gone blank with terror, his carbine still slung, his bridle-hand limp. But that is not all I saw.

There were two in that saddle.

One moment so—and with a shriek of pain the mare was off, headed for the mouth of the *arroyo,* her neck stretched out, her ears laid back—a gaunt image of sinewy speed; while Jim rolled loosely in the saddle, and the other—one with Jim from the saddle down and one with him at the hands—crouching low to the tossing mane as one who rides a race.

The firing ceased and the whole troop gazed thunderstruck.

It was like a dream, brief in the memory, but endless in the passing. The flying mare became a shadow, vague against the deeping gloom. And then out of the mouth of the *arroyo* the yelling Sioux burst forth upon us. We fell back upon the main column, fighting as we went.

THE ART OF HATE

MANY tales have been told of noble sacrifice for love, and I have seen such in my time; but I have in mind an instance in which a man reached a sublime height through the least exalted of human passions—hate.

There are some who argue that love is born at first sight. However that be, I am certain that it is often thus with hate. I have seen men in my time the first sight of whom was an insult to me—sudden, stinging like a slap on the cheek. It is a strange thing, and I have never heard it explained satisfactorily. Sometimes in my own case I have attributed it to even so slight a thing as a certain turn of the nose, a curve of the lip, a droop of the eye. And again I have felt that it was due to nothing visible about the man, but rather to some subtle emanation from the very soul of him, that maddened me as though I had inhaled the fumes of some devilish drug. Have you ever felt this?

Well, I am telling you about Zephyr Recontre.

He was a little, wiry half-breed, with a French father and a woman of the Blackfeet tribe for a mother. Quite a promising combination, if you think it over! I came across him 'way up at Fort Union in the early '30's, when I was in charge of a keel boat of the American Fur Company. He was employed at the Fort as interpreter, being a fluent speaker of several Indian tongues as well as English and French.

His forehead was a narrow strip of brown between his wiry black hair and the continuous streak of black that was his eyebrows. His eyes were large and black and quiet. His cheek bones were prominent and his jaw was so heavy as to throw his whole face out of balance, as you might say. The face of a stayer, you know. Never said much except as his duties demanded, and then he went straight to the point with a quiet directness that left little need for a question.

Superb little animal he was, too; had the maximum strength with the minimum weight, and a cool head to run it with. I never saw him impelled by sudden anger except once, and that is where the story begins.

In the spring of '39 I took charge of the steamboat *Yellowstone,* as captain. We were loaded with supplies for the American Fur Company's posts on the upper Missouri, and carried a number of *engagés* of the Company, and a certain Frenchman, Jules Latour, who had been appointed *bourgeois* of old Fort Union, and was going up to take charge.

If there ever was an emperor in this country it

The Art of Hate

was J. J. Astor, the head of the Company at that time, and his empire was spread pretty much all over the white space on the map of the West as it stood then. The *bourgeois,* masters of the trading posts, were the proconsuls, and they acted the part.

The *engagés,* humble servants of the empire, were as dogs about the feet of these Western princes, who stalked through their provinces, mountain-high in aristocratic aloofness.

Latour outprinced princeliness. He felt his dignity and dressed it; his presence on the boat was like a continual blowing of trumpets going before a conqueror. A capital "I" swaggering in broadcloth—that was Latour!

Recontre was going back with us, having dropped down to St. Louis the fall before on Company business. I happened to be near when master and man first met on the forward deck. They stared upon each other for only a moment; but there were years of hate condensed in that bit of time, the master casting a contemptuous glance from beneath lids scornfully drooped, and the servant meeting this with a sudden glare of black fire.

Not a word was passed; Recontre made no sign of obeisance, passing on with a sullen swing, his jaws set firmly, his eyes brilliant as with a smouldering fire blown by a gusty wind into a baleful glow.

It was a plain case of hate at first sight. A week later, after we had passed St. Mary's, I was standing on the hurricane deck, gazing downstream where the colors of a quiet sunset swept the waters. I heard an angry snarl below me, and looking down, I saw Recontre lift the struggling Latour in his arms and hurl him into the river.

I immediately stopped the boat and ordered a crew to man the yawl and rescue Latour, at the same time having Recontre seized.

Latour came aboard coughing and spitting, a most ludicrous object. But to my surprise, he immediately commanded that Recontre should be released. I wondered much at this at the time; but ten years later I had a talk with Recontre, which threw some light on the subject. He was leaving the country, and, as we had become close friends, he did not hesitate to tell me what he had kept a close secret for years.

We were taking a friendly glass together at a St. Louis bar, when I purposely brought up the name of Jules Latour, who had starved to death some years before in a mackinaw boat that got caught in the ice far up the river. I had heard stories of how Recontre, who was with Latour on the trip, had shown a faithfulness to his master equalled only by the faithfulness of a dog to a man. This had always seemed strange to me, and so I brought up Jules Latour.

At the sound of the name I saw the black fire grow up in my companion's eyes, just as I had seen

The Art of Hate

it ten years before on the forward deck of the *Yellowstone*.

"You got that story, too, did you?" he said dreamily, staring straight ahead of him as into a great distance. "Well, it's all over now, and for the first time, I am going to tell the truth about the death of Latour and my great faithfulness. When I first saw that man, I felt as though he had struck me between the eyes with his white fist. I hated him as I had never hated before, and as I hope never to hate again. It hurts to hate; it eats into a man like some incurable blood disease.

"You saw me throw him into the water. I can hardly explain why I did that; only, the man spoke to me in a way that insulted me more than if he had blackguarded my mother. It wasn't in the words, for I have forgotten what he said.

"We hated each other. I knew how much I hated, but I did not know how great was his hate until he smilingly ordered my release. I knew then that his hate was a great hate—stronger than love can be. And also I knew that this hate would grow until one of us was killed. And it did."

"What!" said I; "did *you* kill Latour?"

Recontre smiled one of his enigmatic smiles and said quietly: *"Nature* killed Latour; *I* merely helped Nature!"

And then he laughed softly, while the black fire grew again in his eyes.

Recontre led the way to a table in the back of the room and we sat down, when he began talking rapidly, never hesitating in his story, and seeming, at times, wholly unconscious of my presence.

"When we arrived at Fort Union," said he, "no one could have guessed the hate that we nursed for each other. Being a new man in the country, Latour consulted me upon many phases of the business, and we were much together. The whole post considered me a most favored person; little knowing, as I did, that hate can bind two persons as closely as love.

"My hatred for the man made his a most fascinating personality to me; and I often found him studying my face with a diabolical fondness.

"Latour heaped favors upon me, and I received them with a strange gladness of heart that even now I cannot explain. One day in November he sent for me to come to his office. I found him in a mood seemingly most agreeable. His face beamed with a light that any other would have taken for kindness. I saw in it the ecstatic anticipation of triumph. And when he spoke I knew that I was right.

" 'My dear Recontre,' said he, 'it seems that I am forced to fall back upon you for everything. I have a difficult task on hand, and you are the one man to perform it; I know of no other so peculiarly fitted for it. I shall carefully lay before you the dangers of the mission I have in mind, leaving you free to consent or refuse just as you see fit. Perhaps the undertaking is impossible. It may be that no man is sufficiently equipped with strength and daring to do what I wish. You shall decide.'

"You see he imagined that he was wheedling me through my vanity. He then stated that he wished to open trade with the Blackfeet tribe. He drew strongly upon his imagination to explain the great dangers in store for him who should undertake the task. The Blackfeet were at that time deadly enemies of the whites. They had killed and mutilated a number of traders. I would of course stand a poor chance of coming back alive. He was convinced of that.

" 'Will you go, Recontre?' said he, staring steadily into my eyes.

"I was dumfounded at the audacity of the man. I saw the light of doubt wavering in his eyes; but I did not wish to flinch before my enemy.

" 'Certainly,' said I; 'and I will go alone!'

"I saw the triumph glisten in his eye.

" 'Very well,' said he; 'you may start in the morning. Make your own arrangements. I give you full power to transact the business in hand as your wisdom may dictate.'

"And I started in the morning. Two weeks later I returned, successful beyond all hope. I not only brought back a band of the leading men of the tribe for a council, but I brought also a young woman for my wife. I called her Pelagie after one of my sisters.

"As I think of it now it seems miraculous that I succeeded. I am half convinced that I was inspired from out the profundity of my hate to do and say the right things.

"Latour played skilfully the part of gratitude and joy, but I saw, nevertheless, the deep, devilish disappointment that he felt. And I was very glad, for I had conquered in this first combat; and also Pelagie was a pleasant woman.

"As the winter deepened, Latour and I became more and more friendly. We outdid each other in acts of seeming kindness, until all the post was jealous of my intimacy with the master.

"They little guessed how we played a ghastly game that would be finished only when one of us could smirk and flatter no more.

"The winter grew bitter; heavy snows fell. And I wondered much what great honor Latour would heap upon me next, seeing that I was so capable and willing. Near Christmas Latour called me to his office, and the light of anticipated triumph was upon his face.

" 'My friend,' said he; 'I do not wish to impose upon you, but I have in mind a great service that you may render me, as a friend, mind you, Recontre. I am sure that you will succeed unless you freeze to death or get killed by the Indians. None but a brave man would attempt what I shall mention. I have a very important communication to forward to the office at St. Louis. It must be there before the middle of March or the Company will suffer heavy losses. If you can get this there at the time stated, you shall be advanced considerably, with a raise of wages. Now how would you like being my private clerk?"

"I stared into Latour's eyes and saw all hell deep down in them.

" 'Give me a good dog to carry my bedding,' said I, 'and I will be at St. Louis by the middle of March,' and then I thanked him extravagantly for this last and greatest of favors. All the time I hated the man more pitilessly than ever before because of his shallowness in hoping to flatter me into getting myself frozen to death.

"I started the next day with 1700 miles of frozen prairie before me. I felt a strange joy at the thought of my hardships. Once again I would have the joy of seeing disappointment in the eyes of my enemy, and my soul could laugh again. I say I was glad to go, even though I was obliged to leave Pelagie behind at a time when the post was ravaged with smallpox.

"It was a trip to make one love hell by comparison. Nothing but my hate sustained me. On March 10th I delivered the written message to the official at St. Louis. He read it wonderingly.

" 'What!' said he; 'have you walked from Union to deliver *this?*"

"I stated that I had and he shook his head, frowned and dismissed me. I never knew what was in that message. I surmise that it was nothing of much importance.

"When the first boat started up the river for the North I went with it and arrived at Fort Union in late June. Latour was at the landing when the boat pulled in. He threw his arms about my neck and actually kissed me upon the cheek. He then and there made me his private clerk with my former salary doubled. He treated me as a brother.

"But I saw in the depth of his eyes the soul-fret of a wounded beast.

"When we reached his office walking arm in arm, he gently told me of the serious sickness of Pelagie, and how he had looked after her like a brother through the hard winter.

"I hurried to my home. I found Pelagie delirious with the fever of smallpox. All that night I sat beside her, my heart aching, for I felt that she would die.

"And for the time I forgot my hate for Latour, until, in her feverish tossing about, she threw her bare arm over the side of the bed. Then I saw that which made me shiver with a desire to kill. There was a scratch on the arm, and the flesh about it was swollen and blue. It came to me that Latour had caused her to be inoculated that she might die before my return, and thus make my heart sore that he might see.

"I grasped a dirk and ran wildly out of the house in search of Latour. I reached his door. Then I faltered. It was not fear that made me falter. It was that I knew my revenge could not be completed in this way. I wanted to see him suffer more than I had ever suffered. Also I wished to come away with clean hands. I did not know how it could be done then, but I trusted to some mysterious power that had seemed to be with me all through my terrible winter tramp.

"I stole back to the bedside of Pelagie. She died at dawn.

"Latour mourned with me. He wept and spoke touchingly of his own wife. I gritted my teeth and strained every nerve to keep from choking him.

"The summer passed. Latour was so kind that I often found it an effort to keep alive my belief in his treachery. And at other times, I was obliged to leave him abruptly, feeling a madness in my blood for striking him down.

"Oh, all the great actors have not appeared upon the stage! I must confess that Nature and Zephyr Recontre killed a great actor!

"The fall came, and our friendship did not abate. I began to fear that my chance would never come, and I should be obliged to kill him as one brute kills another. Many nights I lay awake shaping impossible schemes of revenge that were rejected in the sanity of the morning.

"In the first week of October I had occasion for a great joy. Latour called me to his office and stated that certain conditions of the trade which had been wholly unforeseen, made it necessary that he should be in St. Louis before the winter set in. Unfortunately, the last steamboat had left Fort Union for the South, making it necessary that the trip be made in a mackinaw boat. Would I, his dearest friend, consent to accompany him on the trip?

"With a studied reluctance that hid my insane joy, I consented. Latour left a clerk in charge of affairs, and we started. We made very slow progress, as we depended almost entirely upon the current, having no oars, and there being little wind to fill the square sail we carried.

"This was as I wished it to be. I kept longing for the ice to come down and shut us in. Time and again I managed to run the boat aground on bars in order to kill time. Latour seemed not to notice this. In fact, he was unusually pleasant in his bearing toward me.

"We had a small hut built on the mackinaw, fitted with two bunks, and a small box stove for cooking. When we tied up to the shore for the night and turned in, I was often obliged to choke back laughter at the comedy that we played—a grim comedy. Each of us would at once feign deep slumber, ever now and then opening our eyes to see how the other slept. Once our eyes chanced to meet in the dim candle light of the room, for Latour insisted upon the candle. We both grinned and rolled over.

"Our understanding seemed perfect; and yet, owing to the devilish refinement of our mutual hate, neither really feared any vulgar act of violence from the other. We knew that the thing would not be done in that way.

"We had made about five hundred miles down stream into the very heart of the wilderness, when the ice began running. Within twenty-four hours after that, we were frozen in. A heavy snow began falling and continued for a week. It lay three feet deep upon the level, and was so light as to make it impossible to take the trail.

"Latour and I merrily set about to chop wood, not knowing how long we might be forced to live in the little cabin of the mackinaw.

"We had brought only about half enough provisions for the trip, having depended upon hunting for much of our food, as there was a great deal of game in those days. The deep snow made it impossible to get much game, so that in less than two weeks our little supply of lyed corn was almost exhausted.

"One morning Latour said that he was sick, and remained in his bunk. At first I looked upon this with suspicion, thinking that he thus sought to throw the duties of seeking game wholly upon me, who had proved myself so capable and willing. But the next morning I knew it was no sham, for he had a high fever, and was delirious at times. You see, he had been used to luxury, and his feeble constitution had not been equal to the thorough soaking we got while chopping wood in the deep snow.

"Often in his delirium he linked my name with bitter curses. At last he had betrayed his hate, and I smiled, knowing that he would lose the game at last, since he no longer had the cunning to continue it.

"Again it began to snow; it was a hard winter. Much as I might have wished to seek game for my sick enemy, I could not even seek it for myself. Nature had taken a hand in the game; I began to feel her master-touch in the bitter scheme of things. She seemed determined to starve us both; but I knew that I could last longer than Latour with his constitution weakened by too much easy life.

"So I blessed the snow as it deepened. Latour would die before my eyes; and then afterward I too would die, the winner of the game. It would be a most sublime revenge, it seemed to me; for I think I was hardly sane when I was near Jules Latour. It would be like Samson crushing his enemies and himself together. No one could blame me, should our bodies be found. I would have had my revenge and still none could blame me.

"There was a small quantity of lyed corn left. I ate sparingly of this, carefully saving Latour's share for him when he should wish to eat.

"One morning he awoke from his delirium; he asked for food.

"'I have saved your share for you,' said I. 'I might have eaten it, for I think we shall starve to death in a week or so. The snow is too deep and soft for hunting. Still I have divided fair with you, remembering your great kindness to Pelagie, remembering your great kindness in allowing me to distinguish myself among the Blackfeet, remembering your generosity in allowing me to take your message to St. Louis. Do you remember?'

"He groaned, and his eyes became cold and savage, like a starved wolf's.

"I gave him his lyed corn and he ate. His delirium returned. He cursed Recontre bitterly. He clenched his feverish, white hands about the imaginary neck of Zephyr Recontre; and I smiled.

"In two days more all the lyed corn had been eaten. In the meanwhile the surface of the snow had hardened with the intense cold. I could have hunted, for I was not yet too weak, and there was a gun and plenty of ammunition. But I did not go hunting. I saw Latour weakening rapidly. He might die during my absence, and I would thus lose the sweetness of my revenge. It seemed to me that this would be like selling my birthright for a mess of pottage.

"I could have taken the gun and gone south over the snow to Fort Pierre, several hundred miles down the river. But I did not go. Latour had not died yet. After he died, if I could still walk, I might go.

"All day I sat beside the little box stove, gazing upon Latour. At night I slept lightly, awakening often to see how fever and hunger dealt with Latour. He might die while I slept.

"One day in December, I cannot remember just when, for I myself was often delirious with hunger, Latour again awakened from delirium.

" 'Food, food!' he gasped. 'For God's sake, Recontre, don't let a man starve like this! Let's make it up between us; only give me something to eat!'

"His voice was thin like a sick woman's. His face was the face of a damned man.

" 'Make what up?' I said sweetly. My voice was also thin. I struggled continuously with a terrible giddiness. I felt as one in a nightmare. I, too, was starving.

"Latour stared upon me with tears in his faded eyes, and groaned. I, too, fetched tears; it was easy to weep in my weakened condition.

" 'I have no food,' said I; 'neither can I go in

search of any. I am starving, and the snow is deep. Would I not go if I could? Would I not go for *you?* Can I forget Pelagie and the Blackfeet trip? Can I forget the winter trip to St. Louis?"

"Latour fainted. I shouted feebly with an insane joy; I thought he had died.

"In a few moments he revived, and again begged piteously for food. I wept, and said there was none. Then he became delirious and cursed me like a devil. I never heard such cursing before nor since.

"And the strange thing about it all was that I pitied Latour. But my hate had become a mania; I could not relent.

"What passed after that hour I cannot remember with distinctness. Dreams were real, and reality was a dream. I only remember in a vague way, as though it had happened in a nightmare, that Latour died cursing me; that I sang and shouted; that I crawled out of the hut on my hands and knees, laughing and shouting, and that I saw a band of men coming over the frozen snow from the direction of Fort Pierre. I remember hearing them call my name as with the voices of a dream. I remember that I cried out, 'Latour has just died!' I remember that these men gave me food, warm food, and that after a long sleep I awoke and saw a Jesuit missionary kneeling at my bedside.

"It was then that I tasted the full sweetness of

Indian Tales and Others

my triumph. The priest was blessing me! He spoke of the Christ-like kindness of Zephyr Recontre, who had not deserted his sick master.

"I did not see Latour again. The Jesuit's party had chopped a hole in the ice and given his body to the river."

BEYOND THE SPECTRUM

B UT is Frank Steel dead? I do not know.
I can only tell what seemed to happen.

In the fall of —— my friend Steel had expressed his intention of "becoming invisible for an indefinite period," as he put it; and from that time until the April of the following year I had not the least idea of his whereabouts, although I fancied that he had betaken himself to some hidden corner of the world for the purpose of elaborating in solitude some unique conceit.

Steel was a young man, and bore the unmistakable characteristics of a rare genius, which, owing partly to his peculiar reserve, and partly to the extreme grotesqueness of his thoughts, had become known to only a few select spirits. As for me, I had been his companion from his earliest youth; at least as much so as any human being of my rather matter-of-fact disposition could have been.

All through the last winter of his life—or *was* it the last?—I had wondered much about my friend; and my anxiety for his welfare, knowing as I did the dangers of so unusual a temperament as his, was only in a small measure offset by my firm belief in the work of rare beauty which would doubtless be the result of his winter's meditation.

Imagine my joy when in the latter part of April I received an envelope addressed to me in the handwriting of my friend. The postmark was one of those modest, self-effaced affairs, denoting a town of no importance, a comatose village painfully conscious of its insignificance and quick only with meek apology. My friend was somewhere in one of the most lonesome regions of the Black Hills.

I said that I felt joy at the receipt of this letter; but no sooner had I torn the envelope and taken a hasty glance at the whole page within than I felt a sudden depression of spirits that, upon closer scrutiny of the page, increased to a strange dread. For the chirography of my friend had been remarkable for a firm stroke, as bold as his adventuresome spirit, and the writing before me had changed somehow. To be sure, there was still about it that imperial atmosphere, as I might term it, which still gave me, as of old, the sensation of having seen a vivid flash of purple light; but something else was manifest in a scarcely perceptible quivering of line and an unusual thinness of the final strokes.

This is a copy of the rather abrupt note:

DEAR REYNOLDS: I have living with me at present a white cat—most unusual creature—yea, more than a cat! Come at once while same still *consents to dwell in the spectrum!* Be at ——(here the self-effaced village is named) on May 10th. Follow the Chinaman. FRANK.

Beyond the Spectrum

Now, Steel was one of those rare human creatures whose wishes might be termed a dynamic force. This is one of that order of facts against which only the intensely ignorant can produce argument. Knowing Steel as I did, even so common a thing as a white cat took on for me a weird and compelling significance; and in that inevitable self-conscious mood that follows upon the heels of sudden enthusiasm I laughed at myself. Nevertheless, I made the necessary preparations for the journey, and on May 10th I alighted at the wretched little Black Hills village.

It was already late evening. A drab light with an ever-decreasing power of illumination filtered through the melancholy air that oozed with rain, though yet no rain had fallen. I looked about feeling a vague sense of dread, which was but little relieved by the grinning face of the Chinaman whom I at once discovered standing at one end of the platform holding by the bits two ponies. The Oriental face and the odd appearance of the ponies, whose tousled winter coats had not yet been shed, added much to the grotesquerie of a journey begun through a seemingly silly whim exalted by some inexplicable psychic force into a matter of the gravest importance.

Having assured myself that one of the ponies was for me, we mounted, the Chinaman setting out at a brisk trot and I following. As we proceeded, the oozing twilight deepened into an eerie haze through which I saw indistinctly a landscape that has, since the happenings which I shall relate, taken on in my memory the aspect of a land seen in a quinic delirium. But at the time I was not entirely conscious of the photographic accuracy of the picture which was being impinged upon my mind.

About the scarp of a cliff the road ran in tortuous gyrations. Around us in the mist wild crags and fog-swathed summits reared themselves aloft—huge, impalpable shadows, hurled upward as from some subterranean phosphoric illumination. Upon the rocky trail the ponies' hoofs awoke a sullen muffled throbbing, perceptible more as a feeling than a sound; and the immediate space about us seemed as a winged island that should have left us groping in its wake of fog but for a headlong speed that kept us in its narrow confines. Like tapering columns of spectral smoke from innumerable hidden witches' fires, the pine-trees revealed themselves in faded chiaroscuro.

By imperceptible degrees the whole passed into a dull monochrome, a melancholy madness of gray, and a rain began to fall. At first it came as a confusion of many ghostly whispers, the inarticulate complaining of an exhausted grief; then a sighing grew up out of the silence, and a dull wind moaned about the many-folded mantle of the fog. The rain increased, and the wind dragged it across my face

as with innumerable soft mops. It seemed to me a
ceaseless thing; something coeval with Nature; a
melancholy fact, primal and ultimate.

Reaching a space where the trail widened, I
spurred my pony and drew up beside my guide. My
knee touched his, and I felt then, more than I had
ever felt before, the essential kinship of men; for
this region was grotesque and utterly ultra-human,
pressing upon me, as never before, the pitifully in-
cidental importance of man. We seemed as phan-
tasms moving in a mist, and this was my brother.

Wishing to cast off the feeling of dread—a visible
emanation of which the fog seemed to be—I ventured a few questions as to my friend's habits. The
man shook his head and kept silence. I had hoped
to see a human light in his face; but instead I saw
only an ugly mask, dull, and expressive only of some
vague fear—a reproduction of the eternal gray melancholy fact about us.

"I hear he has a white cat," I remarked, with a
final desperate effort to throw off the clinging dread.
The man straightened his body with a spasmodic
thrusting of his hands against the pommel. Peering
through the murky gloom under the dripping rim
of his hat, I saw a pallor flash across his face and
die.

"Well, what about the cat?" I snapped, half
angrily.

The man rocked himself uneasily in the saddle,

and with a perplexed shaking of the head he spurred his pony up the trail.

Like the black shadow of something huge and irresistible moving in the oozing air, the dark bore down upon us. It seemed as the heralding projection of a calamity that should be swift and crushing. With a series of preliminary gusts the wind felt round the gloom as with the tentative thrusting of powerful, slimy tentacles that meant at length to crush.

Then suddenly—like the first stroke of the catastrophe—a vivid streak of purple fire, a writhing sword-blade coruscant with the fires of hell, leaped from the scabbard of the night! Once, twice, thrice the blinding stroke descended! It slit the inky mantle of the mist, revealing in the more than noonday brilliance of its flame the sinister naked bodies of the crags! And from beneath the inward rushing of the murky flood that followed hoarse roars of giant pain surged up and died in chaos.

Faster and faster we took the trail ahead, the nose of my terrified pony clinging tenaciously to the tail of its galloping companion. Great grotesque night-dogs barked incessantly at our heels. Spiteful spirits struck me in the face with slimy whips. I caught myself clinging to the pommel and shouting, "Damn the white cat!" Over and over I shouted the words with little care as the order of them. They seemed somehow a part of the dread eternal fact that whipped my face with snake-like ropes of water, and yelled at my back, and smote the howling night with burning, ghastly wounds.

But at length, lifting my eyes with no hope of seeing aught, I was aware of an upright rectangle of steady light ahead of me. It was the open door of a cabin, and at once the figure of my friend grew up in sharp silhouette in the midst of it.

I leaped from my pony and, giving the reins to my guide, hurried to the door. As I approached, a white cat leaped from the shoulder of my friend where it had been perched, and disappeared.

It seemed to me that the greeting I received was hardly commensurate with the manner of my arrival. In a perfectly matter-of-fact way, as though he had parted from me but the moment before, Steel led me into a dingy room almost bare of furniture and offered me a seat in front of a fire that burned cheerily in a rude open grate.

"But, Frank," I said, "I'm wet to the skin and deuced uncomfortable!"

"It is quite probable that I shall be very busy to-night," replied my friend; "so be careful to make yourself comfortable. Your bed is in the next room. Tolerable tobacco on the shelf. John will see to your supper. Rather above ordinary courtesies to-night, old man, as you see."

With that Steel left me, entering a room to my left, and locking the door behind him. I set about to make myself comfortable, as I had been bid, and very soon John, the Chinaman, came in and set me out a very good supper.

So accustomed had I become to the occasional oddity of my friend's bearing that I was not at all offended with his seeming coldness; for many times had I proved the warmth and manliness of his nature. But I was worried about a change in his facial expression. There was a transparent look about his features and the eyes were over-serious. Settling myself comfortably before the fire I thought over the whole affair, and went to bed with a feeling that my sense of dread and the weirdness of the night and the changed expression of my friend's face bore some cryptic import. Also I thought of the cat and the momentary terror I had seen in the face of John.

II

My sleep was not the sleep of rest. It was rather to be described as a state of narcotized intellect and stimulated imagination. The mountain storm without invaded the thin upper air of sleep and was no longer a strife of physical forces, but a psychic cataclysm. At times the dream thunders took on the sound of exaggerated purring, howls of feline rage, and died off down the infinite mist-mantled valleys of sleep like the sullen goblin moaning of a mad and couchant cat. And now the chaos of the fog developed feline forms. Huge, milk-white panthers fought with lions white as snow, and the flashing of their eyes was lightning. Sinuous forms of terrible beauty, whirlwinds visible they seemed! And then like a flood of impalpable soot the night rushed down, and knives of rapid fire rent the gloom with hideous gashes that dripped with bloody flame, and closed and opened and closed. And after ages of darkness and flame and sound, a golden glow grew up that seemed more a blowing of melodious horns than a light. And I awoke; the quiet mountain dawn was in the room.

I dressed hastily, and seeing no signs of life about the place, went out. The cabin, built of pine logs and much more commodious than I had thought it to be, sat upon a knoll overlooking a panoramic landscape, lyric in its riot of light and shade and epic in its vastness. The early sunlight, falling aslant across a bald summit reared in severe grandeur against the rain-washed sky, dipped the tops of the taller pines in liquid gold. A diaphanous purple mist flowed down the long ravines and turned the quiet valleys into strange, enchanted lakes. No trace of the tempest of the night was there—only an Olympian calm through which a miraculous blending of light and shade raised up a visual hymn of peace. Somewhere far off swift waters leaped and laughed and smote thin bells of joy among the gulches hidden by the pines. The subtle wine of Spring ran sparkling through the thin, crisp air.

Finding a narrow trail that led upward among the crags, I set out leisurely for the sun-smitten summit. Absorbing the youthful vigor of the time and place with all five senses, I was suddenly aware that the inexplicable dread that had clung about me since the receipt of Steel's letter had all but passed away. I smiled as I thought of it. But why should I have felt it at all? I have always been blessed with a sunny temperament, and my health was perfect. Why, then, should I have felt a strange sinking of the heart at the sight of the letter? Could not a slight change in a man's penmanship have been the result of any one of innumerable trivial causes? A slight coldness of the hands, an over-indulgence in tobacco? Even though it were due to close confinement at study—what of that?

But why had I, who am ordinarily phlegmatic in temperament, been so thoroughly terror-stricken by an ordinary fog, followed by an ordinary thunderstorm? And the face of my friend—had I seen any material change in it? And the cat—ah, the cat! Had not the Chinaman's face clearly expressed fear at the mention of the cat? Or was that also a fancy of mine? Or—the thought struck me with peculiar force—could my brain have received some psychic impulse from the brain of Steel itself, that filled me with foreboding and gave to every thought an uncanny significance?

Thus occupied with introspection, I was suddenly aware of Steel beside me.

"Quite a color-scheme, is it not, Reynolds?" said he cheerily.

I looked into his face and felt a shock at what I thought I saw: an unutterable weariness of the large blue eyes, as though they had gazed too long into great distances; a translucent appearance of the skin; deep horizontal lines in the forehead, and the least hint of shadows in the cheeks. He seemed as one who had passed a night of debauchery; and yet—this was not the result of a debauch of the flesh.

"Indeed a marvelous picture," I replied, still scrutinizing his face. "I can scarcely believe that this was only last night the scene of a perfectly hellish tempest."

"Was there a storm?" asked Steel dreamily.

"A storm? Where in the world were you, man?"

"A storm is merely a physical phenomenon, is it not?" he replied; and he added hastily, "What are you seeing in my face?"

"Unspeakable weariness, Steel! You've got to get out of this."

"Do you know why you see that in my face, Reynolds?" he asked. "Because it's there! Any-

body could see it! And as for getting out of *this*"
—he indicated the vast panorama with a sweep of
the arm—"I *shall* soon, perhaps; very soon, perhaps!"

The voice of my friend was soft and even more
musical than I had ever known it before. There
was in it not the least suggestion of the cynic, not a
single note of harshness. Doubtless, one who was
not acquainted with the essentially poetic nature of
Steel would have thought of incipient insanity. So
far as I could discern, there was absolutely no trace
of it.

We strolled on side by side in silence, and reached
at last the summit smitten into gold with the slant
morning. We sat down upon a boulder to rest, and
I had drawn my friend's attention to the purple and
gold that rimmed the far horizon, when he produced a glass prism from his pocket.

"You are still seeing with your eyes, I perceive,"
said he; "a very wretched habit to fall into, I am
sure! Look!" He turned his back to the sunlight
and smoothed the skirt of his coat across his knee.
Holding the prism in the sunlight he cast the seven
prismatic colors upon the shadowed cloth. "Do
you know what you are seeing here on my knee?"

"The seven colors of the spectrum—the primary
colors," I answered, a little piqued, I confess.

"The world in epitome!" he said, with an air of
one who corrects a child. "You are looking upon

the naked truth about a thing in which and for which you toil and sweat and suffer! Look upon it carefully! There it is—the whole monotonous and inconsequential scheme of life in the flesh! Believe me, the eye is an imperfect instrument capable of receiving only those vibrations which blind it! But to proceed"—Steel was now seemingly unconscious of my presence and had the manner of one rehearsing a speech—"to proceed. Man is a creature of illusion existing between a violet ray and a red one. Time is an illusion caused by the contiguity of seven visible rays which, viewed together, produce a sensation of change. But so perfect is the illusion to man that we may, speaking in his language, define Time as being that portion of motionless eternity which falls within the narrow confines of the spectrum. Violet upon one hand and red upon the other, man is a prisoner reveling in the illusions of his prison.

"Born in the violet—the ray of germination— he passes in turn under the influences of the indigo, the blue, the green, the yellow, the orange, and is snuffed out in the tempestuous vibrations of the red. His life, as he terms it, is a color-scheme, the combinations of which are controlled by Chance or Fate or God, just as you wish to put it. Health is merely a perfect blending of complementary colors, and disease is merely a combination of colors that cannot vibrate in unison.

"Now it has been demonstrated, even by physical methods, that beyond the violet and the red are other rays. Beyond the violet the invisible rays that foster germination; and it has been demonstrated that these are most in evidence in the spring months. Beyond the red are the visible rays that foster growth; and these are more in evidence in the summer months. Do you catch the significance of this—the wonderful, illuminating significance? The red, last of the visible rays, lies next to the invisible rays of growth. Death is a mere passing through the red ray into the ray of growth. There is no dying; there is only a passing out of the spectrum into infinite development!

"We are souls passing through a motionless, colorless eternity, and it is only in the path of the seven rays, here cast upon my knee, that we become visible, like particles of dust floating athwart a sunray in a dark-room!

"Co-existent with the seven visible vibrations are the audible vibrations—eleven or twelve octaves of them. Beyond these, what? The inaudible vibrations of the Infinite!

"Now, the ear is an imperfect instrument capable of receiving only those vibrations which deafen it!"

Here I broke in upon the volubility of my friend. "What in thunder are you driving at, Steel?" said I, for, as I have stated, I am a most matter-of-fact individual. "When are you going to laugh and put up that prism? To be strictly scientific, there is at present in my interior inwardness a kaleidoscopic process incident to a lamentable intertanglement of invisible rays, which bids fair to send me ramping through the visible red into the regions of infinite development before I have even finished with the violet, which, as you well know, it having been demonstrated, is entrusted with the delicate process of germination. To speak in vulgar terms, commonly used by the laity, I'm hungry and I want my breakfast!"

It was my intention to arouse the sense of the ridiculous in my friend, well knowing that nothing is so healthful as an occasional laugh at one's own vagaries. I confess that my attempt at facetiousness was but a melancholy affair, but is it not the duty of a friend to laugh at the intention even though the joke be flat?

Anxiously I scrutinized his face for the least glimmer of light that should proclaim his sense of humor still alive. But a shuddering passed through my limbs as I gazed into his face, as though I had unwittingly laid my hands upon a corpse in the dark.

With the same intense seriousness, he waited until I had ceased speaking, and when my melancholy effort at good-natured laughter had been made he proceeded rapidly; and never have I heard a more musical voice than was his.

"We are like shipwrecked wretches huddled on

an infinitesimal point of land in an infinite sea. Faintly we catch the thunderous music of the reefs. We stare hard into an impenetrable fog and our hearts grow sick. We cannot see beyond the narrow limits of the sea-girt speck of earth. And some of us go mad. Think of it, Reynolds! A little patch of tense skin is all we have with which to catch the grand musical utterances of the outer sea. Another little patch of skin on which to catch the beauties of the Infinite. Poor heartsick slaves of the spectrum and the gamut are we!

"But listen! What if we should find within that portion of us which is the child of the Infinite a latent sense not limited to a certain number of vibrations per second? What if we should discover an inner eye, the eye of Psyche—an inner ear, the ear of Psyche? What could we see? What could we hear? Less than an octave of color, less than twelve octaves of sound? Ah, my friend, then there would be for us the twinkle of the romping satyr's hoofs in every woodland shadow! In every silver stream the bodies of the Nymphs would be revealed, diaphanous and splendent with gems of dew! We would see the saucy Echo flitting through the purple shadows of the gulches and peeping coyly 'round the stern gray crags! For us no longer the pages of the poets, and Homer's songs would be forgot. For we ourselves could stand in dread-hushed Aulis and feel the ominous silence of the windless sea! We could see the idle sails drooped listlessly as from some awful sickness of the heart! We could see the altar and the fearsome huddled faces of the Argive host! We could hear the shrieks of Iphigenia piercing the tragic silence even as the sword had pierced her virgin breast; and in the dread hush of eternity would grow up the ceaseless dripping of her blood! We could see the mighty Achilles lying sullen in his tent; and 'round the visible walls of Troy would fly for us the pitiless charioteer trailing in the dust the body of the fallen Hector! Before our eyes Cambyses's futile unreturning host would march into the deserts of the West and round the huddled legions we could see the awful pillars of the sand reared skyward in the whirlwind! The flood of nations driven northward by the breath of Xerxes's pride would roll before us! Lured by kinder scenes, we could stand unseen among Thessalian meadows and hear the tender words of Lais and her boy. Or with the ancient jury we could feel the overpowering beauty of the breasts of Phryne.

"Helen would walk before us, changeless, even as she walked for Paris; and for us would be the maddening allurement of that face 'that launched a thousand ships and burnt the topless towers of Ilium'! We could know the songs the sirens sang! Through the sullen days of August we could read upon the golden face of the sunflower by the dusty road a more than Homeric epic! And in the quiet nights of moon and star when winds were lulled with perfumes, we could hear the passionate lyric of the crimson rose!"

At this point in his impassioned outburst Steel drew out his watch and stared blinkingly for a moment upon its dial.

"Ah," said he at length, "breakfast is doubtless cold by this time!"

III

"At least," said I, as we sat down to the rude table, "we can perfectly agree as to the urgency of hunger. That is also an illusion, is it not?"

For a moment I had hopes of awakening the old self that I still believed to be sleeping in my friend. For a moment, I say; for there was the least glimmer of the light of old times in his eyes.

But just then the cat came!

The light died. The face of Steel suddenly took on a deeper seriousness, an almost worshipful aspect, as the white puss entered the room with a majestic stride, leaped upon a high-chair and sat up with an air of regal dignity that, at any other time, would certainly have seemed ridiculous. But somehow laughter in this strange world, which I had lately entered, died on the lips or perished in a throaty cackle.

In the oppressive hush that fell the Chinese serv-

Beyond the Spectrum

ant entered and to my surprise, leaning over the cat said gravely: "Will madame have an omelet?"

I must confess that as I stared upon the mock scene I actually listened for the answer of a human voice! I am not, I think, given to hallucinations; but in that strange moment I seemed to see *through* the white cat, as though I were gazing into a great distance at the end of which the vague outlines of a most charming woman appeared. The hallucination—or was it such?—was accompanied by a momentary giddiness which I cannot explain; and then I heard a soft *meow,* and I was again staring upon a most ridiculously grave cat and a most ridiculously obsequious servant.

When we had all three been served I was aware that my hunger was indeed no longer a reality. I trifled with my omelet, dawdled with my coffee and broke my toast into innumerable pieces. Steel, however, gave evidence of a very good appetite; and this fact in a measure reassured me as to his mental condition, for I have read, having had no personal experience to guide me, that mania is very often accompanied by a loss of appetite.

Throughout the meal, which progressed in the most profound silence, my friend was ever on the alert to anticipate the wants of my feline hostess, and more than once I fancied that I saw creeping across his face the unmistakable light of love.

As I look back over all the meals that I have

eaten, I am forced to single out that breakfast as the most tedious, though certainly the most significant of them all. I say "significant," for in a sense it was so, but with a vague and bewildering significance. At length it came to an end in a manner which should have been ridiculous, but, for some subtle reason, was not.

The white cat, having finished her meal, gave forth a series of purring sounds. Strangely enough, it seemed to me that this was no ordinary purring, but a sort of exquisitely musical speech the meaning of which flashed rapidly through my befogged brain only to be forgotten immediately. Such speech the reader may have heard in the delirium of malarial fever. Exquisitely musical, delightfully caressing it seemed; and as I watched and listened I experienced a momentary hallucination similar to that upon the creature's first appearance at the table.

When the cat had ceased purring (or should I say "speaking"?) Steel began speaking (or should I say "purring"?) very softly. Again I caught the vaguest shadow of a meaning which instantly left me. If indeed he was speaking at all, it was in no modern tongue. Only one sound in the musical flow of sounds which he gave forth bore any resemblance to any sound with which I am familiar. That sound was not unlike "Cleo." From the manner of its use I judged that this was the name of the cat, although I confess that this is merely a conjecture of mine.

When Steel had ceased, my hostess gracefully left her high-chair and disappeared. Whereupon I felt as one suddenly relieved of a great weight. Such a feeling has no doubt been experienced by the reader upon the departure from the room of some celebrity of strongly magnetic personality. Although I am of an extremely skeptical turn of mind, I am half convinced that some powerful personality *did* leave the table with the departure of the cat.

I immediately regained my composure and my hunger.

During my renewed attack upon the omelet I felt obliged to speak to my friend in no equivocal manner.

"Steel," I said, summoning what I could of a naturally small stock of severity, "this is an utterly idiotical proceeding and I, as your nearest friend, feel obliged to protest! It would pain me beyond measure to be convinced of mental decay in you; but this is indeed an insane proceeding, and I insist upon your laughing at once and being so kind as to point out to me forthwith precisely where the humor in the situation may lie!"

So violently did I hurl these words at my friend that I could say no more, but fell upon the omelet in a manner so savage that I thus discovered a hitherto

Indian Tales and Others

hidden phase of my nature which alarmed me. But in the suavest of manners and in a peculiarly musical voice my friend answered: "As I have said, Reynolds, you have the common habit of seeing only with your eyes and hearing only with your ears! Please do not disclose your limitations quite so freely; at least until the *end of this!*"

When I had finished eating I arose from the table and announced my intention of again climbing to the summit; and feeling somewhat ashamed of my heated words, asked Steel if he would accompany me. He stated that with my permission he would remain in the cabin, as it was his habit to do a certain amount of reading at that time of day. I went out much perplexed at what I had seen.

When I returned an hour later I found Steel deep in a book. Having inquired as to what he was reading, he answered: "A rather clever work of art, as art goes; but a most ridiculous bit of history— Shakespeare's 'Antony and Cleopatra.'"

"I believe the Master-Poet consulted Plutarch for his history, did he not?" said I.

"My friend," said he, "Plutarch was a mere credulous boy, hearing only with his ears and seeing only with his eyes!" This astounding retort was uttered in that musical voice and with that suave manner which were beginning to wear upon my nerves.

"Steel," said I, with considerable coolness, "I

Beyond the Spectrum

recommend that you begin at once to rearrange the world's store of facts!"

In the most matter-of-fact manner he replied: "And who would believe my version if I should?"

"Oh, I'm sure I don't know!" I answered, with a sickening sense of being unable to arouse my friend. There was a silence for some time, during which I was possessed with a wild desire to snatch my poor friend out of this mad swirling stream of thought that seemed bearing him rapidly toward a fate far worse than death.

"O Steel! My friend!" I cried. "For God's sake be as you were of old! *Can't* you arouse yourself! *Don't* you see the inevitable end of this?"

With a smile of ineffable pity he met my passionate appeal. "Reynolds," said he quietly, "my good friend, you cannot possibly understand. And something is about to happen which shall further mystify you. But have no fear; I am not insane. On the contrary, I have discovered the great secret of life and death. In a foolish burst of confidence this morning I attempted to reveal to you a portion of this secret. You are incapable of receiving it, and I advise you to keep silence as to what you hear and see in this place, lest your own sanity be questioned.

"Reynolds, listen! I have discovered the psychic ear and the psychic eye! As to my statement concerning this rather ingenious drama and the history upon which it is supposed to be founded, it might

[251]

be interesting for you to know that *only last night I was at the court of Cleopatra!"*

As when one watches through a long anxious night beside the bed of a friend stricken with a mortal illness, and will not give him up until the death rattle has passed and a chilling quiet falls in the room, so had I watched and hoped. But now my heart sank. I was convinced that Steel—the chum of my boyhood, the companion of my maturity, the genius of rare promise—was stark mad!

And yet—since it is all over—I have thought much on the subject, and am almost prepared to reverse my decision, hastily formed in that most hideous hour.

IV

I hesitate as I find myself about to narrate the happenings which ended that week of mystification; for those happenings were so thoroughly out of proportion with our ordinary ideas of things that I fear, from those who shall read this, even a more serious charge than that of mendacity. But as to my soundness of mind I wish to state with becoming modesty that I was only recently chosen by a large majority of my fellow-citizens to discharge the duties of an important county office.

During the day preceding the night on which the end came Steel was much occupied; in fact, he left his room only once. I noted with additional alarm that he seemed to have all but lost his senses of sight and hearing. When I spoke to him he gave no evidence of having heard, but stared through me, seemingly, as though I were transparent.

I went to bed that night with the firm intention of making an effort the very next morning to remove him to some private sanatarium, for I still clung to the idea that he was mad. At no other time had I experienced such a heartache, and it was only after several hours of tossing about that I fell into a feverish sleep.

I judge it must have been at about four o'clock in the morning when I was snatched violently out of my slumber by a peculiar cry. It seemed to come from a great distance; and while I thought it to be the cry of a woman, there was about it something that suggested the moaning of a cat.

Thoroughly frightened, I sat trembling on the edge of the bed and listened. The strange cry died away as though swallowed up in great spaces; and then there came ever so faintly a sound not unlike the complaining of a rough sea, though it seemed to me at the time like the hoarse shouting of a far-away multitude.

Suddenly the same cry that had awakened me grew up again. It seemed to emanate from Steel's room. A wild, unearthly sound that made my flesh crawl and gave to my scalp that prickling sensation so often described as a standing of the hairs!

Shivering as with a chill and tottering like a drunken man, I made my way to the door of Steel's room. I shouted his name aloud, but received no answer. A silence fell; a silence even more terrible than the cry, because of something awful latent in it!

I remember shrieking with fright when John, the Chinaman, appeared with a lamp. I remember the ghastly appearance of his face in the sudden light, the chattering of his teeth, the terror-stricken eyes.

Then there came from the room a final cry that chilled my brain as though an icy wind had blown upon it; a cry wild and piercing at first, but dying away into a pitiful minor wail.

I hesitated no longer. Throwing myself violently against the door, I found myself staring into *an empty room!*

Empty? Yes, and no. Steel was not there; but *something was there!* Something that was a sound, yet not a sound; a light, yet not a light.

For I was aware of a ghostly sort of sound, beautiful beyond the dreams of musicians; a something like and unlike light, exquisitely pleasing. For a moment I stood entranced. I seemed no longer in a room; the place seemed without bounds. It was neither dark nor light, neither silent nor containing sound.

But instantly the strange sensation left me. With that instinct of all frightened animals which drives them to their kind in moments of danger, I turned to the Chinaman. I could see neither him nor the lamp! I called to him, but could not hear my own voice! I stepped to the place where he had been and my hand fell upon the hot globe of the lamp. I could feel the vibrations of the heat above it, but could see no light, though I knew the lamp to be still burning. I felt about in the dark for the face of the man. I touched his mouth. The lips were moving rapidly, but I heard no sound!

Had my senses been momentarily paralyzed by those invisible, unheard vibrations of which my poor friend had spoken? Had I stepped for a moment *beyond the spectrum?*

After a lapse of time that seemed an age the dim outlines of the lamp and the Chinaman and the room began to grow before me, and I began to hear again. By daylight my senses were again quite normal.

All that day we two searched for Steel in vain, and the cat did not appear. Several years have passed since then, and still in spite of the most diligent searching I have found no clue to the disappearance of my friend.

No clue? At least none that could be accepted as such by the reader or, I confess, by myself. I have in my possession a few scraps of paper upon which certain incoherent notes are scrawled in the handwriting of my friend. The greater part of the writing is illegible, and judging from the numbers on the pages, many sheets have been, for some reason, destroyed. Below I submit to the reader all that I can decipher of these notes. At times I seem to catch a vague significance from them, half believing that I can imagine what the illegible words are. I do not insist that they are the notes of a sane man; neither do I wish to commit myself to the contrary.

FRAGMENTS OF STEEL'S NOTES

(page 3)

. . . perhaps the greatest discovery of all time; one which . . . all hitherto accepted archeological . . . but . . . and . . . coming of the cat

(Here as indicated by the numbers, five pages are missing.)

. . . can no longer doubt that . . . and nothing has ceased . . . merely passing out of the range of the five physical senses of man!

. . . coexists with us, though invisible, and . . . kingdoms . . . as one might say, between seeing, hearing, tasting, touching and smelling . . . often entertaining unawares historical personages . . .

(Here four more pages are missing.)

Many hitherto unexplanied psychological phenomena . . . pageant of history has not ceased but is continuous . . . myself seen the heterogeneous . . . driven . . . Xerxes . . . into Greece . . . Strymon(?) . . .

(Ten missing pages here.)

. . . when I have at last . . . shall become free . . . shackled . . . with Cleo(patra?)

(The next page is utterly illegible with the exception of a few words in the last sentence.)

. . . once more . . . shall not return into the . . . illusions . . . spectrum!

Beyond the Spectrum

I have given as much of the notes as I could decipher. They seem to have been jotted down under great nervous strain, many lines appearing to me like a continuous stroke of a quivering pen point. How much would I give for the complete notes in legible form!

THE NEMESIS OF THE DEUCES

FRENCHY called for two cards and reached for a glass and the bottle. His head swam dizzily. The clinking of glasses at the bar smote upon his ears like gongs. He was about to risk upon one "show-down" the realisation of a five-years' dream. He felt certain of losing; that was the strange thing about it. Yet somewhere in the buzzing back of his head a compelling little devil whispered and he obeyed.

He drank three big ones straight, and for a moment things stood still and the buzzing ceased; but in the sudden silence the hissing of the little devil increased to a roaring like the river's in the June rise. *"All on the deuces! All on the deuces! Every damned cent!"* That is what the little devil in the back of his head was howling now.

"But if I lose it all—and wanting to go back home in the spring?" That was the question his pounding heart hurled at the insistent little devil.

"You won *once*—didn't you—*didn't you?*— DIDN'T YOU?" howled back the little devil jeeringly.

"Five hundred," said Frenchy quietly. His bronze face had grown livid; his black eyes narrowed and glittered with a steady stare. With a hand that betrayed the least perceptible tremor, he pushed the chips to the centre.

The next man tossed his hand into the discard. The next hesitated, carefully studying the face of Frenchy with a furtive lifting of the eyes under his hat brim; he too laid down his hand.

"Raise you two hundred," said the next with quiet cheerfulness.

"Two hundred more," said the next nonchalantly, drumming a devil's tattoo with his fingers on the table.

The fifth drew a long breath, grinned nervously, showing his teeth like a hungry wolf—and tossed his hand into the discard.

It was now up to Frenchy.

"Pardon me," said he, "but did you call me?"

His face had turned a dull, ghastly green, but his voice was quiet and clear.

"Raised it."

"Oh, certainly," said he, smiling. "Thinking of something else—trip home, I guess." His voice lowered until it was almost audible. This absent-mindedness was unusual for Frenchy.

An oppressive silence had fallen in the barroom of the "Big 6." There was no longer any clinking of glasses or hum of maudlin voices. The loungers drew up in a hushed circle about the table and stared with fascinated eyes. A "big game" was on—and it was up to Frenchy. Frenchy was no quitter; he was a gambler to his finger-tips. "Frenchy? He'd bet on which'd be the last breath of his dying mother!" That was the way the popular legend ran, and the man lived up to it.

"Stake it all—stake it all on the deuces—*the deuces*—THE DEUCES!" The little devil in the back of his head was shrieking now and stamping red-hot heels into Frenchy's brain.

"But the trip home—I've planned five years ———" urged his pounding heart.

"You won on them *once*—didn't you?—*didn't you?*—DIDN'T YOU?" reiterated the little devil.

Frenchy quietly poured out another glass and downed it. Then he pulled off his boots, produced a bunch of bills from the bottom of each, put on his boots again and looked at his hand.

"Come two thousand more!" he whispered.

A sound of deeper breathing grew up about the fascinated circle of on-lookers. Frenchy had gone into his boots—they knew what that meant. Would the others stay? *Would they?*

The place became uncanny with stillness. Nothing moved in the room. The circle of eyes stared steadily upon the three who sat with expressionless faces blanched with the pitiless struggle that was going on. For a minute that seemed endless the soundless battle continued. Psychic forces exchanged invisible sword-thrusts across the table.

The Nemesis of the Deuces

Nerve wrestled with nerve that cowered but still fought on.

The whole scene vanished for Frenchy. It seemed to him that he was the center of a silent hollowness; only a voice, that was rather an ache felt than a sound heard, kept up a pitiless jeering.

"They'll stay—they'll stay," shrieked the little devil; "your bluff won't work—you're a dead horse and they're crows—crows—crows!"

"They're weakening!" beat the heart of Frenchy.

"Deuces—ha, ha! Deuces! And they've both got face cards—deuces—ho, ho!—going home, eh? —win on deuces?—ho, ho, ho—deuces!' The insistent devil laughed spitefully.

"Raise you five hundred more!"

The words echoed and re-echoed in the lonesome hollowness. Frenchy stared at his cards.

"Five hundred more!"

Frenchy winced and shivered. It seemed to him that a long, thin-bladed knife had reached out of the silent hollow that surrounded him and stabbed him twice in the breast.

"Ho, ho, ho!" went the little devil at the back of his head. "Stay with 'em! Put up the horses— everything on the deuces—ho, ho, ho!"

"But I can lay down now and save the horses," urged the sick heart of Frenchy.

"You won on the deuces *once!*" shrieked the little devil; "didn't you—DIDN'T YOU?"

Frenchy now heard his own voice growing up out of the hollow. "Taken: my five horses and outfit are good for it."

Then he emerged from the soundless hollow and was aware of the circle of glittering eyes staring down on the field whereon he had just staked five years of his life and his last cherished dream.

"Full house—aces on queens."

Frenchy heard the words and grinned exultantly. The little spiteful devil was silent.

"Four kings!"

Frenchy dropped his cards face up and reached for the bottle. "Ho, ho, ho!" went the little devil, dancing all over his brain; "everything lost on the deuces—dead horse for the crows to pick!—he, he, he!"

A ripple of exclamations ran about the circle of loungers as they leaned forward to see the hand upon which Frenchy had staked all that he owned.

"Deuces! By the jumping—four dirty deuces!"

"Deuces?"

"Four of 'em."

"How's that for a bluff?"

"Fool play!"

A buzzing undertone of comment filled the room and steadily grew into a chattering as of crows about a spot where something has just died. Frenchy seemed not to hear; he was busy filling and refilling glasses. The man with the four kings quietly raked in his winnings. "And the horses——?" he suggested.

Frenchy set the drained glass down with a bang, and with a snake-like forward thrusting of the head leered hideously at the winner. *"Can't you shut up about the horses?"* He forced the words menacingly through his shut teeth.

A hush fell upon the loungers as they looked upon the pinched, malignant face with the upper lip lifted quiveringly and the close-set teeth showing beneath. This was no longer the Frenchy of legend; that Frenchy had always been known as one who lost or won large sums with the utter nervelessness of a machine. This was no longer the face of Frenchy—the gay, careless, haughty face of him who flirted with Fortune. This was a new Frenchy —a terrible Frenchy; with a coiled snake lurking just behind each glittering eyeball. This face sent a shiver through the crowd—like the sight of an ugly knife unsheathed in anger.

The loungers with affected carelessness began to move away. With a lightning sweep of the hands Frenchy drew his guns and banged them down violently on the table before him. "Stay where you are, gentlemen!" he said; "I'm going to talk and I want an audience. When I'm done talking, I'm off on the long trail and the first man that moves goes with me!"

There had always been a winsome something in

the voice of the man. It was now commanding, irresistible. The loungers stood still and stared dumfounded upon this terrible new version of an old
legend.

Frenchy picked up four cards from his hand and
held them up fanwise before his enforced listeners.
"Look at 'em!" he shouted hoarsely. "Look at
'em! Let 'em burn through your hides into your
souls! Oh, you don't see anything, eh? Don't one
of you dare to grin!"

One hand fumbled nervously with the guns.

"What do you see? I say, what do you see?
Four deuces? That all? I'll tell you what *I* see. I
see the red, warm hearts of two friends! I see
diamonds that are cheap beside such hearts! I see
a club—a black, brutal, treacherous club—that
struck down a friend! And I see the devil's spades
that dug his grave! That's what I see! Look
hard!"

Frenchy seemed to exercise an uncanny influence
over his hearers. Not one moved—all stared upon
the four upheld deuces.

"It's the devil's story, gentlemen," he continued
in a low, husky voice. "It's hung by me for three
bloody years—it haunts me! I've got to tell it."

He passed his free hand over his forehead beaded
with sweat. Then he whispered a question to the
spellbound audience:

"Did any of you know the Kid—Kid Smith?"

The Nemesis of the Deuces

A momentary expression of infinite kindness softened the face of Frenchy, only to give way immediately to deep quivering lines of anguish. He continued tremulously.

"I knew him—the Kid. Had the biggest, bravest heart that ever beat in the God-forsaken white spaces of a map. One of that breed of fellows that the world nails to its crosses—the Kid was. And we were friends; that is, he was a friend. He gave and I took, and he was happier in the giving than I in the taking. That's the way it always goes: one gives and one takes—and God pity the man that only takes!

"Why did I bet on the deuces? Oh, the damned, dirty deuces! Don't I know the game? By God, I know every card like a kid knows his mother's face! Didn't I know it was the last ditch for me and no hope? I tell you, gentlemen, I didn't play 'em. The Devil played 'em for me—the black Devil of the dirty deuces with the fiery feet that have been kicking me hellward for three years!

"Look at the cards! Look at 'em! There's blood on every one of 'em, and they stink with the writhing flesh of a friend in the flames!"

Frenchy took another drink and his manner changed. The violence of his delirious outburst gave way to quietness. He spoke in a low, penetrating voice, and the black flame of his eyes held his hearers.

Indian Tales and Others

"The Kid and I had been riding across a big stretch of brown grass for two days, and our tongues were thick with thirst. I remember how he gave me the last drops of water we had with us, cussing and damning a man who got thirsty. 'I can go without water with the biggest camel that ever stuck a hoof into the sand,' said he. And I took the water; I always took and the Kid was always giving.

"And along in the evening we struck a little water hole and camped. How the Kid did drink when he thought I wasn't looking! Oh, he wasn't such a camel for carrying water with him! It was his big heart that carried the water—the sweet, pure, sparkling waters of friendship.

"Along about sundown a dull gray cloud grew up in the west—smoke! But the wind was against it, blowing soft and dry from the east where the river lay thirty miles away. 'Think we'd better ride on?' says the Kid. But I was tired and wanted sleep, and the Kid gave in. Says he, 'Horses need a rest, I guess'; didn't lay it onto me, you know. Giving again, and I taking.

"So we lariated the horses and rolled in. Do you know how a man sleeps after he's been burning dry for days and fills up at last? I plunged into ten thousand fathoms of soft, soft sleep—deep, deep down, where the cool sweet dreams bloom in worlds of crystal. And everywhere in my sleep there were bubbling springs and I drank and drank and drank, and every gulp was sweeter than the last.

"Then the dreams changed and the many bubbling water holes of sleep went dry, and fine hot dust sprayed up out of the chinks where the water had flowed. Then the wind of sleep grew hot and hotter. It scorched my face and sent thin needles of fire into my brain. And then I was standing up coughing and rubbing my eyes and the Kid was beside me. What did we see?

"The wind had veered about while we slept. All hell was climbing up the west and a booming wind swept howling devils through the smoky twilight. Above the unnatural dawn, long black ragged arms reached out into the zenith and cloaked the stars. I heard a horse snorting and tugging at his lariat.

" 'Good God, Kid!' I wheezed; 'let's be off!'

"The Kid turned his face upon me and smiled— that slow, brave smile haunts me night and day.

" 'Your horse is gone——' He waved his hand toward the miles of dark that stretched toward the river. 'Pulled his stake just before you woke up; heard him go.' The Kid's voice didn't even tremble.

" 'Quick!' I yelled; 'the matches! Start a back fire!'

"Then a big, cold hand gripped my heart; the Kid had given me the last match that day; I had wanted to smoke.

Indian Tales and Others

"All hell behind us and a horse for two! A thirty-mile heat with the mustangs of the Devil, and double weight to carry! It made me sick— dizzy sick. I forgot everything. Oh, gentlemen, when you face hell fire you'll know if your mother bore a coward.

"For a minute we stared into the west—a minute years long. Big pink waves of smoke rolled into gulfs of purple and disappeared into holes of murk. Above, the blood-red surf frothed and sparkled and fell in yellow showers! Great blankets of dense gloom dropped from the sky and smothered out the hellish morning, hurling momentary night down the howling wind! Then keen zigzag blades of fire ripped through the belly of the night!

"I felt the Kid's hand grasp mine. O God! the feel of his hand! 'One horse for two, Frenchy,' he said, quiet as a man who proposes another drink at the bar. 'One of us makes a run for his life; and the other——' He motioned carelessly toward Hell. 'One more deal of the cards, Frenchy, and the last for one of us. High hand takes the horse; low hand—produce the deck.'

"I produced the deck—greasy and dog-eared; for many's the social game the Kid and I had played with 'em together. We squatted on the prairie in the red twilight, and the Kid dealt. Not a tremor of his perfect gambler's hands! Cool as though it was a game of penny ante.

The Nemesis of the Deuces

"I drew three deuces! *Deuces!* Oh, the damned, dirty deuces!

" 'How many?' says the Kid pleasantly. For the first time in my life I forgot to guard my hand. A deep rolling thunder had grown up out of the burning west. It seemed I could feel the prairies tremble like a bridge under a drove of sheep. 'Listen!' I gasped. 'It's the critters coming,' said the Kid; 'cattle and buffalo and elk and deer and wolves —the whole posse. How many cards did you call for?—*two*, wasn't it?"

"He thrust two cards into my hand. One of 'em was the deuce of hearts! O God! It wasn't only the printed heart he gave me; it was the warm, red, beating heart of a friend."

Frenchy dropped his head into his arms on the table and groaned. When he lifted his face again his eyes were wet.

"Four deuces—and they burn holes in the dark whenever I shut my eyes! And all day I see four pairs of devils dancing in the sunlight till my head swims!"

Frenchy dropped his head upon his chest and breathed deep, uneven breaths for a space.

"The Kid had only a pair of face-cards," he continued; "a dinky little pair of face-cards. And for a second the man in me came to the surface, and I threw the four hand down and stamped on it and said I wouldn't leave him. And what did the Kid do? Began with all the blackguard adjectives of the language and ended with 'coward' and threw the bunch in my teeth. 'You're the first man that ever called me a quitter, Frenchy,' he said. 'I played my hand, didn't I? What would you do to a man who'd ask you to take your money back when you'd lost? If I'd won, do you think I wouldn't leave your carcass here to stew, you cussed fool?'

"And then something in the back of my head woke up and howled: 'You won—it's yours—a chance for life—fair play—he'd go if you lost—he'd go!' And there was a roaring in my head and the flaming night whirled 'round, and the bitter words stung me, and my heart hardened—and—I—went.

"I found the Kid's horse saddled and bridled. I cut the lariat and leaped astride. I jabbed the spike spurs into the frightened brute till he roared with pain. I had forgotten everything. I was a fear without a body flying through a darkness that coughed smoke and spit light. And then at last things quit whirling, and I felt the steady *lift, lift, lift* of the good brute racing with all the devils down a heart-breaking stretch for the river.

"I turned about in the saddle. Half the sky had turned into an open furnace! Above me a great stormy ocean of blood rolled on into the twilight of the east! Blood!—a seething, billowy sea of red blood, with great, red, purring cat-tongues lapping it greedily! Gaudy giant flowers—purple, yellow, red, green—bloomed for a moment in a strange garden of dreams, and nodded in the wind and fell and bloomed again and fell! The infernal beauty of the thing fascinated me for a moment. Then I heard the rumbling—the unceasing thunder. It was louder than before. I though of the ten thousand sharp hoofs gaining, gaining, with whips of fire lashing them in the rear. And then I thought of the Kid back there.

"My heart sickened. The hot wind that scorched my face accused me; the choking air accused me. I could see him lying on his face even then with the mad hoofs beating him into a pulp; I could see the writhing of his body as the heat increased; I could smell his sizzling flesh!

"I reeled in the saddle, yet the mad wish to live lashed my hands to the pommel. But this was only for a moment. The meanest worm that ever wriggled in a dunghill holds fast to his life. I forgot the Kid again; I remembered only myself and that I must ride to win. I pulled the horse down and held him steady. Never did I throw a leg across a better horse than the Kid's—honest, rangy, clean-limbed and deep in the chest! My heart leaped with joy when I heard his long even breathing. I had a great delirious love for the big-hearted brute as I felt his long, even reach, the tireless rhythmic stride that throws the miles behind. The drifting red sea of smoke above cast the wild glare down upon the prairie and made the footing sure. I threw my guns away; I stripped off my coat and gave it to the wind. I knew what an extra pound might mean.

"An elk forged slowly past, his wide antlers tipped with light. An antelope sprang up and bounded away into the twilight ahead. A coyote leaped from a shoe-string clump; he cowered and whined like a whipped dog with his tail between his legs, then raced away down the wind. Snorting shadows began to move to right and left in the further gloom and disappear in the smoke-drift. I was now a part of the ragged edge of the flotsam tossed up by the approaching lip of the flood. I gave my horse another inch of rein and held him steady. The thunder in the rear grew louder; I could hear dimly the wild confusion of animal cries. I was the fox hearing the yelp of the hounds and racing for cover.

"Years and years of flight with the breath of an oven to breathe! Years and years of rising and falling, rising and falling, and my throat was tight with the driving smoke. The good brute began to wheeze and cough. I felt the tremor of his wearying muscles, the slight unsteadiness of the knees. I prayed for the river—prayed like a kid at his mother's knee. I begged the brute to keep his legs; I cursed him when he tottered; I called him baby names and damned him in a breath.

The Nemesis of the Deuces

"And after years the day began—a sneaking shadow of a day, shamed out by the howling western dawn that met it on the run. A storm of sound was all about me. Neck and neck I raced with a buffalo bull that led the herd; his swollen tongue hung from his foaming mouth; his breath rumbled in his throat. Wheezing steers toiled up about me. Deer and elk raced side by side, slowly forging into the van. Gray wolves bounded past, whining and yelping. And my good brute beat away bravely at the few remaining miles. I felt the dry rasp of his lungs and the breaking of his big, strong heart. He stumbled—I gave him the spur to the heel; he gave no sign of pain. He was dying on his feet.

"And the cheap, dirty day crept in through the smoke—and I thought of the Kid, and lost heart and cared no more about the race. But by and by I saw the river ahead, and we plunged in—a howling, panting flood of beasts, struggling for the farther shore.

"The sky and the river whirled about me. I felt my horse totter up a sandbank and fall. Then the day went out, and I forgot.

"O God, I wish I'd never wakened! Why didn't the buffalo and the steers beat me into the sand? Why did I wake up?"

Frenchy covered his face with his hands and the tears trickled through his fingers.

"But the dead horse parted the herd, and I woke

up and the fire was dead and the sun looked like a moon through the smoke. Three aching years ago, it was; and I've dragged my carcass about and tried to look like a man. But night and day the deuces have followed me and tortured me. They burn holes in the dark whenever I shut my eyes; four pairs of devils dance before me all day in the sunlight till my head whirls."

Frenchy picked up the four deuces and held them tremblingly before the staring crowd.

"Look at 'em! Let 'em burn through your hides into your souls! There's the blood of the Kid on 'em. The damned dirty deuces! They've got me in the last ditch! I'm done!"

Frenchy crushed the cards and dashed them to the floor. He arose unsteadily to his feet, took his guns and staggered out of the barroom of the "Big 6."

THE REVOLT OF A SHEEP

"OH, shut up, Hank! Damn it! Hain't you goin' to let a feller sleep none? How can I be strong enough to keep from snivellin' in the mornin', if I don't get my sleep?"

A small man with a thin, weak face, that might have suggested the vacuous countenance of a sheep had it not been for an expression of anguish and childish petulance, sat up among a bunch of furs in the corner of the cabin. He supported himself tremblingly upon an arm and stared with watery, haggard eyes upon Hank, who regarded him wistfully.

Hank was a big man and raw-boned. His big, quiet, hirsute face contrasted strongly with the face of the other. About his waist hung a belt containing a pair of six-shooters. Since the dark had fallen he had been pacing nervously back and forth across the cabin floor, his eyebrows knit, his face twitching, now and then offering a soft word of comfort to the little man who lay among the furs in the corner breathing fitfully.

"Cuss your hide, Hank! You know I hain't

slep' none for a week, and you go on a-trampin' and a-gabbin' till you got me all on needles! Why can't you leave me be? O damn it!"

The last words were more like a sob than a curse; and the white, thin face and quivering lips seemed too feeble for the words. Hank stopped pacing up and down, and with his fists resting upon his hips he stared at the little man.

"Now, Sheep," he drawled kindly, "you hain't got no call to talk that away. Hain't I tryin' to be your friend to the finish? I was just thinkin' to cheer you up so's you'd make a respect'ble, manly hangin'. I didn't go to rile you."

The little man thus addressed as "Sheep" drew himself up into a shivering bunch among the furs and groaned. The big man shook his head slowly and sat down, leaning against the wall of the cabin. "Pore Sheep," he muttered.

For an hour he sat with his chin in his hands, staring with pitying eyes upon the huddled little man, who now and again shook with shuddering sobs. The candle flame flickered dismally in the night wind that came in through the chinks in the wall.

At length a series of stifled groans grew up among the furs, accompanied by a spasmodic jerking of the limbs of the little man. With a deep sigh he sat up. With an imbecile droop of the lower jaw, and eyes that burned feverishly with utter horror, he stared at his companion.

The Revolt of a Sheep

"O cuss you, Hank!" he broke out querulously, "why can't you talk none? You goin' to let me keep a-slippin' down, down, down right into hell and never say a word to me? What you settin' there like a bump on a log for?"

"W'y, Sheep," said the big man kindly; "thought you was tryin' to snooze."

"Snooze! How can I snooze with a million little devils runnin' up and down my backbone and a-dancin' all over my head? You knowed I couldn't sleep! You knowed I hain't slep' for a week! Snooze! O damn it! Hain't I goin' to get plenty of snoozin' when they drag the cart out from 'n under me in the mornin'?"

Sheep's voice broke; the fire went out of his eyes; his teeth chattered as though a sudden gust of winter had struck him.

"Now, Sheep," said Hank, "don't be so riled up like. I know it's hard to go out that away; but it won't last long, and it can't hurt much after the first jerk. I reckon it don't matter much how a feller goes out after he's gone."

"Oh, shut that up!"

The little man leaned against the wall and closed his eyes. After a considerable silence the big man produced a flask of liquor and spoke soothingly.

"Want a drink, Sheepy, old man?"

The little man leaped up with a glimmer of hope in his eyes.

" 'Course I do! What made you keep a-hidin' it when you knowed all along that's what I been wantin'?"

He grasped the flask and drank with great eager gulps until it was empty. Then he sat down against the cabin wall, staring fixedly at the candle flame. The empty, sheepish, cowardly face began to gain expression as the liquor mounted to his head. A light of fearlessness began to grow in his eyes. Lines appeared and deepened in his thin face, suggesting at once a certain degree of mastery and infinite malevolence. The wolf that lurks somewhere in the fastness of every man's soul had come forth and routed the sheep.

"What in thunder you doin' with all that heavy artillery hangin' to you, Hank? Take 'em off! I don't need no guards. Who said I was thinkin' of breakin' camp? I hain't tryin' to run, am I? Damn me, I'm glad I done it and I'm a-goin' to walk right straight into hell a-grinnin'! Sheep, am I?"

The little man laughed a strange laugh that had the snarl of a mad wolf in it; a moment since he had been bleating like a scared lamb.

"You set there and listen. Sheep, sheep, sheep! That's what they all been a-callin' me, but when I get done tellin' you about it, I guess you won't call me no sheep. Hain't a danged one of you big fellers as would 've done it up better 'n me!

"You've knowed me quite a spell, Hank; and you

The Revolt of a Sheep

never knowed no bad of me till now, did you? And I hain't had any easy trail most of the time neither. When I was jest a little feller goin' to country school back East, the other fellers always picked onto me 'cause I was so easy to pick onto. Never had a fight in my life. Always scared to death of fightin'; sucked it in with my mother's milk, I guess. Used to get off alone and bawl 'cause I couldn't make myself fight.

"Never was a real boy; always a kind of a stray sheep, bleatin' around in lonesome places. Guess I must look like a sheep; anyway the boys called me that; and it stuck. Pretty hard bein' a sheep amongst wolves, Hank!

"I was always shy and easy scared, Hank. I never owned it to a livin' man before; but a man is like to say things just before he goes out for good that he wouldn't say before.

"You knowed ol' man Leclerc, didn't you? *Her* dad, you know. Used to live down-river half a day's hard walkin'. I reckon that ol' man was about the best friend I ever had, 'ceptin' you, Hank. Kind of seemed to understand me like. Wonder if he's hearin' me now! Don't give a damn if he is! He knowed it wasn't in me to be bad, and he knows I done right. I tell you, Hank, I ain't scared, nor 'shamed nor nothin'. Damn me, I can see Donahan a-dyin' yet, and it does me good, Hank! Does me good!"

The little man's eyes blazed, and his face seemed to take fire from them. But the light died as quickly as it was kindled, like a fire in too little fuel whipped by a wind too strong. A soft light of reminiscence lingered where the fiercer glow had died.

"Used to go down there pretty often when I could; part to see the ol' man, and most to see his girl. Nice little thing, Hank; awful nice little thing! Don't you think so? Good as an angel, too, but weak like a woman can be. I hain't nothin' again' her, Hank—so help me God, I hain't! I wasn't the man for her. She'd ought to 've had a big, strong, quiet feller what wasn't afraid of the devil. Some feller like you, Hank—or Donahan.

"Oh, let the hottest fires in hell eat Donahan!"

The little man shook with a passion that seemed grotesque, because it was too big for him.

"And I kep' goin' down there, and goin' down there, till I begun to be happy, Hank. Begun to thinkin' part of this world was made for me. Begun to thinkin' about havin' a woman and babies; and somehow I got to feelin' bigger and stronger, and not sneakin' any more.

" 'Peared like the girl liked me. Never had nothin' to do with no woman 'cept my mother, you know. Oh, Hank, why can't a feller be a man when he wants to so bad? I dunno. I tried.

"Well, one time I went down there and ol' man Leclerc was pretty sick. Said he was a-goin' to die sure thing. Wheezin' already and pickin' at the blankets. Calls me up to him, and after he got done tellin' me what he was goin' to do d'rectly, he says: 'Sheep, my boy, I've brought her up as near like a French lady as I knowed how. She hain't able to hustle for herself, and—well, ain't she a pretty girl? Why the devil don't you ask me for her?'

"And I asked, and the ol' man said 'yes,' and that was his last word, 'cept 'God be with both of you.' Took all his breath to say that.

"And so I saw the ol' man under ground and come up here with the girl. Got the missionary, Father Donahan, to do the tyin'. (Oh, damn him!) And then I begun to be happy. Seemed like God heard the ol' man for a spell, tho' his voice was weak when he said it. Now I guess mebbe he didn't hear. Does he always hear, Hank?"

"Dunno," muttered the big man, who sat with his face in his hands; "seems like He ain't out here 't all, sometimes.'

"Oh, shut up, will you?" peevishly snapped the little man. "Le' me talk! *You* got plenty of time for talkin'! Le' *me* talk, will you?"

The big man sighed, and the other continued rapidly in a sort of a dazed sing-song voice with little inflection in it, like a man in a trance.

"Big change come over me then; better man all 'round. Factor saw it and sent me on some long trips; seemed to trust me more'n before. But I always done the longest trips in the shortest poss'ble time. Doted on that girl wife, and I guess I was about the happiest feller that ever cussed a pack mule. Used to like to set around the cabin when I could and watch her skip about the place makin' things comfort'ble like a woman can when she's a mind.

"And by and by I was happier'n ever. That was when the little boy come. Cute little feller, that boy was. Don't you mind? Had blue eyes, and that tickled me half to death, 'cause black eyes is the rule in my fambly and hers, and it seemed like God was tryin' to be kind to me.

"When Father Donahan christened the young'n, I drawed his attention to them blue eyes and Donahan (no, I ain't going' to call him Father no more, 'cause if he was a priest, he was a priest of the devil!) What was I sayin'?"

At the sound of Donahan's name upon his own lips, the little man's face writhed into malevolent contortions.

"What was I sayin'?" he repeated dazedly.

"Blue eyes," suggested Hank.

"Quit breakin' in onto me that way!" snapped the little man peevishly. "And when I showed him the blue eyes, Donahan grinned and said, 'Yes, God had been very kind.' And it did look like it, didn't it?

The Revolt of a Sheep

"Donahan named the boy; asked me if I'd let him. Called him James for a front name and Donahan for a middle one. Well, things went along smooth until one day the little feller died. Made me feel pretty bad—like to tore my heart out. But Donahan he come and cried too, and that helped. Always helps to have somebody feel bad with you; don't you think so?

"After that things dragged on like they have a way of doin'. I kep' on tryin' to be like a man. But the girl, she seemed to be takin' it pretty hard. Got stranger and stranger toward me, like as if she didn't care for me no more. Donahan used to come in often and console her, and she seemed to brighten up at them times—'cause she was always strong on the religion business. That's what made her so good, I guess.

"But by and by there was goin' to be another youngster, and I kind of got into the way of whistlin' again somehow. Got to thinkin' how it'd be a boy with blue eyes like the one that died. About that time the Factor sent me off on a long trip. Hated to go, but it couldn't be helped. You'd ought to seen me travel, Hank! Wantin' to get back, you know; 'feared all the time mebbe she was sick and a-wantin' me. Made a quick trip—quicker'n most big men could, Hank. And when I come in sight of home, I was that glad that I couldn't feel my feet and legs achin'.

Indian Tales and Others

"It was night when I got back, and I thought I'd just take a peep in at the winder before I went in; light was shinin' out so home-like. You know how a boy looks a long time at a big, red apple before he eats it; gettin' his eyes full of it before he fills his belly? That was like me.

"I crep' up and looked in; winder was raised a little. I could see Donahan inside and he was talkin' soft and low.

" 'Hope it'll have blue eyes,' he was sayin'; 'blue eyes like mine.' And that made me love Donahan more, 'cause it was just what I was a-wishin' myself. Talked along quite a spell, and me watchin' outside, all the time pityin' Donahan 'cause he couldn't never have no little woman like that and a youngster with blue eyes.

"And the talkin' growed into a mumble and hum like as if I was a-dreamin' it all in a happy dream; until all to oncet some of the words leaped out of the hum, and stood out clear like so many candle flames a-burnin' into my head, and a-scorchin' my backbone, and a-settin' the whole world afire with bloody light.

"I held onto the winder sill to keep from fallin' down, and this is what I heard: 'Sometimes I feel sorry for the pore sheep; and I've spent many nights prayin' to God about it and askin' him to forgive me. Then when I see you again, it all comes back and the prayers are no more than so many curses.

The Revolt of a Sheep

What'd you ever marry that sheep for? Curse the day that I was made a priest!'

"And then the words seemed to get muffled, only now and then I could hear some of 'em plain, and every one of 'em was like a big man's fist drivin' into my face and a-beatin' my eyes full of blood."

The little man covered his face with his hands and sobbed.

"O, I ain't a-blamin her, Hank," he blubbered. "Never was a better woman. I ain't blamin' her."

He rocked himself back and forth for some time. His sobbing ceased. Suddenly he raised his face and the flames of hell glittered in his tear-washed eyes.

"I'm a white-livered coward, so I didn't go in and kill him. He was a big man, and I ain't no fighter. I run; don't know why. Didn't feel sore nor achy in my legs no more. I run and run and run till my breath give out, then I fell down and the stars swum 'round and went out. Then after awhile I was up and walkin', and nothin' would stand still. Things danced round and round me and the air was full of little spiteful, spittin' lights and sounds like devils a-laughin'. And by and by I come to ol' man Leclerc's place. Don't know why I went there. Nothin' there but the *place*.

"I went in and laid down on the floor all broke up. And when I went to sleep, I dreamed of killin' Donahan. I woke up and it was mornin'.

Indian Tales and Others

"First thing I heard was the rattle of some Red River carts goin' north. I guess it was the devil that whispered somethin' in my ear then. I run out and told a big lie to the bull-whackers. 'Man-a-dyin' in here! Go as fast as you can to the next post and tell Father Donahan to come down to see the pore devil through with it!'

"Guess I looked like I'd been sittin' up for a week, so the bull-whackers believed it and went on north a-whackin' their bulls into a swingin' trot.

"Well, Donahan come all right."

Here the little man lapsed into a stubborn silence. He leaned against the wall and for several hours there was no sound in the cabin but that of heavy breathing.

At length Hank got up and walked over to the little window. A dull gray blur had grown up in the East. It would soon be time. Hank sighed.

Suddenly the little man was aroused from his lethargy as though he had heard a shout. He began talking rapidly.

"I stood behind the door of the cabin, and when he come in I——"

The little man hesitated. Suddenly an expression of supreme terror came over his face. The wolf was dead—the frightened sheep looked out of his eyes. There was a sound of footsteps. The shabby light of early dawn had already cheapened the glow of the guttered candle.

The Revolt of a Sheep

The door opened—a priest entered.

The little man gave a yell of terror and shrank into his corner.

"*Take it away, Hank!*" he screamed. "*Take it away!*"

Hank spoke a few words into the ear of the priest, who muttered a prayer and went out. For some time the little man stared appealingly into the eyes of the bigger man. When he spoke his voice was husky and low: "Won't you look after the woman a little, Hank? If it's got blue eyes——"

There was was now a sound of other footsteps approaching.

The footsteps were very near the door. The little man became quiet, biting his finger-tips.

THE MAN WHO SAW SPRING

IT was late in October when the *Jennie Lucas* cast off her cables at the Fort Union landing, swung out into the Missouri, and under high pressure went grunting and snoring southward. Old river men about the Fort watched her trailing cloud of smoke until she had disappeared, then shook their heads and muttered dark prophecy. For, although she was the lightest and fastest boat in the upper waters at that time (for which reason she was chosen to carry a very important message from the Fort to St. Louis), yet no boat is so swift as the prairie winter—and the winter was coming early that year. The old men read warnings upon the face of the heavens and sniffed treachery in the damp south wind. They recalled other Octobers when the winter had swooped down suddenly; they spoke of blizzards; they recalled the names of companions who had perished.

But the *Lucas*, laden heavily with an ever-decreasing cargo of firewood, and groaning through all her strained machinery, raced into the south.

She had made only a hundred miles when a bolt head in the boilers gave way under the abnormal

The Man Who Saw Spring

pressure of steam, and it became necessary to lay up for repairs.

Jim Hanway, the head engineer, worked upon the boilers with a nervous haste that attracted the attention of the captain.

"Take your time, Jim," said the captain; "there's no hurry."

"No *hurry?*" Hanway grinned with twitching lips at the captain. "Take a look at the sky, will you? By God, if we don't all turn up in some coyote's belly before spring, you can thank me and this engine!"

The captain endeavored to laugh pleasantly, but succeeded only in producing a dry cackle. Certainly something had come over Hanway. The tall, gaunt, good-natured engineer was no longer good-natured. There was a drawn, set look in his face, and the whole engine room seemed filled with some strange disquieting influence, some subtle emanation from overwrought nerves.

The captain went up on deck. "Jim's got a case of cold feet," he said to the pilot; "nerves all frayed out to a ragged edge. Talks about us all turning up in some coyote's belly before spring! What do you think of that for Hanway?"

"The way he's been giving her the whip so far, he'll be blowing us to kingdom come more likely," said the pilot. "I yelled down the tube for less speed a dozen times, and he went right

on slapping the steam to her. Want to look after
him a bit, captain!"

Meanwhile Hanway worked nervously at the
boilers. He reinforced them with other bolts and
belted them wtih iron hoops, all the while muttering to himself. A deck hand, tottering under a
log of wood, ventured to joke with the engineer.
Hanway turned upon him and snarled with a savage lifting of the upper lip. "If you roosters don't
get this engine room full of wood before we start,"
he said, "I'll brain the last one of you!"

The "rooster" deposited his load and withdrew
at a trot.

On the morning of the second day of the delay,
the *Lucas* again started south. Hanway bawled
up the tube to the pilot at the wheel. "Don't go
yelling any more instructions down here to me!
This boat is going somewheres!"

In the late evening the *Lucas* ran foul of a snag
and came off with a shattered paddle wheel. This
required two days for repairing, during which time
it began to snow with great, wet, lazily tumbling
flakes, that fell melting upon the deck like soft
kisses of betrayal. Hanway grew more and more
nervous as he helped at the repairing of the paddles.

"Are you sick, Jim?" asked the captain kindly;
for Hanway fumbled the tools with shaking hands
and dropped them often.

"No, not sick, cap," answered Hanway with a

The Man Who Saw Spring

strange tremor in his voice. "But it seems like I can feel something coming."

"Oh, this is just a little flurry," said the captain soothingly. "Too early for real winter, Jim. Better go to bed a while and let the second engineer run her to-night. You're worn out."

When the damage had been repaired, the *Lucas* again started south with the second engineer at the throttle. The *Lucas* was now running night and day, for something of the dread of Hanway had come upon the captain.

In the middle of the night Hanway awoke with a start from a heavy sleep. He arose at once and went on deck, for he had not undressed. The snow had ceased falling and a northwest wind with a keen knife edge smote him in the face. He listened for a moment to the *chug chug* of the revolving paddle wheels, the sigh of the waters about her sides, and the asthmatic snore of the exhaust. Suddenly he thought he caught the tinkling sound of small ice particles. He rushed to the thermometer and, striking a match, gazed for a moment horror-sticken upon the mercury. It registered 31°!

The match flared and went out. Hanway shivered in the sudden darkness as though he had just gazed upon the face of a corpse. He glanced at the pilot house and saw the pilot swinging a free arm about him to warm his numbed fingers.

Hanway ran down the aft stairs and burst into

the engine room. He rushed past the second engineer and glanced at the steam gauge. It registered ten pounds less than he himself had been carrying.

"Get to bed!" he hissed to the engineer.

"I don't go off till morning, Jim," replied the other kindly.

"You go off *now—d'you hear?*"

Hanway grasped the second engineer by the shoulders and, with the aid of a vigorous foot, hurled him bodily through the door, which he bolted. Then he strode over to the lounging firemen and lifted each to his feet with a violent kick.

"*I want steam!*" he growled. "What d'you think you're tending—*a tea kettle?*"

The firemen fell to work sullenly and soon the *Lucas* felt the feverish will of her new master throbbing through her timbers. Hanway stood before the steam gauge with his gaze fixed upon the rising indicator. She now carried fifty pounds. With the reinforced boilers he figured that she could carry fifty-five; after that she would probably blow up.

Fifty-one—fifty-one and a half—fifty-two—fifty-three—fifty-four—fifty-four and a half——

Hanway, with his gloved hand on the lever of the safety valve, muttered to his engine: "One quarter more, old girl! Hang on! You can't go back on me now! It's a good race and we can win—we can win—if——"

Hanway lifted the lever and the steam howled

out through the valve, filling the room with vapor. The indicator had crept up within a hair's breadth of fifty-five. It now dropped back to fifty-four and a half. Hanway closed the valve, and again the pressure mounted slowly toward the danger mark. Backward and forward crept the indicator between the half and the number upon which Hanway gazed transfixed, his hand clutching the lever.

He was racing with the winter, and the whips of his own dread goaded him. In his overwrought imagination he saw the pitiless Spirit of the North bearing steadily down upon the fleeing little *Lucas*, like a great white bird of prey.

"Here, one of you!" he bawled to the firemen. "Scramble out on deck and tell me how the mercury stands!"

One obeyed and came back with chattering teeth. "Twenty-nine," he said.

"Work lively with that wood there!" snarled Hanway, again turning to the steam gauge. The indicator had crept a hair's breadth across the danger mark. He set his teeth and held the valve down until the needle registered fifty-five and three-quarters. "She'll stand it!" he muttered with a nervous grin. "She's good for fifty-six."

As a man who rides a thoroughbred in a race for life and loves the good brute for responding to the spurs, so Hanway loved his engine. Curiously enough, he felt that he and the machinery were one being, and he caught himself gritting his teeth and groaning with the intense strain under which the engine sobbed and whined.

The boat was now quivering through all her length; so much so that the captain rushed down the aft stairs and through the engine room door which had been left unbolted by the fireman.

"For God's sake, Jim!" he gasped. "You'll blow us sky high! She's shivering like a man with the ague and running like a scared jackrabbit! How much are you carrying?"

Hanway turned a haggard face upon the captain. "I'm a licensed engineer, ain't I?" he said. "This is the biggest race of my life, and I'll win if I don't blow us all to powder! Do you hear that? Jim Hanway is running a thousand-mile heat with the winter!"

"But Jim," pursued the captain, endeavoring to reason with the engineer, for river engineers in the old days were very often autocrats below decks; "how much steam——"

Hanway, who was again staring at the indicator, threw his hat over the gauge and grasping a stick of wood, turned upon the captain. His face had a nasty look.

"*Go to hell, will you?*" he snarled. His eyes had narrowed into two steely points of light in the dark sunken sockets that told of tense nerves and sleepless nights.

The Man Who Saw Spring

The captain withdrew—and Hanway held the steam at *fifty-six*.

Morning crept in through the dirty little windows, and still Hanway stood with his hand on the lever and his haggard eyes fixed upon the gauge. When the second engineer came down to go on duty, Hanway coolly knocked him through the door. After that the crew fought shy of the engine room.

"This is my first trip with the devil for engineer," explained the recently ejected, walking the deck and nursing a bruised jaw. "But he's sure making the *Jennie* dance!"

All day Hanway stood at his engine, carefully scrutinizing every part and holding the steam up to the danger point. The boat tossed and groaned like a man with a fever. With an occasional snarl of command, he kept the weary firemen at work fetching wood from the decks and feeding the furnace. Ever and anon he asked for the reading of the thermometer. The mercury fell steadily.

27°—25°—24°—22°.

His tireless pursuer was gaining upon him slowly, surely. But a strange exaltation seized upon Hanway. The rage of the born fighter mounted to his head like a strong liquor, and a sense of superhuman might ran through his muscles.

In the evening a fireman, tottering under a load of wood, volunteered some information, "It's down to ten degrees, sir; and the ice is running a bit!"

"You're a liar!" snarled Hanway, lunging at the man with a savage blow that sent him sprawling under his load.

"Would she stand fifty-seven pounds?" muttered Hanway to himself; "the last reading was twenty-two. We've lost twelve—twelve what? Twelve years—no, twelve miles—no, *degrees*——"

By a curious mental process at which he himself wondered vaguely, it seemed to him that zero was death. Why zero? He didn't know—but somehow, zero was death.

Turning to the firemen, he ordered one on deck to see how the mercury then stood. The man returned sneakingly.

"How is it?" asked Hanway.

The bearer of ill tidings withdrew to a safe distance before he ventured to answer as one who confesses his guilt. "It's no better, sir—it's worse, sir —it's dropped to nine, sir."

Hanway seemed not to hear. His eyes were riveted upon the gauge. The indicator had just touched fifty-seven.

At midnight the pilot bawled frantically down the tube for less speed. Hanway stuffed a handful of waste into the tube. A minute later there came a grinding, slushing sound. Then the *Lucas* shook herself, shrieking and groaning through all her body, reared like a frightened horse—and stopped stock-still.

The Man Who Saw Spring

Hanway was thrown to the floor. In a dazed mechanical way he scrambled to his feet again, shut down the engine and released the steam. Then, vaguely realizing that the race was lost and his adversary upon him, his legs gave way, and the light in his brain went out quickly like a snuffed candle.

When he awoke, the dirty day was filtering through the grimy windows. He was alone in the engine room. He lay still for some time, blinking at the wan light. He could hear voices of command up on deck and the creaking of windlasses. For a moment it seemed to him that he was already dead, and these were sounds above his grave. Then realization of the situation came upon him. The *Lucas* was on a bar, and the crew was making ready to spar her off.

He staggered to his feet, and with a mighty effort of his enfeebled muscles, shoved wood into the furnace. Then he set the pumps to work. They would need steam, he thought—steam for the capstans. *They* would need steam. As for *him* —he had lost. He no longer felt any interest in the affair. He had fought a good fight and he had lost.

He tottered up the stairs and went on deck. Considerable ice was running. The bow of the *Lucas* was thrust far up onto a bar and the ice was already lodging about her. He went to the thermometer and found the mercury at five degrees below zero.

He grinned as it occurred to him that *he had now been dead five degrees!*

All night the crew heard the grinding and chugging of the ice about the *Lucas*. It was the forging of the chain. The fugitive had been captured, and the captor was fastening manacles upon the conquered. In the morning the river was jammed with ice from bank to bank.

For a day the crew scarcely stirred from the engine room, where they sat about sullenly. They were beaten, and they did not care to see the completeness of their defeat.

With the beginning of the second day the temperature raised; a fine dry snow began to fall.

Hanway went about as a man stunned. He ate mechanically and seldom spoke.

The matter of food now became a problem, as the supply aboard was not sufficient to feed ten men more than six weeks; whereas five months lay between them and the spring break-up. Accordingly, the captain proposed a big hunt, and five volunteered—four deck hands and the head pilot.

So when the snow ceased falling, these five went forth. The five remaining men watched their com-

The Man Who Saw Spring

panions dwindling into the great white prairie till they disappeared over a ridge; and there was a muttering on the boat, for a strange dread had grown up out of the hush.

In the afternoon a gusty wind blew up from the northwest, sending long, snakelike streamers of snow writhing and hissing down the valley. Hour by hour the wind increased, and the remaining five peered anxiously into the steadily contracting circle of the storm; but no hunters appeared. And the night crept in through the thickening snow haze, scarcely perceived.

The five men sat huddled about the furnace in the engine room, listening for the voices of their returning companions. The wind boomed down the smokestacks and shrieked through the supporting cables.

Late in the night the captain proposed a game of poker. All except Hanway sat in. But though they staked their summer's wages recklessly, the gaming spirit was dead. Once, when a big jack-pot had been opened with all hands staying, a violent gust of wind beat at the door and howled hoarsely about the boat like the shouting of a desperate man. The second engineer dropped his cards face up, and, leaping to his feet, cried: *"There! They're coming! They yelled!"* Then he dropped into his seat and looked foolish.

And when the second pilot called an unusually stiff bet with a pair of treys, the captain closed the game.

Morning came—a travesty of dawn. The day passed—a writhing, howling gray shadow. And the night came—a mere deepening of the twilight, felt rather than seen. On the evening of the third day, the storm fell and the yellow sun went down smiling cynically upon the ghastly storm-swept spaces.

There were now only five men in the ice-bound *Lucas*—the captain, Hanway, the second engineer, the second pilot and a deck hand.

The temperature fell again after the storm; it reached twenty below zero, and the snow became crusted. In the long nights the dread-ridden crew heard the coyotes bewailing their empty bellies and the ache of their frosted feet. All night the cables, drawn taut with the intense cold, sang dismally in the frozen hollow that was the world, and the contracting timbers popped and groaned.

One night in late November the captain dreamed a pleasant dream. It seemed to him that the winter had broken up; the spring rains fell; the good smell of the earth, mixed with the odor of wet grass, filled his nostrils. He felt the lift of a flood beneath him. He heard the snoring of the engines; felt the eager trembling of the boat as she nosed the flood and took the swirl of the current southward.

Then suddenly it seemed that the *Jennie Lucas*

The Man Who Saw Spring

shook herself like a wet dog, and he awoke with the sound of splintering wood in his ears. The boat *was* vibrating! The machinery *was* moving!

He leaped out of his bunk and ran on deck, for he had not undressed. There was a light down the aft stairs. He rushed down into the engine room and found the boilers sizzling with heat and the machinery working under forty pounds pressure, which was steadily mounting, for the safety valve had been tied down.

He cut the cords that held the valve, and shut down the engine. Then he looked about for Hanway, but he was not in the room.

"Where is that idiot?" muttered the captain; "he's busted the paddle wheels! I'll——"

He had reached the top of the stairs when a strange wild moaning cry, like and unlike that of a coyote, pierced the silent night like a pang. The sound seemed to come from the after deck. There the captain ran and beheld Jim Hanway on his hands and knees in the snow, with his haggard face lifted to the sky, sending forth doleful answers to the coyotes.

"What the deuce, Hanway——" began the captain.

Hanway raised himself to his knees, and turning his drawn face upon the captain, pointed off down the white river and said with a weak, expressionless voice: "I told you she'd have supper ready, didn't I, cap? Seems like I did—let's see. She's sitting up by the fire waiting—and I'm not coming home because, cap, I can't get the throttle open somehow. Throttle's busted, somehow."

Hanway passed a shaking hand across his brow and fell to sniveling like a frightened boy.

The captain put Hanway to bed and explained matters to the others who had turned out: "It's nothing but Jim—just a bit off his head—thought he was driving her south."

But the captain placed the deck till dawn, muttering to himself. He was haunted with a premonition that he would never see spring.

The dawn crept like a shivering thing across the white expanses, and the sun lifted a pale face above the ghostly bluffs. Hanway slept heavily in his bunk, and the captain did not appear. The three others fried the bacon for their breakfast and ate in silence. Then they sat about in the engine room and waited. Waited for what? They did not know; but the monotonous winter hush seemed ever about to bring forth some unutterable horror. The perishing of their five companions in the blizzard and the madness of Hanway were having their effect.

Conversation seemed impossible. A question called forth only a laconic reply. Late in the afternoon the second pilot leaped to his feet and with clenched fists paced up and down the engine room. "Why don't you talk?" he growled. "Why don't

The Man Who Saw Spring

you talk? Hang you, why don't you sing or yell or talk?"

His two companions turned blank faces upon him for answer.

"You're all infernal lunatics—that's what you are!" whined the second pilot, pacing the floor. "The devil's got it in for the *Lucas!* I tell you, you're a parcel of——"

Just then the great outer silence was broken by a wild song sung in raucous tones. The three leaped to their feet. Who had dared to shout so loud into that terrible stillness? It seemed like a challenge to some invincible sleeping enemy!

They rushed out on deck, and high above them on the curved roof of the pilot house they beheld the captain, looming huge against the sky. He was without coat and hat, and his hair fell in tangles about his bloated face. He was evidently very drunk.

Upon the slippery edge of the roof he stood, balanced upon his toes like a ballet dancer, leering down upon the suddenly appearing audience.

Then he suddenly began his song again and swung off into the dizzy mazes of a rowdy dance. He clogged, he shuffled, he pirouetted, he chasséd. Keeping time with one giddy foot, he kicked high for the edification of an imaginary bald-headed row.

Louder and wilder grew the song; faster and faster he danced. Then, swinging too near the slippery edge of the roof, he went off in a whirling spray of snow, struck the hurricane deck, and bounded off, landing at the feet of the three spectators.

He lay still. A sluggish stream of blood oozed from his head and reddened the snow about him. The three gazed horror-stricken. This was the *something* that had been waiting about them in the silence.

For many minutes they stared upon the quiet face that seemed to them the visible center from which emanated the awful hush. At length they carried the body into the engine room; but the captain was dead.

In the evening they chopped a hole in the ice and thrust the body into it. There was no ceremony; they wanted this quiet thing out of sight.

The next morning only two men appeared on the boat—Hanway and the deck hand. A fresh trail wound southward down the valley. The second engineer and the second pilot, taking the last gun and the greater share of the grub, had fled in the night from the evil-starred *Lucas*.

Of the two who remained, one had lost his reason, and the other kept continually drunk; for having despaired of following his deserting companions, since there were no more guns, he consoled himself with a keg of liquor which he had discovered in the captain's room.

The Man Who Saw Spring

The wolves, grown bold with hunger, came close to the boat at night and filled the darkness with wailings. And through the day the two men stared vacantly down the white valley into the south. They seldom spoke to each other.

In the latter part of February a sudden change came over Hanway. He seemed as one who had been aroused from a long sleep. In a vague way he again realized the situation, and a longing to live and see the spring grew upon him until it was an obsession. Now, for the first time, he knew that the grub was running short; that there was only bacon left and not enough to feed two men until the spring thaw. But there was enough for *one*.

He would be that one!

The will to live grew big in his weakened brain and filled it full, until there was no place for pity. He got up in the night, seized the bacon and the liquor and hid them in the engine room. All the next day he sat in the engine room with a stick of wood in his hand, guarding the priceless stuff which alone could enable him to see the spring.

And the deck hand threatened and cursed and begged piteously by turns—but Hanway guarded his treasure. He would see the spring again.

But in the middle of the third night, the deck hand, grown desperate, was creeping stealthily down the aft stairs when Hanway awoke from a momentary doze. They met on the stairs.

[305]

"Great God, Hanway," begged the deck hand, "give me just a rine to chaw at, and I'll go away —please, Jim!"

Hanway laughed hideously in the man's face. And they fought.

At length, Hanway tottered to his feet and fled into the engine room. He bolted the door with palsied fingers. But the other lay quiet on the stairs.

Then there came a confusion of sounds as of a thousand devils swooping in upon the boat. The wolves were fighting over the thing on the stairway.

But Hanway, shrieking with fright, piled log after log against the door. *He would keep the devils out. He would see the spring!*

In the middle of March a steamboat from Sioux City, forging its way up the stream that still ran ice, met a pitiful ghost of a boat. Both her paddle wheels were shattered, and she was scarred from stem to stern with the ice. Idly swinging about with the swirl of the heavy spring current, she came down like a floating corpse.

When the crew boarded her, they found the stripped skeleton of a man on deck. They went through the cabin and discovered no one. But, after much battering at the door at the foot of the aft stairs, they entered the engine room.

In a corner of the room a gray-haired man crouched and whimpered.